THE EMBATTLED ROAD

&

EMBATTLED HEARTS

BY
J.M. MADDEN

Cover by Viola Estrella

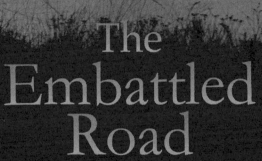

The
Embattled
Road

THE LOST AND FOUND SERIES PREQUEL

J.M. MADDEN

THE EMBATTLED ROAD

By
J.M. MADDEN

Acknowledgements~

My deepest thanks to Bruce McDonald for the insightful information that has made this book as true to life as possible. You've brought a dimension to the story that may not have been there otherwise. THANK YOU.

Donna and Robyn, you're awesome cheerleaders and perfectionists. You guys rock! Kally, thank you for the idea of the prequel itself, not to mention the tips and encouragement.

And most importantly, to all the service members who have given up any part of themselves to serve this glorious country, I thank you from the bottom of my heart for securing our safety and that of my family.

A Note from J.M.~

I've had the idea for this series for a long time. But I had a lot of doubts about whether I could convey the message I wanted to.

As we go about our daily grind, it's easy to forget that there are men and women dying every day as they fight to ensure our freedom. When they come home, no matter what shape they are in, they deserve our utmost respect and appreciation for doing the job they volunteered for.

Every soldier that has served overseas will carry some type of scar, either internally or externally. It's our responsibility, as their support, to make sure that those scars are seen as marks of courage, not something to turn away from when you pass them on the street.

I sincerely believe there is a soul mate for everybody. The external package doesn't matter when it comes to the heart. The same goes with friendship. There are people you come across that you just click with, and know they will be a part of your life forever. When men serve together in combat, there's a special bond created that surpasses everything.

That bond is what I tried to at least touch on here. There are no heroines in this book because the men had to be solid with each other before I could introduce the girls in the coming books. I hope you'll be patient as we follow all of their journeys.

Chapter One

June 2007

Duncan could not wait to get the fuck out of this sand pit. He had grit in his junk, his armpits, the creases of his eyes. It didn't do any good to try to rub it away because all you did was scratch yourself.

Fucking desert.

Jungle fighting would be welcome right now, and that said a lot. He hated the jungle.

Three more months before he reached the end of his tour and could go home. His last tour. He'd already decided to go on drill instructor duty when he was done, so he could train recruits at Parris Island in relative comfort instead of here. He'd served his time. Perhaps he and Melanie could actually build a life together.

The Humvee rattled over a rock, bouncing him in the seat.

"Monroe, you gotta hit every damn rock on the road?" Bates groused. "My ass is killin' me."

The driver grinned and glanced behind him at the other two Marines. Bates always complained. "Dude, you've been here long enough to know the damn rocks breed like crazy. Scrape 'em off and they're right back with a new layer. I'm following the tracks exactly."

The men snorted in the back and Duncan looked out the window. The monochrome, hilly landscape stretched for miles, leading to the mountains in the distance. Rocky outcrops dotted the land, interspersed with scrub grass clumps, perfect ambush points they had to pass to get to the northern base, where they were due to relieve the current MP force rotating out.

The convoy had been traveling for hours. It was slow going through this rough terrain. Driving in Iraq wasn't like driving in Colorado. You had to be aware of everything and follow in the path of the truck in front of you. Too many men had died already by IEDs this year, and more died every day.

Beauchamp had been the most recent. Blown to hell by a young Iraqi on a motorcycle that pulled alongside his window while he was talking to a group of kids. Three of the kids had been blown away as well, but insurgents didn't care about them. They were supposedly blessed by Allah for dying a glorious death. He wondered if the mothers felt the same way as they gathered up pieces of their children.

The radio squawked to life with men yelling. His ears were hit with a reverberation of sound and he knew immediately that an IED had been triggered. Duncan gripped his weapon, ready to jump to the ground as he searched for the source of the explosion. Monroe slammed on the brakes, sending the Humvee skidding in the loose gravel. Duncan glanced in the side mirror. The vehicles behind them had disappeared in a cloud of smoke and fire. Burning debris rained down in chunks on their vehicle. Black smoke swirled upward. Duncan saw the vehicles were still there, but heavily damaged, all shoved askew. The men's screams reached his ears before they were drowned out by rifle fire.

"Out of the vehicle! Bates and Clark, cover fire! We've got men down!"

He threw himself out of the Humvee and shouldered his M16. There was a copse of rocks several hundred yards to the west. The attack seemed to be coming from there so he fired in that direction. Smoke obscured his vision as he took cover behind the truck, but he could still hear men screaming. "Monroe, get on the horn and make sure we have air support coming!"

Crouching, Duncan ran across the open expanse of ground between his vehicle and the one behind him in the caravan, the M16 barking in his arms. Bates and Clark laid down cover fire as he ran. The first Marine he reached was already gone, a gaping hole in his sternum. Duncan circled the truck, which sat at an odd angle, flipped with the roof to his side. The front passenger's side wheel was in a hole, but the ass end poked in the air. He tried to follow the sound of screaming while staying under cover.

At the back of the truck, he found another young Marine trying to crabwalk around the vehicle. The distinctive chatter of the enemy's AK-47s echoed through the air, and the answering response from the Marines. Ignoring the heat of the smoldering truck, he surged to grab the kid beneath the armpits and drag him around the vehicle. Bullets struck the dirt in front of him and he jumped, rolling with the kid out of the line of danger. Monroe was there, then, laying down cover fire as Duncan dragged the Marine out of reach of the bullets.

The passenger-side door of the Humvee fell open just above them and two men tumbled out to the sand. One hustled to the front of the vehicle, raised his weapon and started to fire. The second fell to the ground and didn't move. Duncan glanced down at the kid he'd just helped. His tag said Fallon. He gasped for air but Duncan didn't see any obvious blood or breaks. "Hey Fallon, looks like you skinned by with this one. You're fine, you just need to breathe. Just breathe. I'm going to check on your buddy."

Fallon blinked and nodded his head. He still had his helmet on.

The Marine who had fallen to the ground did not. Duncan scrambled across the sand, ever conscious of how close the little puffs of dust around him reached. Some were within inches of his feet. The insurgents had planned this ambush perfectly. Before he rolled the kid over, he felt for a pulse. There, but faint. Again, he didn't see any obvious blood but in situations like these what you couldn't see was more dangerous. The impact of the percussion to the body and then the body against the vehicle could kill a Marine in minutes. Not an easy death. He called for a corpsman, but all he saw was swirling smoke.

Pulling the kid over enough to look at his face, Duncan leaned in. *Shit.* Parker. Newest of the bunch. He'd only been here two weeks. Poor kid had a hell of a dent in his head that Duncan hadn't seen at first.

A bullet pinged off the undercarriage inches from his face and he knew he needed to move him whether he wanted to or not. Slinging the rifle around to his back, he grabbed him by the pits and pulled. Parker didn't rouse at all. Bad sign.

The corpsman dropped down beside him as he lowered Parker to the ground, twenty feet from the overturned Humvee. He motioned to the young Marine's head. "Head wound!"

Scrambling back to the truck, he pulled his weapon forward and took position behind Monroe, firing toward the rocks. The gunfire slowed and he wondered if the enemy had retreated.

Eventually the firing dwindled away. Duncan stayed put. Sometimes the enemy stopped shooting and waited till the Marines relaxed, then set in on them again. This time, though, they seemed to be gone. Or dead. Several bodies littered the outcrop.

He clapped Monroe on the back, impressed that the young grunt had done exactly what needed done.

The medic shook his head when Duncan returned to him. "I don't know if he's going to make it or not First Sergeant. He's got serious swelling on the brain. I've called in a 9-Line Medevac but I've got other wounded to eval."

In other words, there was nothing more he could do for him.

Duncan nodded and waved the man away. Monroe helped Fallon over to sit with Parker. Fallon still wheezed and held his gut, but he'd probably be fine. Duncan followed Doc to the next vehicle in the convoy, obviously the epicenter of the blast. Bodies lay strewn behind the burning carcass of the Humvee. The transports were armored, but only to a certain extent. Obviously, this one had been deliberately targeted, fired upon repeatedly after it had hit the IED. Did they think he had been in it? The driver's side was ripped open like the lid off a can, with its guts strewn everywhere. The men in the fire team were all men he knew and had spoken to hours ago. Now, they were all gone. The gruesome sight was enough to turn his normally cast-iron stomach. It had been his responsibility to get the men in these squads to the camp safely.

His throat tightened as he went man to man, cataloging names when he could see them. Six dead, total, from two different teams. Six families he'd have to call when he got to base. Sorrow threatened to drop him to his knees, but he had to shove it aside.

The third Humvee affected by the blast had little to no damage and the men were fine, though banged up. One had a bullet hole through his leg but was conscious and calm as Doc bandaged him up.

Duncan sent out a squad to secure their position. A few minutes later he heard the distinctive thwop-thwop-thwop of the Medevac. Shielding his eyes from the sun, he watched the chopper roll in.

It was a couple hundred yards away when a surface-to-air rocket blasted out of the hills from the west and struck the side of the massive two-rotor machine, sending it floundering in the air. Rifle fire sounded, three short bursts, but it was lost in the whine of the overtaxed engines as the pilot tried to recover the craft.

Too close. The thought registered as his feet began moving. He tried to get the men up before the chopper came down right on top of them.

Even as he started shoving Marines out of the way, he knew it was too late. The monstrous machine hit the ground behind him and blew. For a heartbeat of time, everything stopped—sound, motion, thought. Then the blast struck him in the back, flinging him into the air. It seemed like he flew forever before landing with a sickening crunch on top of one of his men. Heat seared his body from shoulders to toes.

His burning world went dark.

Duncan jerked awake, then realized all he did was open his eyes. Reality smacked him in the face as he focused on the beige tile floor. Yep. Still at Walter Reed. Landstuhl Hospital's floor had been pale blue with darker flecks in it. He remembered that much. Somebody had turned the page of the automotive magazine for him, but he was still strung up like a marionette, arms stretched out to his sides, in the medical contraption immobilizing his spine and protecting his burns. The mattress beneath him was hard. After three weeks in the same position, you'd think he'd remember. But no. Every time he woke up, he wondered why God hadn't just killed him and gotten it over with. At least then the pain would end.

One of the nurses squeaked her way into the room. Pink rubber Crocs stopped beside his bed. What was her name? Lacey? Or Lainy? Something like that. He glanced into the edge of the mirror not covered by the magazine. She smiled at him, that professional nurse smile meant to conceal how very desperate his situation actually was.

"How do you feel today, First Sergeant?"

He rocked his head as much as he could and closed his eyes. If she was going to ask stupid questions like that he wasn't going to answer her. She circled the bed and he felt her tug at the sheet over his burnt back. "How is your pain right now?"

He sighed. She wouldn't leave until she answered her. "About a seven."

She hummed under her breath and moved to the IV stand, adjusting something there. Within seconds he felt a blessed wash of numbing heat roll through his body. Seemed like the only thing that made him happy anymore was morphine. He closed his eyes and tried to sleep his life away.

August 2007

"That fucking hurt!"

The grey-haired doctor at the foot of his bed grinned at him. "Good."

Duncan reeled against the mattress, in spite of the pain the movement caused his raw back. It had *hurt*. "Do it again," he demanded.

Richards ran the weirdly shaped roller up his foot and for the first time in two months Duncan felt something. "It's about fucking time. Why did it take so long?"

The doctor shrugged. "Well, in addition to the spinal shock you had the burns and the cracked vertebra. Your pelvis was broken in two places. It took time for all that to heal. Now the nerves are fixing themselves. I think a couple more months and you should be up and moving."

"Months?"

"Yes, at least. Because I want you to take it easy. We can't rush this, or it could set you back right where you started. You'll end up in the chair permanently if we're not careful of your recovery."

Duncan let the information sink in, shocked. He would be fine, it would just take a while. He could stare at the walls a little longer.

His heart raced at the first glimmer of good happening to him in months. A huge chunk of his company—those valiant men— were gone and his career fried, literally. Uncertainty yawned before him like an abyss. But finally, that one little tickle had changed his life.

*****

That following Saturday, anticipation thrummed through his body as he watched the clock. Sixteen thirty-four. Melanie would be here any minute. He'd debated calling her to tell her the news, but decided he wanted to see the happiness on her face when he told her in person. In spite of the doctor's assurances that she could handle whatever happened, she'd been slowly withdrawing. Maybe this could also be her galvanizing spark.

As if in answer to his thoughts, the hospital room door swished open and Melanie walked in, looking beautiful as always in the tan coat that matched her hair so perfectly. Her pale cheeks were flushed and her blue eyes glittered. She crossed to kiss him like she normally did but moved away from his side, instead choosing to stand at the end of the bed, hands folded in front of her. She kept her jacket on.

His gut twinged in warning.

"Melanie, are you okay? How was your drive from Columbus?"

"Fine, Duncan. A little busy but not too bad. You're looking good."

"Thank you," he murmured. He'd shaved the stubble from his face and gotten his hair cut this morning, expecting her.

Narrowing his eyes, he cocked his head. Obviously she had something on her mind to talk about. Some instinct made him hold his own news close and wait as she fidgeted. Finally, she looked up at him with tears welling in her eyes. "Duncan, I can't do this anymore. I can't be here for you anymore."

Chills rippled over his skin. "You mean here at the hospital? That's fine. If it's too much of a drive you don't have to do it."

She shook her head, biting her bottom lip. "No, I don't think I can be here for you." She waved a hand at the medical equipment around the bed. "At all. With all of this."

Duncan stared at her, hard, until she shifted uncomfortably. She dropped her eyes to her white-knuckled hands. "I know you'll get better, eventually, but I need to move forward with my life." Straightening, she stepped to the side of his bed and held out the engagement ring he'd given her a year ago. Dazed, he took the ring, folding it into his palm.

She folded her hands against her stomach, drawing Duncan's gaze. White-hot anger exploded when he realized what the swell beneath her hand meant. She'd worn the jacket to try to conceal it.

"Ahh, it all makes sense now. So, who's the lucky guy? Or do you even know?"

Melanie sucked in a breath. "Don't be like that," she implored. "What did you expect me to do? Go without companionship for nine months while you were gone who knows where?"

He looked at her incredulously. "Yes, exactly, just like I did. And are you serious? I was in Iraq fighting in a goddamn war!"

She broke into harsh sobs, but he didn't—couldn't—soften. She looked to be a few months along, so, just before he got injured. Hell, even if he hadn't gotten injured he'd have come home to find her knocked up by some other guy. Betrayal turned his stomach.

Something had nagged at him about the relationship anyway. She'd been remote since he'd gotten back, not very communicative. She'd moved to her parent's house in Ohio. Hell, she'd only been up to Maryland to see him a few times since he got back in the States, and only called a few times besides that.

Melanie was needy and spoiled. He'd known that a long time ago. Honestly, in his heart of hearts, if he was honest with himself, he'd kind of been expecting this.

He looked down at his motionless legs. It was probably a hell of a downer for the party girl to think she was going to have to take care of him the rest of her life.

The fact that feeling had begun to return to his legs didn't matter. It wouldn't change the outcome tonight, so he kept the information to himself.

His *ex*-fiancée continued to weep beside the bed. Her audacity spiked his fury.

"Okay, Melanie, you can stop with the water works."

She looked up at him from tear-drenched eyes that did nothing for him. She'd chosen her path.

"I'm sorry, Duncan. I wish things had turned out differently."

He wasn't interested in her platitudes. "Yeah, well, drive safe back to Ohio. Ship my stuff to my parents in Colorado."

Her eyes widened at the dismissal, and she opened her mouth as if to argue. Instead, she snapped her jaw shut, turned on her heel and disappeared from his life.

The amount of relief he felt that she was gone surprised him. They'd been a little rocky to begin with, before he ever left for Iraq, but he didn't think she'd betray him with such a flourish. He was a little regretful that he didn't have anybody to share his news with other than his parents, who were on the other end of the country.

Lacey walked in just then, as if she'd heard his thoughts. She gave him a cautious smile. "I saw your honey leave. She didn't look happy."

He snorted. "She's not my honey anymore. Guess she got tired of waiting for me. She's pregnant."

The nurse winced. "Ouch. Nice. Let me guess, she was lonely and needed companionship?"

Duncan looked at her, surprised. "How did you know?"

Lacey shook her dark head. "Sad to say, but it happens a good bit in here. You guys are long term, and a lot of people just can't deal with the way their lives have to change." She shrugged. "I've been doing this several years, and the ones that hang around the first few months post-injury will likely be around for a long time."

He mulled that over as she fiddled with his IV. Some of the guys had family at the hospital day and night. Others didn't have anybody. One Marine down the hall hadn't had any family visit. Ever.

His parents had just left for home in Colorado. They'd been here for most of his recovery, until he'd told them to get back to their lives. They'd been reluctant at first, unwilling to leave him alone, but he'd persuaded them, promising that he'd relocate back there. It was the first time his father had left the family print shop for any length of time. Sam, his brother, was running it while they were gone.

He had to be honest with himself. The Marines had no use for a grunt in a wheelchair. Even a career man like himself. The thought of trying to find a job while restrained this way absolutely nauseated him, but no other option was available. His father had reassured him that there would always be a job available at the shop, but that would be the same as taking welfare.

It made him that much more determined to get out of the chair.

Lacey paused beside his bed, an earnest look on her young face. Her pretty eyes were soft with understanding. "You need to know that when they walk out like that, it's not the patient's fault. It's a failing in them, not you guys. I've been a nurse here for six years, and it always happens the same way. But the Marine always conquers and adapts."

Duncan snorted at the way she dropped her voice and puffed out her chest for that last part.

"Well," he admitted. "I'll let you in on a secret. I'm not that upset. I think I kind of knew it was coming."

Lacey grinned and nodded her head. "I thought not. Besides," she said as she turned to leave, "you've got much bigger things to think about."

She wiggled his blanket-covered toes before walking out the door.

*****

A week after he started getting sensation in his feet, they moved him out of the single unit room into a double occupancy. The threat of infection had passed, for the most part, and they needed the room for more wounded rolling in. His new roommate was Gunnery Sergeant John Palmer, incomplete spinal cord injury, or SCI, paralyzed from the hips down and angry at the world. It took Duncan a week just to get a "fuck you" out of him. He eventually realized this was the guy that had no family, and it made Duncan all the more determined to connect with him, in spite of his surly attitude.

Duncan watched two young nurses just out of school leave in tears because they tried to talk to the paralyzed Marine and had been ripped to shreds. The only nurse not outwardly affected by his nastiness was Lacey. She grinned when he cussed her out and shook her dark head. "If you weren't so cute, Gunnery Sergeant, I'd smack that sour look off your face."

"Fuck you," he snapped.

She grinned that much more and sailed out of the room.

Duncan felt slightly offended on the sweet nurse's behalf.

"Dude, they feed you. You better cut them some slack."

"Fuck you," he snarled, with no regard to rank.

Duncan didn't try to correct him because he understood where the man came from. A week ago he'd thought he would be in the chair permanently, and it hadn't been a good feeling. The tiny, living, feeling area that had stretched up to his ankles had reignited all his desperate hopes for a normal life.

Chapter Two

A week after Duncan moved in with Palmer, Chad Lowell rolled into the room, pushed by an orderly. His left arm was bandaged and there was a stump below the knee of his left leg, but Duncan grinned in spite of himself and gave a yell. He leaned forward as much as he could and almost fell out of bed clasping arms with his ex-Sergeant, genuinely glad to see his buddy. They'd been on two tours together in the desert and they worked together well, though Duncan was several years older. Chad had been injured months ago while they'd been on patrol, walking next to the Marine that had stepped on the mine, Mike Dodd. Dodd hadn't survived but Chad had, in spite of the traumatic injuries to his entire left side.

He grinned and Duncan was relieved to see the easygoing character still in there. Though his eyes were haunted, his spirit still seemed strong. Duncan shook his head at the younger man. "I never expected you'd still be here. I asked a couple weeks ago but nobody would answer me. How the hell are you?"

Chad shrugged and motioned to the orderly standing behind him. "Fine. Getting the royal escort." He looked up at the orderly. "Mind if we hang for a while? I'll holler when I'm ready to go."

The orderly gave a laid-back wave and left.

Chad looked him over. "You look like crap, Dunc. When I heard you were part of that messy 'copter crash, I knew it was going to be bad. What'd they tell you?"

Reaching above himself, Duncan used the bar hanging over his head to shift his weight on his hips. He was starting to feel when he'd been in one position too long. "I'm okay. Busted pelvis and a few burns. Spinal cord shock was the biggie. But my feeling is starting to come back." He grinned in spite of himself, and Chad grinned with him. "What about you?"

"Ah, well..." Chad paused to clear his throat. "You knew my

leg was gone. Luckily I still have the knee joint. I'm going to be fitted with a prosthetic next month." The young Marine looked where his leg used to be. "Damn strange nothing being there."

Duncan couldn't imagine. As he looked at the Marine in front of him, changed for the rest of his life, it was hard not to get pissed at the country and all the suits that pretended to run it.

"The arm had third-degree burns. I've had several grafts that have taken well, but I may need more. The ones on my neck didn't need to be grafted." Chad touched the skin of his neck and grimaced as if he didn't like the feel of it.

Duncan nodded in support. The grafting process was as painful as the actual injury sometimes. They'd taken skin from his thigh to graft to his back. The pieces seemed to be attaching fine but he still took meds to combat rejection and infection.

Chad looked across the room at Gunnery Sergeant Palmer, who was flipping channels on the TV. "Hey, Gunny."

"Fuck you."

Chad winked at Duncan. "Yeah, nice to see you too, buddy."

"I'm not your buddy, Lowell."

Chad made a comical face at Duncan. "Gunny and I were in the same airplane for a while, weren't we? Then we shared a rehab room for a while."

Duncan looked at Palmer. He'd refused to talk to anybody unless it was to berate them. This was the first time he'd heard the man talk to anyone without having a "fuck you" attached. And though he was flipping channels on the TV, Duncan thought he seemed to be paying more attention than he normally did.

"But don't worry," Chad continued. "His bark is worse than his bite."

Palmer snorted but didn't remove his eyes from the screen. "Come within reach of this bed, you little shit, and I'll show you how bad I can bite."

Chad laughed and wiggled his chair with his right hand. "Sorry, Gunny, I can only make left turns right now. Maybe another day I'll let you take a chunk out of my hide."

"Plan on it," he murmured.

Duncan was in shock. The downright belligerent Gunnery Sergeant had berated and insulted all who stepped through the hospital room door, including Duncan himself, but he apparently had a soft spot for Lowell. The sharp kid was easy going and a bit of a cut-up. He'd been the perfect balance of tough and fun to work with the new pukes when they came in. Apparently the same approach worked well with Palmer.

They sat and talked for the better part of an hour before the orderly returned for Lowell. "Grub's coming, sir."

Chad nodded and made his goodbyes. "I'll be back tomorrow."

Duncan wasn't going to hold him to the promise, but when he rolled into the room the next day he was very glad to see him.

They settled into a pattern of hanging out together unless one of them had rehab. Sometimes they scheduled their rehab at the same time, so they still hung out and encouraged each other.

Palmer unthawed enough to talk to him, but he seemed reluctant to mention his wounds. Duncan couldn't blame him, even though it was the great purple elephant in the room. He'd overheard enough conversation between the doctors to know that the other man's injuries were not recoverable. Yes, he might feel things occasionally, but he'd never walk again. Guilt that his own feeling was returning but Palmer's wasn't nagged at him, and he debated whether or not to request to be moved to another room, just so the other Marine didn't have to watch.

But he put it off the more connected they became. Palmer even gave him congratulations on the feeling moving up his legs. Duncan wished he could share his good fortune with the other man. They hadn't been in the same unit, but he'd come to be partial to his grumpy ass.

*****

Gunfire erupted right next to Chad's head and it took everything he had not to clap his hands over his ringing ears. Instead, he tightened his fists on the stock of the M16 and tried to sight down the barrel. They were running low on ammunition. Every bullet had to count. "Short and controlled, men. Don't waste your ammo!" Half a dozen "yes, Sergeants" bounced back to him.

He squeezed off two rounds and the return fire coming from across the street stopped. His ears had gone beyond ringing to numb and his head ached from the percussion of the gunfire in the confined space, but he grinned. They were pushing the bastards back.

He glanced at his watch. Only an hour since they'd rolled into this damn little village. They'd only engaged the enemy less than ten minutes ago. Ten minutes in Iraq's Diyala Province was longer than ten minutes anywhere else on the Earth though, and he knew he probably had injuries in his squad.

"Sims, you got air support coming?"

The Marine didn't respond. Chad craned his neck to see through the dust and rubble of the bombed-out building they were in. Sims was in the corner of the room, mic clutched in his hand. The radio box was sitting on the floor beside him and he was twisting dials but not talking. "Shit!"

Scrambling across the floor on his belly, he snatched the com out of the Marine's grip and keyed it. Static filled the air. Calling out his location, he prayed that somebody would hear him, but it stayed quiet. Sims turned the box to the side, showing him the bullet holes in the back.

Fuck.

Heavy gunfire erupted across the street again, pelting the front of the building they were taking cover in. Apparently the bad guys could get backup but the Marines couldn't. What the hell! First Sergeant Wilde was somewhere to the east. Surely by now he'd heard the explosions and knew that his Marines needed him.

The men he commanded were returning fire, but unless they got reinforcements or air support, the entire sitch would swing the other way.

As if in answer to his prayer, M16 gunfire sounded from the east. "Oorah! 'Bout time, First Squad!"

He repositioned himself behind the weapon with new

enthusiasm, firing at everything that moved. Seemingly too easy to believe, the two squads overwhelmed the few insurgents left in the village. They were quickly dispatched or ran away, and the silence rang through the heat of the day.

Chad scrambled to get care for his wounded and met up with his commanding officer. Wilde slapped him on the back for maintaining their position. It was high praise from the First Sergeant.

The men were all giddy as they started back to base, and he couldn't really blame them. The numbers had not been in their favor. But they'd all managed to walk out of the situation alive.

As the group fell into loose formation, he went from man to man checking to make sure they were tight. He had a lot of new blood in his squad. Sometimes, the newbies had to go through a meltdown before they could get on with the job. It was tough, shooting people for the first time. Usually, especially in close quarters, there was a lot of puking their guts out and moaning over going to hell. Not this time, though. They all kept their shit together.

Private Barnes seemed more quiet than usual. "You all right, Private?"

The young grunt nodded. "Yes, Sergeant. Just thinkin'. There was a lot going on all at once."

"Well, that's kind of the way they work around here."

Barnes grinned and nodded, looking a little more comfortable in his skin. "Yes, Sergeant." He moved on.

Chad pulled to the side a bit and waited as the men trooped past. Dodd paused in front of him and locked up at the position of attention. "Sergeant, my rifle malfunctioned a couple times during the fight. It wasn't reloading correctly. I had to clear it manually before I could fire again."

Chad took the rifle from the Marine and ejected the clip, clearing the weapon. The squad marched on. With one eye on his men and the environment, he examined the M16. Structurally, it looked fine.

"Was it misfiring when you had it to your shoulder?"

Dodd shook his helmeted head. "No, Sergeant. Only when I was holding it away from me."

Understanding dawned on the young Marine's face as he worked out the problem in his head. "I know what it was, Sir. I didn't have enough stability behind it to jack another round."

Slamming the clip home, he handed it back to Dodd. "You got it. Always keep your shoulder tight to the butt. The rifle needs that stability to send the bolt back with the next round."

Grinning, Dodd chambered a round and turned to follow the group, who was disappearing over a knoll. They picked up their pace to a jog, Dodd looping around a rock.

"Dodd, follow..."

...the footprints.

Chad's world went supernova. Blazing heat seared his body, blinding him, and he went spinning through the air. He landed on his pack and floundered, trying to find up. His brain blanked out. Adrenaline pumped through his body and he managed to pull his weapon around, even though he couldn't see a damn thing. His eyes refused to focus.

He heard voices to the right of him, and it sounded like a group of men. He brought his weapon to his shoulder but couldn't find a target.

First Sergeant Wilde's voice broke through the melee. "It's just us, buddy. I've got your weapon, Chad. Let go, buddy."

He didn't want to let go. That weapon was his life and death. He slept with it, kept it in the latrine beside him. First Sergeant was asking for it, though, and of all the men in the unit, he trusted him the most. The weight of the M16 left his arm.

The world was slowly coming back into focus, and there were a ring of faces hovering over him. Warmth was spreading across his lower legs. It felt like there was wool in his ears. The feeling was similar to the aftereffects of a hard shoot when he didn't use his hearing protection.

"I need a tourniquet above that knee!"

Nothing on earth could make a grunt focus like those words. "What...tourniquet? Wait..." He rolled his head forward enough to try to focus on his legs, but all he saw was a blur of gore. Oh, fuck. Oh, fuck no. That much red couldn't be good. Panic clutched at his insides. He reached out to his friend.

Rough hands released Velcro and buckles, pulling his pack away, and he dropped flat to the ground. His helmet thumped against a rock, but it didn't really bother him. The heat that was licking up his legs and rolling up his left side was bothering him more. He shifted on the ground, trying to get away from the burning, but it followed him, making him grit his teeth. "First Sergeant, what's going on?"

Duncan's rough face leaned over his own, making solid eye contact. "Chad, you got issues, buddy. Dodd stepped on a mine. Your left leg's a mess, but we're taking care of you. Medevac's on its way, but it'll be a few minutes."

Chad fought to untangle the words and keep focus on the face above. "Fuck. My legs?"

First Sergeant nodded. "Looks like just one, though. The side that was closest to Dodd. Your other one looks good."

"Are my nuts still there?"

First Sergeant grinned at him. "Well, I'm not going in to check, but from the outside it looks like you lucked out. You've still got your nuts."

Chad allowed himself to relax back against the ground. There were two sharp pinches in his arms, and the roaring heat on his left side kind of started to ease. The sunlight straight up above was hard to look at, so he rocked his head to the side.

Dodd's young face was surprisingly clean considering the mess the rest of him was in. His eyes stared unseeingly. Chad knew that wasn't good. "You guys take care of him."

There was a warm, soft wave blocking the blaze of pain from his side as it was tugged him into sleep. With a sigh, he let his worries fall away.

The next time he opened his eyes, he was in the hold of a Medevac. His stomach somersaulted as they surged into the air.

Chad jerked awake, clutching the rail of the hospital bed. His left hand banged into the other side, sending agony roaring throughout his body. Nausea twisted his stomach. The dream had seemed so real. Even his left foot was aching. The same images pestered him every night. Dodd, wide-eyed from his first engagement with the enemy asking about his rifle. Then Dodd in pieces. The doc told Chad he'd died instantly, but that didn't ease his guilt. It was his responsibility to train them up to be good Marines.

Sometimes, in his dreams, he'd be the one to step on the landmine rather than Dodd. And he was okay with that, because when he woke up he didn't feel nearly the same amount of guilt. He'd been a Marine for years. He knew what the risks were. Dodd had been so eager, just starting out his career. He hadn't deserved to die.

Over the months of being in the hospital, his images had changed sometimes. Since he'd reconnected with First Sergeant Wilde, he'd had flashes of helicopters landing on him. Talking to his roommate Swenson, his mind created scenarios of being mowed down by an AK-47. The way he died changed every night, but he always flashed to *his* injury just before he woke up. The counselor he talked to said that was pretty normal, and that eventually the dreams would fade. Yeah, okay. It'd been six months already and they were just as vivid as if he were there yesterday.

Squinting, he tried to see the clock on the wall. Zero two seventeen in the morning. Swenson snored away, undisturbed. At least this one hadn't been loud enough to wake him up. He looked down at his legs and was shocked all over again when he remembered the left one was gone. Every morning he was surprised it wasn't there, because it still ached. And itched. God, the itching was the worst. The docs said that would probably go away too.

Chad pushed himself upright on the bed and dropped to the floor on his right foot, balancing. The wheelchair was right beside the bed, but he tried not to use it any more than he had to. Pushing away from the mattress, cradling his left arm to his stomach, he hopped to the bathroom, catching the rails just inside. Avoiding looking at himself in the mirror, he did his business and hopped back to the bed, grabbing his robe at the end. Once he was covered, he dropped into the wheelchair. Using the heel of his right foot, he pulled himself out of the room.

Though it was ass-crack early, he wasn't the only one up wandering the halls. More than one insomniac avoided his eyes as he rolled down the hallway to the elevator.

One of the nurses looked up from her paperwork and smiled at him, used to his nightly wanders. He dragged close enough to steal a peppermint from the bowl behind the counter, then a second, winked at her and moved on. When the elevator arrived he pressed the button for fifth floor where the SCI ward was. Dragging himself down the long hallway with his foot, he peered into room 523. Duncan appeared to be sleeping, his gray head turned away from the hallway, but Palmer's bed was empty, as he'd expected. He turned down another hallway and pushed out through a glass access door. At the far end of the balcony, Palmer had parked his chair in his normal spot to look out over the hospital grounds. There wasn't much to see other than yellow mercury-vapor parking lot lights, but they didn't mind. It was one of the few places they could get away from the sights and sounds and smells of the hospital.

He parked himself next to Gunny. "Hey."

"Hey."

They didn't say anything for a long time. Chad's breath fogged the air. He pulled the blanket from the back of his chair to cover his lap. "You wanna share?"

Palmer snorted. "Fuck no. I'll freeze first."

The Gunnery Sergeant was only wearing a black t-shirt in the forty-degree weather, so Chad thought it was definitely a possibility. Though it didn't seem to affect the big, muscled Marine. Many a night this fall they'd sat out here just breathing, waiting for the next sunrise. Most of the time they didn't say a word. The conversation wasn't what they met for.

"They're kicking me out next week." Palmer sighed. "Knew it was coming, but didn't think it was going to be so soon."

Chad felt like he'd had the rug pulled out from beneath him. The Gunny could be a royal pain in the ass, but he still counted him as a friend. "North Carolina?"

Palmer nodded. "I guess they have an awesome VA down there that would 'better suit my needs'."

Chad winced. Basically, he was being shuffled away. "Hell, Gunny. I thought they'd give you more time."

Palmer shrugged his big shoulders. "Other soldiers need the space, I guess."

They sat in silence until the morning sun crested. Chad didn't sleep at all once they finally went back to their rooms. Though the Gunny played a good game, Chad knew he had to be upset. In the entire time he'd been in the hospital, he'd only seen him have a few visitors. The first was an aide who came to deliver his medical discharge paperwork. The second was his commanding officer. And the other few were grunts he'd trained and served with. All of the visits were painfully short.

Chad felt bad. His family irritated the crap out of him, but they were still blood. They still came for visits and brought cookies and news from home. Still kept him in the loop, even though he was a thousand miles away. They were already making plans for him to return to the ranch in Texas.

He honestly didn't know what he was going to do when he got out of the hospital. Ranching just did not appeal to him.

Palmer had no family. No parents or siblings or even cousins. Chad had made the mistake of asking him and had his ass handed to him. The only thing waiting for him at Lejeune was an empty rack.

After physical therapy, Chad rolled himself down to Duncan's room. Palmer was sitting at the window and a nurse was holding Duncan's chair as he transferred into it. Once she left, they all agreed to go out to the balcony. Palmer rolled out first, anger in every movement he made as he shoved his chair down the hallway. Duncan went next, pushing the wheels of his chair more calmly.

Chad got there last, of course. His left hand wasn't recovering as quickly as they'd hoped, so the thing was wrapped like crazy. They were talking about shipping him to Brooke Army Medical Center in San Antonio, where they specialized in burn treatment. It didn't help that he banged it in the night, sometimes undoing the work from whatever surgery he had last.

So his one leg didn't drag as fast as their healthy arms pushed on the wheels of the chairs. He couldn't wait to be fitted with the prosthetic. Then he could get out of the chair and use a cane or crutches at least. How sad was it that he was hoping for a cane.

It was cold outside, but nobody felt it. Palmer stared off in the distance, refusing to make eye contact with either one of them.

"So, what's your itinerary?" Chad asked him finally.

Palmer glanced at him. "I fly out Friday. A volunteer will meet me at the airport and take me to my old barracks. Collect my stuff. I'll be in a step-down program before I'm released completely into the world. Then I guess I'll get an apartment and stare at the walls."

Chad cringed in sympathy. The scenario was something they all could be facing. "Are you going to go to school?"

Palmer shrugged. "I've been an MP for years. Have no frickin' idea what I'd go to school for." He snorted. "Fuck, I barely made it out of high school. And I'd be older than everybody there."

They were each lost in their own thoughts for a while, because it was a reality they all could envision. Having no purpose in life other than to collect a disability check from the government. It gave him chills to even consider it. "We may not have an option."

Gunny shot him a furious look.

"You know," Duncan said, "we all have experience. We trained Marines for years. Military Police, no less. We have leadership abilities, decision-making skills, armory experience, and a boatload of other things the government considered us valuable for. No, we can't drive anymore or run around shooting people, but somebody has to need what we can offer. We just have to find them."

Palmer looked unconvinced. His dark brows were furrowed

over his black eyes and Chad knew that nothing was sinking in right now.

He was ashamed to feel relief that he wasn't the one leaving the hospital first. It had become a haven for all of them, where they'd been through similar things and experienced similar losses. Worry tightened his gut. Palmer had no family to rely on, very few friends and slim prospects for recovery.

But he knew guns like nobody's business.

The thought of never seeing his friend again sent a chill through him. At least here, Palmer could bitch at the two of them. It was a relationship, whether he wanted to admit it or not. So many Marines had not been able to integrate back into civilian life. And the suicide rate was even higher for wounded servicemen. John Palmer *so* fit the profile.

"We need to make sure we stay in touch," he told them.

Snorting, Palmer shook his head. "Yeah, okay."

"I'm serious. We're Marines, we stick together."

"I'll move on and somebody else will take my place. It's how it works here. You'll forget about me by lunchtime the day after I'm gone."

Chad shook his head at the man's stubbornness. "No, I won't. You're a brother. I won't forget that. Just like I won't forget any of the other men I served with."

Palmer stared at him hard for a couple of seconds, then turned to look out over the parking lot without saying anything. If Chad didn't know any better, he'd think the Gunny had just gotten a little emotional. He glanced at Duncan, who gave the tiniest shake of his head.

It was hard to convince somebody who had never been cared about that you actually cared.

Chapter Three

John refused to acknowledge the pain that rolled through him from Chad's words. Didn't it figure? He'd looked for acceptance all his life. The Corps gave him that for a while, and, sadly, being in the hospital even more so. He'd served with these men on the front lines, and even though it was an adopted brotherhood, it was more than he'd ever had before.

He felt pretty salty right now, though. He'd served his country faithfully, through all conditions and three deployments, and they were turning him out like a relative who had stayed too long.

Panic made his heart race and his hand slipped to his hip automatically, looking for iron confidence. But it wasn't there. Hadn't been there for almost half a year now.

Hell, maybe it was time to move on.

There wasn't a lot of stuff at Lejeune. Which was good, because he had no idea how he was going to get it anywhere. He'd say goodbye to some people and reminisce a bit, then be gone. If those meetings were anything like the few he'd had here in the hospital, they would be quick and final. The able-bodied grunts didn't like to see the wounded because it reminded them of their own mortality. Any one of them could step on a landmine or drive over an IED.

He looked at the watch on his wrist. Twelfth of the month. Three more days and he'd be out of here.

In a way he was relieved to be moving on, before he became any more attached than he already was. Chad talked a good game, but he'd forget him eventually too. The kid had family that appreciated his service and were already making plans to welcome him home, with a parade and everything. The Lowell family had made a concerted effort to always have somebody at the hospital every week. In spite of the trek from Texas, his parents came out every month like clockwork. They'd have a heck of a surprise when they came out this month. Their boy would have his leg back.

Genuinely, he was glad for Chad, but he couldn't help but be envious at his recovery. The damage from the Humvee panel landing on his own back in the IED explosion was permanent, and no hoping in the world was going to change that. Yes, there were drugs and trials they could try, he was told, but there was no guarantee. Yes, every once in a while his leg twitched. Oorah.

His dick remained a useless lump. It pissed like it was supposed to now, and that was it. No arousal even when he tried to imagine fucking a woman. Or, God, getting a blowjob. He'd deliberately tried to get hard several times with no result. He wouldn't be trying again.

All his life, he'd prided himself on being a good lover. It was a great cosmic joke that the thing he would miss most would be denied him.

Rolling forward in his chair, he looked over the balcony. Five floors up probably wouldn't do the job. Rather than killing him it would only injure him. Yet again.

Fuck.

Their rumbling stomachs eventually chased them indoors to find food. Chad left for his room and promised to be back in a while so they could watch Jeopardy together.

John hated the thought of dragging himself back up into that hospital bed. He was so sick of it. If the nurses wouldn't constantly nag at him he'd just sleep in the chair. He angled it near the window, facing the door.

Duncan turned Comedy Central on while they ate, but they didn't laugh. They were both dealing with crap and the chatter in the background sometimes helped drown out what cluttered their minds.

"If the three of us went into business together, what would we do?" Duncan asked, flicking the mute button on the remote.

John stared at him in surprise. "Are you asking seriously?"

Duncan nodded his head, running his hand through his too-long hair. It had gone grayer in the time he'd been here, John noticed. "I am."

John squinted at him and shook his head. "Hell, I don't know. Wheelchair test pilots. Medical disability collectors."

Duncan glared at him. "If you have to go out and try to get a job in three days, which you *do* have to do, I might add, what are you going to look for?"

The question aggravated John because he had not the foggiest inkling. "I don't know. I guess I would look at working for the city as a police or fire dispatcher or something."

Duncan seemed surprised to get a straight answer. "Huh. You know, that's actually not a bad idea. With your MP experience that actually fits really well."

For some reason, Duncan's praise eased some of his worry. Though he hadn't known him long, he trusted the man's opinion implicitly. If Duncan thought he could do it, he probably could.

Chad rolled in just then carrying a colorful tin box on his lap. "What's not a bad idea?"

"Palmer being a police dispatcher."

The kid's eyes widened. "Hey, I can totally see you doing that. Although you may have to unlearn the word 'fuck'."

John flipped him the bird.

Laughing, Chad rolled over to him. "Sign language, huh? That may be okay. At least the public wouldn't hear you. Here, have a cookie, sourpuss."

John peered into the tin. Obviously, Mrs. Lowell had been busy. He selected two chocolate chip cookies, appreciating that Chad had shared. He bit into one and chewed slowly, for the first time in a long time appreciating the flavor of something. "These are damn tasty, Lowell. Tell Mom she did good."

Chad grinned, his mouth full. He held the tin out to Duncan, but was waved away. Duncan looked too contemplative to chew anyway as he surveyed Chad sitting in the chair. "Chad, what do you see yourself doing three months down the road? When you've got your leg and are mobile."

Swallowing, the younger man sat back in his chair. "Well, I guess it depends upon how mobile I am with the prosthetic. I know I'm not going to stay in the Marines. Obviously. Desk job just doesn't appeal to me. As much as I hate to say it, I may go back to the ranch and see what I can do there. Mom and Dad would love to have me back in the house." He shrugged. "Not sure, really. As good a place to start as any, though."

Duncan nodded at his answer. Then Chad turned the tables. "What about you, Dunc?"

The First Sergeant crossed his arms over his chest, wincing. John knew it had to hurt to stretch the recovering skin that way, but he knew Duncan did it anyway just so he could hold his favorite position. Countless talks were given to new recruits when they landed in Wilde's company, he'd heard. Procedure, tactics, hygiene—you name it, they talked about it. And learned. Chad had told him he'd never had a Company First Sergeant more knowledgeable about all things tactical, procedural, statistical. He'd compared Duncan Wilde's brain to a computer more than once.

John hadn't served under him, but Chad said he had always stood in the same position. He called it his thinking pose. Personally, John thought it was a way for Duncan to appear more intimidating than he already did. The dude was big without flexing his biceps and chest. Duncan was five or six years older, but in their prime they probably would have been pretty equally matched in a bar fight. Well, before they'd gone to war and been kicked in the ass.

"Honestly, I'm in the same boat. Not sure exactly what I want to do. Or can do."

"Where are you going with this, Wilde?"

Duncan looked at him and shrugged. "Nowhere, really. Just thinking out loud. I've talked to a couple of my guys that have been discharged, and it's hard. They haven't been able to find a job. At least nothing more than manual labor, for those that are able. One is going back to school, but it will take time before he becomes productive again. Seems like there should be a way we can help each other out. We have too much knowledge in our brains to sit at home and vegetate."

John could tell the ex-Sergeant was still worried about his men. That was admirable, but ultimately useless. They would all have to find their own way in the world.

Or make a clean escape.

His hand drifted to his empty hip.

When he looked up, Chad was staring at him hard, all humor gone from his expression. "Whatcha thinkin', Gunny?"

"I miss my piece," he admitted, sitting back in the chair. It was the truth, too.

Chad's eyes narrowed. In spite of the fun-loving, good-ole-boy attitude, Chad was damn smart. It didn't take a genius to know that some fights were better given up.

He grinned at Chad. The guy had become one of his best buds. He couldn't worry him right before he left. "Chill, Lowell. I'm cool."

Chad looked away but he still had a frown on his face.

John couldn't help but wonder if he'd be missed at all. Yeah, they were friendly now, but once he left the hospital, these freaks would forget about him. They had their own lives to look forward to. Chad would be heading back to Texas and his ranch, where he had what seemed like thousands of family members eagerly awaiting his return. As for Duncan, yeah, he'd lost his girl, but he didn't seem too shaken about it. The feeling was coming back to his legs now, he was getting more PT and at the rate it was moving he'd be mobile within a couple of weeks. That took more of his concentration than anything.

Bitterness was a hard pill to swallow as he looked down at his own legs. They *looked* the same, damn it. Just starting to lose some of their muscle. Too many times to count he'd woken, rubbed the sleep from his eyes, sat up, braced his arms…and slammed into a wall. His legs were supposed to drop to the side of the bed and support his ass just like they had for the past thirty-four years. But it didn't work that way anymore.

He knew for a fact God had an evil sense of humor when his legs twitched. Duncan's legs did the same thing and he was getting feeling back.

John kind of half wished his own legs had been blown off, or chopped off by that damn door that crushed him. Then he wouldn't have this nagging, ridiculous hope that something miraculous would happen.

The sun had sunk below the horizon and the shadows were creeping in. Two more days and he'd be gone.

*****

Duncan wondered how John would survive in the outside world. He was surly about thirty percent of the time and downright rude the rest, so the general population probably would not welcome him with open arms. He was a true career Marine, from the attitude to the mouth, and it would be an adjustment for him to readapt.

If he even tried.

He'd seen John drop his hand to his thigh many times over the past couple of weeks, looking for his sidearm. And he'd felt his disgusted looks from the other side of the room as the doctors came in every day to measure the pace of the feeling creeping up his own legs. Duncan couldn't help but be happy at his progress, though he knew it hurt John.

In a way, he would be glad when John left, simply because he could enjoy his own accomplishments without being overrun with guilt. But as soon as the thought went through his head he felt guiltier.

Duncan knew only too well that he couldn't save everybody. If he had the ability to save even a few from the trials that he knew they were going to face, he had to try.

*****

Chad kicked their butts at Jeopardy that night, but he knew it was only because the other two were distracted. He had hoped that the nightly ritual of yelling out the most answers possible would help to lighten the atmosphere, but all it did was call attention to it. He depended on these evenings because when he went to his room, it was all he could do to keep from curling up into a ball and pulling the covers over his head. The PTSD flashbacks had gotten worse this week for some reason, and he didn't know why. The counseling group he went to didn't help much, though the counselor had spent some extra time with him recently, as if she knew he felt off.

The fact that his buddy was leaving probably didn't help matters, but he'd only been told that yesterday. That didn't account for the rest of the week. Maybe it was his unease with how Palmer had been acting.

On the plane ride from Germany, Chad had freaked. His sedation had worn off in the middle of the flight. When he'd roused to the thunderous noise of the huge aircraft, blurry eyed, he'd thought he was right back on the ground, fighting. Then he'd looked down and seen his leg gone, and his shit had disintegrated. He'd flailed and fought with the corpsmen, but it had been one voice that had brought him back. Gunny Palmer. He'd screamed at Chad to get his fucking shit together and act like a goddamn Marine. He could laugh at it now, but then it had been mind-blowing. Gunny had yelled at him long enough for the nurses to pump more crap into him to knock him out. When he'd woken, Gunny had been in the bay right beside his. They'd gone to different parts of the hospital, but Chad still saw Gunny occasionally being wheeled in the halls or in PT. It wasn't until they'd been there several weeks that he realized the Gunny was paralyzed.

The shock stunned him for a couple days, because he couldn't imagine the hard Marine living his life in a chair. It was just so wrong. Chad had promised himself that he would go look the man up as soon as he was cleared by the docs. As soon as his arm was safe from infection.

And when he'd found him rooming with his First Sergeant, though he'd been relieved to see Dunc in one piece, he'd been dismayed at the change in the Gunny. His entire demeanor had dimmed. Just looking at him, Chad could tell he was thinking about ending it. Probably as soon as he got out of the hospital.

When Palmer had disappeared out to the balcony that first day, he'd pushed himself closer to Duncan. "Is he okay?"

Duncan smiled, but it hadn't reached his eyes. "I think so. He's been talking to a counselor every day."

Chad didn't know if the counselor was doing any good, though. Or maybe Palmer just wouldn't allow them to help. Every day Palmer seemed just a hair more unstable. A bit more brittle. Last night he'd seemed almost manic, his dark black eyes blazing with emotion and his jaw clenched. Chad felt helpless against what he feared was coming. But how could he blame the guy? Honestly, suicide had occurred to him as well when some of the pain hit at its worst. But he hadn't entertained the idea for long. It was against everything he believed in, and he hadn't survived a damn land mine to blow his own head away. Or choke himself on pills.

Tonight Palmer was quiet, hollow eyed. They only had a couple more days together and Chad felt like he'd already lost one of the best friends he'd ever found in the clusterfuck of his military career. In spite of the totally opposite ways they'd been brought up, he and Palmer had a lot in common. He found himself lingering that night, waiting for an opening when he could talk to him about his fears. The counselors all said it was good to get them out in the open, but as the tension increased in the room, he wasn't so sure. He was on the verge of giving up on the night and rolling out to his own room when the Gunny broke the silence. "You've been stewing on something all day, Lowell. What's up?"

Chad didn't know what to say when he looked at him. He'd been given the perfect opportunity to talk, but his mouth didn't want to work.

"He wants you to promise you aren't going to go blow your brains all over Camp Lejeune."

Blinking, Chad turned enough to glare at Dunc, unable to believe he'd just laid it out like that. "Fuck, First Sergeant, don't sugarcoat it or anything."

Palmer snorted and looked between the two of them. "Is that what you two ninnies have been whispering about?"

Chad shrugged uncomfortably. "Can you deny you've been thinking about it?"

"No." There was no guile in his face, only flat acceptance. "Have I wondered about it? Yes. Have I wondered how to do it? Yes. Would I do it?" He stopped and looked between the two of them. "No. Probably not."

Chad blinked and looked down at the floor, more relief than he ever expected rolling through him. Emotion tightened his throat and he had to fight to keep damnable tears out of his eyes. He pinched the bridge of his nose and looked up at the gunny. "Are you fucking with us like you do everybody else?"

Palmer blinked and sighed. "No, Chad. I've worked too damn hard for too many years for this country to wipe it all away with an eight-gram piece of lead."

Tension eased out of him. Sincerity coated every word out of the Gunny's mouth.

"Okay. If you ever need anything though, to talk or bitch at somebody about something, you need to call us." Chad pointed at his chest, then Duncan's. "We're here." He rolled close enough to hold out his hand. After a long second, Palmer gripped his hand tight, shaking deliberately.

Some indefinable tension snapped inside Chad. He actually felt the release like a belt had been physically loosened. Palmer held his gaze and, for the first time, allowed Chad to see his relief and appreciation for his friendship. Nodding, giving a final shake of his hand, Chad backed away.

"I'll, uh, see you guys tomorrow."

Without looking at Duncan, he dragged himself out of the room, down the hallway, to the elevator doors. His eyes burned with tears. He blinked them away, determined to get to his room before he lost his shit. If Gunny Palmer had taught him anything, it was to keep his act together. Seconds dragged as he rolled down his own hallway to his room and shut the door. Luckily, he was alone as he finally let the tears roll down his face.

*****

"You better not be lying to that kid," Duncan growled. "Or me."

The scene he'd just witnessed between the two men had made his own eyes ache, but he was too much of a hard-ass to let himself show that emotion. Chad's heart was on his sleeve right now, though he was seriously trying to hide it. Duncan hoped he at least made it to his room before he broke down.

"I'm not," John said. "Chad Lowell is a good guy. One of the few actual friends I have. I wouldn't betray him like that." John glanced at him from the corner of his eyes. "Or you."

Duncan smiled at the admission. "Well, I appreciate that. And what he said goes for both of us. If you ever need absolutely anything, call me. Let me know. I may not know you as well as Chad does, but I consider you a brother."

John nodded and turned to look out the window. He coughed and motioned with his hand without turning. "I consider you the same. If you need anything, I'll get my lame, sorry ass up here somehow."

Grinning, Duncan un-muted the volume on the TV. That was a hell of an admission from the Gunnery Sergeant and there was an awful lot of estrogen floatin' in the room, so they needed the distraction. Duncan relaxed back against the bed, sighing as he stared at the beige wall. Just when Palmer got interesting he had to leave. It figured.

*****

The next couple of days were some of the best Duncan had ever had at the hospital and the worst.

The camaraderie between the three of them seemed more open somehow. They laughed more and talked more. Found more common ground. They all cheered when Chad stood for the first time on his prosthetic, then groaned in defeat when he tangled his feet and landed on his face. Chad took the ribbing like a Marine and got right back up between the bars, and by the time they left PT, he was taking a few steps on his own.

When the doctor came in the next morning to test his touch

response, Duncan made them all gasp by flexing his ankles, both at the same time. Exhilaration made him laugh out loud, more happy to be alive than he'd been in a long time. He'd been practicing in the dark of night, but hadn't been sure he'd be able to do it with people watching.

Then the morning came when John had to leave. The three men were all quiet, knowing that their lives were changing yet again. John seemed especially remote as he shoved his few belongings into his duffle and avoided their eyes. When almost a dozen floor nurses and doctors walked into the room bearing a single-candled cupcake, he seemed genuinely shocked. When he read the "We'll miss you, fuck you" note on the side, he burst out laughing.

Duncan couldn't remember him ever laughing like that, not in the several months he'd known him, and he regretted that it was only at the end of his stay that John had finally started to open up to other people.

John looked at those who had cared for him, his expression a mixture of gratitude and contrition.

"I know I never said it, but I appreciated everything you all did for me. I'm sorry I was such a pain in the ass."

They all joked with him and wished him well as they shook his hand and trooped back out of the room. Lacey was the last. She'd been with them the longest. She wrapped her arms around his neck and whispered something in his ear, making him laugh. He hugged her back, burying his face in her neck for a long moment. When they pulled apart, they both had tears glittering in their eyes. She pressed a kiss to his cheek and walked out of the room.

John sat back in his chair, looking like he'd just been shot. Duncan felt bad for him because John was just beginning to realize how much he actually meant to other people, and now he had to leave.

When the orderly came to wheel him out, Duncan rolled himself forward to stop beside John's chair. Reaching over, he gave the man a hug, slapping him on the back as he pulled away.

Chad wedged in on his other side and they reversed the process, holding just a minute longer while both men got control of their emotions. Duncan fought back his own tears as they locked arms, all three of them.

"This isn't the end," he told them. "It may be a while, but we'll get together again, and next time we'll kick ass."

"Oorah!"

The orderly picked up the duffle as John rolled down the hallway and out of sight.

He looked at Chad beside him. Slapping him on the back, he clenched his hand around the other man's neck. Determination settled in his gut. They would see John Palmer again.

*****

Duncan did PT as hard as he was allowed. When he wasn't in the actual PT room, he went through the motions in his hospital room. Feeling slowly moved up his legs. When it reached his knees, they decided he could try to stand between the parallel bars.

The first time was a flop. Literally. His muscles, even with the physical therapy, had wasted and they gave under his weight the first time he tried. They focused more on strengthening his quadriceps and the second time he stood, they held him. The therapist clapped and urged him to take a step. He did, then another, and another. It was strange because though he knew he moved his legs, he could only feel pressure. In order for his feet to move forward, he had to rock his hips from side to side.

But every day he grew stronger, and it seemed as if the more he worked his legs, the more the feeling crept higher up his thighs. Then the day came almost six months after the injury that the feeling was complete. The doctor plucked hairs all the way up his legs, making Duncan curse in happiness.

"It took longer than normal with these types of injuries, but you had a lot of trauma to recover from. Medically, I don't know if I need to keep you any longer. Your pelvis is strong and your last scan was clear."

Duncan sat back, shocked, but damn happy too. He'd been in here so long. Yes, the staff was fantastic, but this wasn't a life. It was time to get out and make his way in the world.

When he told Chad what the doctor had said that afternoon, his combat buddy visibly tried to be happy for him. Duncan knew it would be hard. Chad would be the first one in and the last one to leave the hospital. He'd gotten an infection in his last skin graft and was on yet another round of antibiotics. They were planning to send him to Texas for more specialized care now that his amputation was healed.

They hung like they normally did, shouting answers at the TV and trying to pretend that everything was normal. Chad left sooner than usual, though, and Duncan couldn't help but feel guilty. Nothing could be said to make it easier on him. Chad would get out of the hospital eventually, but Duncan knew from experience that it was difficult to see friends leave before you did. After John left it had taken them both a couple weeks to get used to the lack of his glowing personality.

Chad was strong. Solid. Duncan hoped he got out soon, too, though.

*****

A week later they were saying goodbye again, this time to each other. Chad's transfer to Texas had come through the same day as Duncan's medical retirement papers. It seemed like life was moving them on, whether they wanted to or not. Duncan's packed bag sat at his feet. The ticket to Colorado bought. They stood in the downstairs lobby, reluctant to depart.

With a sigh, Duncan reached out and tugged Chad into a hug, pounding him on the back.

"Take care of yourself. I'll call you next week, after you're settled."

Chad nodded, jaw clenched, as they stepped away.

"Hey"—Duncan cupped a hand on the back of his neck— "don't worry. This isn't the end. Go to Texas and let them fix up your hand. Then we'll get together again."

Chad sighed and grinned. "I will, Dunc. Good luck moving in with your parents."

Snorting, he shook his head. "I'm not moving in. Forty-year-olds don't move back home. I'm stopping for a visit while I find my own place."

Laughing, Chad waved a hand as he turned away, braced on his crutch. "Whatever you want to call it, buddy."

Duncan couldn't help but laugh too as he watched Chad walk back to the elevators, with hardly a hitch in his stride. As much as he hated to admit it, the kid was right. Calling it a visit was just splitting hairs.

He loved his parents dearly but as soon as he walked off the plane, the hovering started. His mother burst into tears when she saw him on his feet for the first time, and, he had to admit, he got choked up as well. Dad hugged him till he could hardly breathe, then pushed him to arm's length to look him up and down. "You look good, Duncan."

But as he headed toward the baggage claim, he could tell they were dismayed at the way he walked. Duncan gritted his teeth as he made his way through the terminal, conscious of other people staring as well, but there was nothing he could do about his gait. He'd only been on his feet a few weeks and he was still getting the hang of maneuvering the cane. Concentrating, he made sure he planted his feet securely every single time.

Dad snatched his duffle off the conveyor belt before he had a chance to and started for the parking area. "Let me go get the car."

"Nope, I'm good."

Actually, his hips were aching like hell and his back quivered. Just walking through the terminals today had been more exercise than he'd gotten in the past several weeks. A pain pill would definitely be in his future. But he wasn't going to let his parents know how worn out he actually felt.

Duncan settled into the guestroom of the house in Arvada. Though welcoming and comfortable, after a few days boredom drove him out of the house. He walked a lot, thankful for the smooth sidewalks in the subdivision. Melanie had shipped his personal possessions so he took a day to go through those. It made him a little regretful that things couldn't have worked out better with her, but everything happened for a reason.

The inactivity and lack of direction got so bad one day he consented to go to work with his father. As soon as he stepped into the family print shop, he remembered how much he disliked it. The smell turned his stomach, but he forced himself to hang out and pitch in. Helping his dad when he was a kid had been torture, and not much had changed. The metal clang of the machines kept him on edge. He couldn't imagine working here for any length of time. His younger brother Sam was there and it was nice to reconnect with him. Sam had taken to the family business with a passion Duncan never had and he was glad for it.

Robert, the oldest, was an accountant in Denver. He'd promised to come home for dinner on Sunday and visit.

They'd never been a close-knit family, but they were certainly close enough to call upon each other when they needed help. His parents had always understood that Duncan didn't fit in with them exactly. But they'd encouraged him in everything he wanted to do.

So when he started looking for apartments in Denver, though dismayed, they helped. He found one he liked and they helped him move in with little fuss. They seemed happy he was within driving distance. He promised to call if he needed anything.

Once he was on his own he began to concentrate on what he wanted to do. For a couple weeks he scanned the want ads, but nothing appealed to him. Though he'd lived a regimented lifestyle for years, he didn't want to work *for* anybody anymore.

He wanted to be in charge and he wanted to help other vets.

He began to plan.

Chapter Four

Seven months later…

The woman was freakin' hot! As she danced in front of him, all his worries about the service faded away. He was on leave for another forty hours and it had been forever since he'd had a good fuck. There was no way he was letting this opportunity pass.

When he asked her if she wanted to get out of there, she giggled and leaned down to pick up her lipstick from the table, giving him a perfect peek down her generous cleavage. Not that it was difficult anyway with the tiny shirt she wore. In the bars surrounding bases, there were certain types of women that came in for the uniform only. And he was good with that. He certainly didn't want any lasting entanglements.

Somehow the scene morphed into one of his old, empty apartments. Seemed like he was deployed all the time, so he never had time to actually furnish it. The girl didn't seem to mind, though. She led him to the one piece of furniture he did have, a king-sized bed, and pushed him down on the edge. Nudging him to lay back, she attacked his zipper, ripping it down and pulling him out. She had crazy long nails, but she was gentle as she handled his erection. Immediately, warm, wet heat engulfed his cock.

"Oh, fuck yeah," he moaned.

The woman was an expert. She teased him just the way he liked, jacking him long and slow, bobbing on the tip of his cock. She teased the slit on the underside with her tongue, then sank down his length as far as she could go.

John tried to reach down to touch her, but she guided his hand to her heavy breast, pressing into his touch. He was okay with that. Her breasts were magnificent. Hell, what was her name? He couldn't even remember. Amber? No. Kimber, that was it. Maybe. She fondled his balls with her second hand, cranking his arousal. Everything around him faded away as she pleasured him, wringing feelings from him he hadn't felt in too long. He tried to shift to take over, but she held him down gently. "I want you to finish like this," she whispered.

Hell, who was he to disagree? Relaxing into the mattress, he let her work his body. The combination of the wet heat of her tongue and the motion of her strong hand had him on edge within less than a minute. With another glance at her heavy, hanging breasts, he was a goner. Pleasure overwhelmed him and he shouted out, almost blacking out from his orgasm as he arched on the bed. She swallowed him down but continued to jack him with her hand, using his own cum as fresh lubricant. His mind blanked as he let the euphoria glide through him.

When John opened his eyes a few seconds later, he was surprised to feel wetness on his hand. He glanced around, not recognizing the dim room at first. He'd been in his old apartment, he thought. Reality slowly sank in and he winced. There was no woman.

Flinging the sheet from his body, he looked down at his receding erection and wet hand and belly.

"Holy hell," he muttered.

He'd just come all over himself. From a fucking dream.

Emotion tightened his throat as he looked again just to be sure. Yep, it was everywhere. He laughed out loud, then sank back on the bed as tears flooded his eyes and rolled down his temples. The aftereffect from the great orgasm made his muscles languid. He'd masturbated in his sleep. Unbelievable. He'd been out of the hospital for months and not been able to even get an erection, let alone jack off.

He laughed out loud and looked back down. Nope, it was still there. He held his right hand up in the weak morning light and watched it glisten. Regretfully, he reached to the bedside table for a handful of tissues to clean himself up, then hesitated. His cell phone was right there; maybe he should take a picture just to remind himself later. *No—that's too fucking weird.*

He hoisted himself into the chair and went into the bathroom to clean up, smiling the entire time. Though it completely creeped him out, he wanted to call Duncan or Chad to tell them what had happened. Chad was always going on about marking milestones and this was definitely a milestone. First orgasm post-injury.

He rolled into the bedroom to dress and noticed his cell phone was blinking. He hit the green redial button when he saw who had called. Excitement built in his gut as he waited for the call to be answered.

"'Lo?"

"Dude," he laughed, "you must have known I was going to call you."

Chad was quiet for a minute, and John knew it probably shocked him to hear him laughing.

"Is this Gunnery Sergeant Palmer?"

"Fuck you, Lowell."

Chad snorted on the other end of the line. "Yep, definitely Gunny Palmer. What the hell's up with you? I don't think I've ever heard you this excited. Did you get that security job you put in for last week?"

"No—well, don't know yet. This is something different. Better."

"Huh. I'm at a loss, brother. What's up?"

John blinked, suddenly attacked by embarrassment. Would Chad even care? Fuck it. He had to tell somebody before he busted his gut trying to keep it in.

"I just came all over my hand."

Silence stretched on the other end. "Uh, okay. Why'd you do that?"

"That's not the point," he growled. "It was the first time since my injury."

It took a minute for the words to sink in. "Oh, no way! Palmer, that's fucking fantastic. Congratulations on your messy hand!"

John laughed, just because he couldn't *not*. More than a fucking year since he'd had any kind of release. 'Bout damn time.

"Was she hot?"

"Ha! Well, she had nice tits, I remember that." He tried to remember the dream he had. "Totally don't remember her face, though."

Chad snorted. "Of course not. Well, I'm happy for you. Maybe now that your body has remembered what to do it'll be easier next time."

If John believed in a higher power, he'd pray for it to be so. "We'll see. So, what's up?"

They talked about inconsequential things for a solid half-hour before they hung up. John was in a euphoric mood, and he knew he probably sounded downright giddy compared to his normal tone. His body felt more satisfied and relaxed than it had for a long time. He knew it was completely psychological, but he didn't feel like a freaking eunuch.

Dressing himself in shorts and a t-shirt, he headed to the gym to take advantage of his burst of testosterone. He was actually excited to get on the machines. For the past six months he'd gotten disenchanted with even trying to look decent up top.

A woman on one of the stationary bikes looked up when he rolled in and gave him a smile. John was taken a little off guard because, for more than a year, he'd been a hurdle for people to work around. Ignored. Most even avoided eye contact. Had his demeanor actually changed that much with just that one orgasm? Hell, he didn't know. But when she drifted over to watch him do flies with the free weights, he talked to her. And relished feeling like a somebody again.

Leaving the gym an hour later, he marveled at how much his life had changed in the past few hours. And it changed yet again when he rounded the corner to his ground-floor apartment. Duncan Wilde leaned against the doorjamb to his place, a slender black cane at his side.

John jerked to a stop, shocked to see his old roommate on his feet. For months he'd lain in the bed beside his own, recovering. John had never actually seen him vertical. Hearing it on the phone and seeing it were two completely different things.

Duncan smiled, obviously relishing the surprise.

John couldn't help but laugh. Today, for some reason, fate had given him bounties beyond what he'd ever had before. As he coasted to his door, he looked Duncan up and down. "Didn't realize you were such a tall fucker."

Duncan slapped him on the back and went so far as to lean down and give him a manly hug. He picked up a carry-out bag from the floor. "I brought Chinese and beer. Open the door."

John unlocked the door and glided inside, cringing at the sight of his unkempt apartment. He certainly hadn't expected company. Shoving clothes off the couch and clearing trash from the coffee table, he wheeled one-handed from mess to mess, cleaning as much as he could. Duncan stepped in behind him and placed the bags on the coffee table, then sank to the couch with a sigh. "You weren't exactly easy to find."

John glanced at him as he parked opposite the couch. "Yeah. I wasn't wild about the apartment they tried to get me into. They wouldn't approve this one, so I left the program. If I'd realized you'd be looking for me I'd have given you my address."

Duncan made a face. "No biggie. I got it from Chad. He said his mom likes to send you cookies."

Embarrassment heated the tips of his ears. "It's the only actual cooking I ever get."

"Well, how about some more take-out?"

He unpacked the bags, lining up cartons in the middle of the table. John retrieved clean utensils from the kitchen and they dug in. It was only late morning, but for some reason the food tasted phenomenal. Or maybe it was the company. John was man enough to admit he'd missed his buddies. Phone calls were fine, but there was so much that wasn't easy to talk about on the phone.

Duncan cracked a beer and handed him one. "Come on, Palmer. You have to drink one."

"Why? I don't normally toxify myself until after lunch. It's a little early yet."

Duncan winked at him. "We have to celebrate opening our agency."

John squinted at him. "What agency?"

"The investigative agency we're going to create."

For several long seconds, the words just did not compute. When they did, a thrill launched through him. "Are you being serious?"

Instead of answering him, Duncan reached into his pocket and pulled out a sheaf of papers, handing them to him. It was a lease agreement to an office building in Colorado. The owner's names were listed as Duncan Wilde, John Palmer and Chad Lowell. He looked at Duncan in confusion. "Why is my name on here?"

"Because you're one of the partners."

John knew he sounded stupid, but he had to ask again. "Why?"

"Because you have experience. Valuable experience that the government gave you and I'm going to take advantage of. Can you still wire a camera?"

He frowned. "Of course."

"Think you can brush up on your surveillance techniques?"

"Yes." He shook his head, numb. "But I didn't buy any part of it."

"Well, would you be comfortable paying for a percentage of it? The caveat being that I maintain controlling interest. I'm not working for anybody anymore."

John was floored that he would even be offered the opportunity to take part in this. If Duncan wanted to run the company himself that would be fine, all the better for him. Emotion clogged his throat as he looked down at the pages again, and his name typed in bold on the top line beside those of the two best buddies he could ever remember having.

The thought of going into business with them and doing legitimate, needed work thrilled him more than the orgasm he'd had that morning. "Are you serious? Have you talked to Chad about this?"

"No, not yet. I wanted to make sure you were on board first." Duncan grinned. "I knew you'd be the more difficult one."

John snorted, glancing at the pages once again. He thought of what was in his accounts and retirement and knew it wouldn't be enough. When he rattled off a number, Duncan shook his head. "No, you're only buying a quarter interest. I'm going to maintain control of the business, but I want you guys there as partners."

They settled on half of what John had offered and he signed the business contract, promising to be in Colorado as soon as he could release his apartment and make travel arrangements.

*****

Chad looked up at the sound of a truck rumbling behind him. The inattention made his weak left hand slip and thirty feet of barbed wire sprang back into a coil.

"Shit!"

He flexed his left hand inside the glove, cursing his lack of grip. Yes, it was his weak hand, but it was even weaker than when he was a kid. Frustrated the hell out of him.

The familiar red truck pulled to a stop a few feet away and a woman got out. Chad lowered his head until his hat covered his eyes and swiped the sweat from his face. He should have known he wasn't far enough away.

With a sigh, he stepped carefully around the fencing materials, dropping the pliers into the leather saddlebag on the ground.

"Hey, Tara. What brings you out this way?"

As if he didn't know.

"Hi, Chad. Well, it's been forever since I talked to you so I thought I would just slip out and say hi. Your momma said you were fencing. Can I help?"

He frowned and looked her up and down. Her blond hair was curled, make-up on, nice boots and low-cut shirt displaying her boobs. Not exactly fencing attire. More like seduction attire.

"Nah, that's all right. I'm about done anyway."

She swayed forward and reached up to kiss him on the cheek. Chad let her, but pulled back when she tried to rest her hand on his chest. The smell of her god-awful perfume reached his nose. Even in the middle of a thousand acres of cow shit, it was enough to set him back.

He turned back to the fence line. If she wanted to hang around and watch him work that was fine, but this hole needed to be patched. He walked to the previous post, placing his left foot deliberately, and reached for the coil of fence. Barbed wire was cantankerous on the best of days with two good hands, let alone his. Finding the end, he pulled, slowly unhooking each barb from the coil behind it. It was slow, tedious work, and more than once his hand slipped.

Tara stood to the side, watching him. One quick glance at her face was enough for him to see the pity in her eyes. And the longer she stood there staring, the more frustrated and angry he got.

"Tara, why don't you head to the house and say hi to my mom. I'm sure she'd love to see you." *Sorry, Momma.* His mother would probably rather walk barefoot on hot asphalt than entertain Tara Johnson, but he didn't know how else to get rid of her. "I'll be home in a bit."

Letting the coil of wire spring back, in spite of all the time he just spent unwinding it, he turned to guide her back to the truck.

"Well, I don't—"

"Tell her we have a new calf from that black cow of hers. She was wondering about it."

Tara's expression brightened when she realized she could be the bearer of good news. "Okay, Chad. I'll tell her. And you'll be home in a little bit?"

He nodded, though he'd already begun fabricating an excuse in his head.

As she started the big truck her daddy had bought her a couple years ago and turned around, Chad wondered how he could foist her off on some other charity case. Before he'd gone to Iraq, they'd dated fairly regularly and gotten along well. When he'd come back, wounded and bandaged, she'd seen a kicked puppy needing care. It drove him nuts. She used to be an awesome girl, but now all she did was mother him and look at him with her sad eyes.

For the thousandth time he wondered if he shouldn't just go

somewhere else for a while. Get away from all the well wishes and concerned looks. He could get physical therapy at any VA. He didn't have to stay in Texas. His arm was healing and his prosthetic fit like a glove, giving him more freedom than he'd ever expected to have. If he put his blade prosthetic on, he could run for miles on a flat surface. Choppy ground was still difficult, but he would adapt.

As much as he appreciated Honeywell, Texas, and its residents, they still treated him like the kid he used to be. They'd given him a hero's welcome when he'd come home, with a parade and his name on the soldier's wall at the courthouse. But it was as if his combat experience was glossed over. To them he was still a kid who needed taking care of.

His parents were the same way. As much as he loved them, they smothered him. It had been months before they'd allowed him to do any work alone on the ranch. Once he'd gotten used to riding again, it had been easier to get away to find something that needed done.

No matter how many times he returned from chores unscathed, they still watched him as if he were going to break at any given moment.

His cell phone chirped in his pocket. Pulling it out, he smiled when he recognized the number. "First Sergeant, how the hell are you?"

Duncan chuckled at the greeting. "I'm fine, Chad. How are you doing? You get hitched yet?"

"God, no! Don't wish that on me. There are women crawling out of the woodwork down here to try to entice the poor, wounded Marine."

He turned and stepped over the fence roll. The horse was tied under a tree and looked content. Chad dropped down in the shade a few feet away and snatched a water bottle from the saddlebags, then allowed himself to lie back against the saddle. He twisted the cap from the bottle and quickly drank half the contents, washing away the pervasive Texas grit.

"They'd love a chance to get me to the altar."

"You're just too purty for your own good, Lowell."

Chad choked out a laugh, looking at the gnarled skin of his forearm that wasn't hidden by the leather glove. "Yeah, right."

"Maybe it's all that sugar you eat making you irresistible. Women love sweets."

"Whatever." Chad dug a piece of Double Bubble from his pocket, ripped it open and popped it in his mouth. "You're full of shit."

"Well, maybe they won't bug you so much in Colorado."

"Colorado. What the hell's in Colorado?"

"Me. And the business I'm going to open up. With your help."

Shock slowed Chad's chewing down. *He was actually going to do it?*

"And what business is that, First Sergeant?" he asked carefully.

Duncan snorted. "I'm not a sergeant anymore, Chad. I'm just a regular guy opening up an investigative-slash-protection service in Denver. And who's looking for a couple of partners."

There was silence on the line for almost a solid minute.

"Chad? Did you hear me?"

"Are you serious?" Chad's heart thudded against his chest wall as he waited for confirmation.

"I am. I already have a list of clients willing to hire us for several jobs."

He was floored. Yeah, they'd kind of talked about it at Walter Reed, but he didn't think Duncan had been serious. Chad should have known better than that. If Duncan Wilde said he planned to do something, then the man was damn well going to do it.

Possibilities raced through his mind. Selfishly, his first thought was that he could get away from all the wounded hero crap that followed him everywhere here. If he left home he'd be able to reestablish himself without all the childhood baggage.

And, more importantly, he'd be able to feel worthwhile, doing needed work rather than the busywork his parents had him doing.

"How much is it to be a partner?" Chad asked, not daring to hope yet that he could afford it.

Duncan named a figure that had to be incredibly low, but Chad jumped on it.

"When and where?"

Duncan sighed on the other end of the line. "I was worried I'd waited too long to get you to take a chance. As soon as you can get here we'll start. I went down and offered John part of the firm too."

Chad smiled."Oorah! This will be exactly what he needs. Did he say yes? If not I'll go down and kick his sorry ass until he does."

"Oh, he agreed. Took a little more convincing than you did."

"Ha! Well, I'm pretty desperate right now," he admitted. "I was just thinking about getting away somewhere."

"Well, now you have a place to go. You can crash at my apartment until we find you a place of your own. Call me when you have flight arrangements and I'll pick you up."

"I will."

Chad hung up the phone and let out a war whoop, pumping the air. He could get out of Texas and away from the smothering. His mom and dad would be disappointed, but he had to make his own way in life.

Rolling to his feet without even a catch in his step, he attacked the fence with new enthusiasm. The sooner he got it done, the sooner he could move on down the road.

One week later…

Duncan looked up at the office building. Big, metal, kind of generic and nondescript, which suited their needs perfectly. They'd rented the fourth floor of the seven-floor building, and they had room to grow. On the east side of Denver, the entire city was spread before them.

"I thought the Gunny would be here by now, " Chad groused. "I want to see inside."

He grinned at the younger man, enjoying his impatience. "He will. He's coming straight from the airport."

As if in answer to their words, a yellow cab minivan pulled up to the curb. The side door opened and a ramp lowered down. Within seconds John, glowering—true to form—rolled to the sidewalk. "I'll be back in a few minutes," he called to the driver. The stress of traveling domestic for the first time was written all over his lean face, and Duncan knew it had to have been hard dealing with the cabs and the airports and planes. Not to mention the public. But, in true Marine form, Palmer had gotten it done.

John wheeled his chair forward to meet them. Chad whooped and grabbed his hand, then leaned down to bump shoulders with him. "It's damn good to see you, Gunny!"

"You too, Lowell." He grinned. "Looks like that Texas sunshine has been agreeing with you."

Chad ran his hand over his chin and grinned. Duncan realized Chad actually did look healthier. Even the few scars on his neck were fading. The arm still had a good ways to go, but Chad seemed to be using it okay. As for the prosthetic leg, well, Duncan hadn't even been able to tell he had one on until he'd lifted his jeans leg to show him. The man moved as if he still had two natural legs, definitely easier than he himself did.

John looked healthier too. His face was lean and he hadn't shaved for a while, but his eyes were direct and strong. He'd switched to a more compact racing chair with slightly slanted wheels that responded to his hands as if it were actually part of his body. There was a frown on his face, but his eyes glinted with humor.

"So are we going to check this place out, or what? I need to start looking for a place to live."

Duncan held the door for him to enter the lobby. He waved at the security guard as they walked to the elevator. "Twenty-four-hour monitoring. There's a physical guard on duty at all times. The top two floors have some kind of medical research firm."

They stepped inside and he pressed the button for four.

"So, you said you had jobs lined up for us?" Chad asked, leaning back against the wall and folding his arms.

"I do," he said. "I have a contact in the Worker's Comp Bureau that needs a couple of cases investigated and another contact that needs records searched at the courthouse."

Chad grimaced. "Record searches? Really?"

Duncan grinned. "Yep. Hey, we're just starting out. In two days I have a lady coming in to talk about finding a son she gave away for adoption twenty-three years ago. We'll get meatier contracts eventually, but we have to start with small stuff."

The doors dinged and they exited the elevator to stand in an empty reception area. A broad door was open to the right of reception. They walked through into an expansive office with a small kitchenette in one corner. "This will be my office."

"So, where's the furniture?" John asked.

Duncan grinned at him. "Well, we have to go get it. Probably tonight and tomorrow."

"We've got customers coming in two days and the furniture hasn't been delivered yet?" John rolled out to reception and down the hallway where the other offices were located, sticking his head in each one. Chad and Duncan followed along. "Is there any equipment at all?"

"Well," Duncan admitted, "I haven't actually bought any furniture yet. Or equipment."

Chad's dark brows shot to his hairline and his jaw fell open. John, on the other hand, looked furious. "You haven't bought a goddamn piece of anything yet? What the hell have you been doing out here?"

Duncan smiled at him, not disturbed by his anger at all. "Well, I've been closing escrow on the building, filing the proper business paperwork for the state of Colorado, getting your forms to be certified as investigators by the state, opening a bank account, making contacts and placing ads. Oh." He reached into his breast pocket for a slip of paper, handing it to John. "And looking for handicapped-accessible apartments."

The heavy frown slipped away from John's face. "Fuck handicapped."

Chad laughed out loud and slapped him on the back. "Oh, Gunny. You've never served under First Sergeant Wilde, so you have no idea what you're in for."

Duncan pointed at a box against the hallway wall. "I did have some letterhead printed up."

Chad crossed to it and flipped up the lid. He pulled out an invoice. "LNF? What does that stand for?"

"Lost 'N' Found Investigative Services."

They all shared a long look. They didn't need an explanation on the title. They'd all *been* lost and found. With each other.

"Sounds good to me," Chad said.

"Yeah, I guess it's all right."

But the look on John's face said otherwise.

"What, John?"

The other man shrugged. "It's just cheesy. I mean, LNF, really? You name anything else around here, Duncan, as your partner, I want a damn say—"

Duncan held up a hand to interrupt him. "We're working with the public, John. We can't use the word 'fuck' in anything. Why the hell do you think I kept controlling interest?" He grinned at the two laughing men, genuinely excited at the prospects before them.

It wouldn't be easy building a business with men like them, but he couldn't imagine tackling it with anybody else. The way he saw it, fate had thrown the three of them together for a reason. It would just take time, a willingness to learn and dogged Marine determination.

Many would say that success would be next to impossible, but then they'd already returned from impossible. "Let's go shopping boys. We've got a lot to do."

###

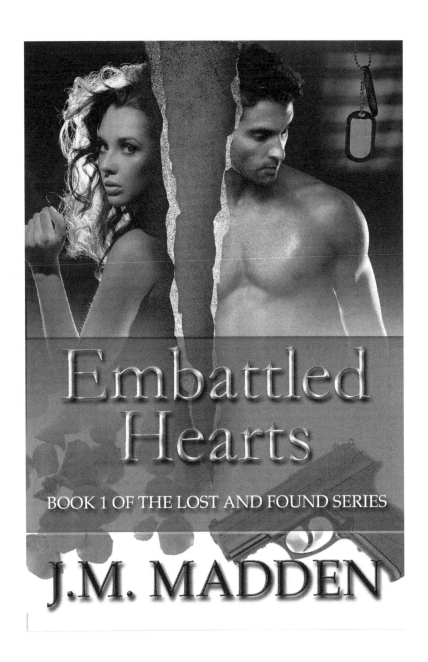

Embattled Hearts

BOOK 1 OF THE LOST AND FOUND SERIES

J.M. MADDEN

EMBATTLED HEARTS

BY
J.M. MADDEN

Acknowledgements~

To my husband, for being ever patient. I love you dearly.

My deepest thanks to Bruce McDonald for the insightful information that has made this book as true to life as possible. I sincerely appreciate your willingness to share. You've brought a dimension to the story that may not have been there otherwise. THANK YOU.

Donna and Robyn, you're awesome cheerleaders and perfectionists. You guys rock! Kally, thank you for the idea of the prequel itself, not to mention the tips and encouragement.

And most importantly, to all the service members who have given up any part of themselves to serve this glorious country, I thank you from the bottom of my heart for securing our safety and that of my family.

A Note from J.M.~

I've had the idea for this series for a long time. But I had a lot of doubts about whether I could convey the message I wanted to.

As we go about our daily grind, it's easy to forget that there are men and women dying every day as they fight to ensure our freedom. When they come home, no matter what shape they are in, they deserve our utmost respect and appreciation for doing the job they volunteered for.

Every soldier that has served overseas will carry some type of scar, either internally or externally. It's our responsibility, as their support, to make sure that those scars are seen as marks of courage, not something to turn away from when you pass them on the street.

I sincerely believe there is a soul mate for everybody. The external package doesn't matter when it comes to the heart. If you are the family of a wounded serviceman, I thank you as well, for being the rock they need through their recovery. The families are just as strong as the soldiers.

Thank you.

Chapter One

Shannon looked down at her rear tire incredulously. "Are you serious? Why today, damn it?"

Snow flurried around her as she stood there, hands on hips, and tried to decide what to do. She'd have to change it, of course. And call Duncan to let him know she'd be late. Grumbling, she stomped up the walk and into the house to change her clothes.

Twenty minutes later, she was positively livid. Not only was the brand new snow tire flat for no apparent reason, but so was the freaking spare. How the hell did that happen? She could hear her father's amused voice in her mind now, as he whispered, "Oh, calamity Grace." Little black rain clouds followed her sometimes and no matter how many pairs of boots she wore or umbrellas she carried, she always managed to get drenched.

Lisa pulled into her driveway a couple houses down just then and waved. Shannon heaved a relieved sigh and crossed the snowy ground to her. "Hey, neighbor."

The pretty strawberry blond flashed a tired smile. "Hey, yourself. Something wrong? You're usually gone by now."

Shannon waved a hand at the lopsided Blazer. "Somehow, I managed to get not one, but two flat tires sitting in my driveway."

Lisa scrunched up her face and laughed. "Really? Oh, Shannon, even for you that's impressive." She looked down at her blue scrubs. "Give me a few minutes and I'll drive you to the garage. Come on in."

Shannon followed Lisa up the walk and waited on her entry rug while she changed. "Wow, nice TV," she called. The flat screen took up a huge expanse of wall space. Looking around, she could see evidence that a man might be staying with her neighbor.

Lisa peeked her face around the corner, grinning.

"You like that? Boyfriend's last apology for being a schmutz."

Shannon laughed and shook her head. Lisa's up-and-down relationship with her boyfriend was more tumultuous than a Colorado snowstorm. "So why do you stay with him?"

Her friend's face closed down. "There are some things you can't change in life; who you're related to, taxes, the nasty boss you'd like to shove off a roof. And you can't choose who you're attracted to."

Oh, boy. Didn't she know it?

Lisa drove her to the garage, then back home an hour later. Shannon couldn't quit wondering aloud about the tire. "If nothing was in it, how did it get flat, then?"

Lisa glanced at her and shrugged, but Shannon could tell her patience was wearing thin.

"Sorry, I know I keep harping on this, but it's driving me nuts. I also had strange tire tracks in my driveway last week."

"Well, do what the mechanic said and drive the truck in and he'll check the other tire too. And maybe the tracks were just somebody turning around."

Shannon nodded and looked out the window. She needed to think about something else.

"I'm sorry I've delayed your sleep. Working swing this week?"

"Nah. Just pulled an extra for a friend with the flu. I'll be back on nights after tomorrow."

"Ah, was it a bad shift?"

Lisa grimaced as she turned into their subdivision. "Bad enough," she admitted. "A three-year-old swallowed two quarters and a nickel, an old guy came in with chest pain, and there was a car crash out east that was flown in. Not pretty. They all managed to survive, though."

"I don't know how you do it, Lisa."

The other woman shrugged. "You get used to it." Lisa grinned. "I don't know how you sit at a computer all day."

"You get used to it," Shannon retorted, laughing.

Lisa stayed with her long enough for Shannon to change the tire, then headed home. Shannon changed her clothes, again, and drove to the garage. The nice little mechanic had the truck ready to go in minutes.

"Nothing in that tire either, ma'am."

Shannon stared at him for several long seconds, and asked him to repeat that. He did, but it didn't make any more sense the second time. She paid the man and walked out to her truck in a daze. What would cause both tires to go flat that way?

Or whom?

Unease tightened her scalp, and she glanced up and down the busy street. Then she shook her head at her craziness. It was a fluke. Had to be.

*****

John gritted his teeth and clenched the wheels of his sport chair in his fists as he listened to the men blather on about how good their lives could be. He wished they would just shut the fuck up so he could hear Shannon in the outer office. She'd come in beautiful but frazzled two hours late and said her tire had been flat. That actually hadn't worried him as much as the unease he had seen in her eyes. She'd tried to laugh the incident off, but he'd been watching her for a long time. Everybody else accepted her explanation, but in his gut he knew something wasn't right.

Something one of the men said snagged his attention. Pictures? Really? He was supposed to be taking part in the meeting, but the proposal was so ridiculous he'd zoned out. He focused his attention on the two...men seated beside him. Were they for real? Yes, they were competent, knew the security business and had plenty of money to throw around, but at the bottom line they wanted the publicity of financing an all-veteran detective agency. His eyes flashed to Duncan's across the desk, and he was gratified to see his boss was as unenthused as he was, with his heavy arms crossed and his brows furrowed.

Time to end this farce.

"Are you fucking serious?" John snarled.

The men looked uncomfortable for all of two seconds, before

they plowed on with their spiel.

As if it wasn't bad enough they were disabled, now these yahoos wanted to publicize them? *No fucking way.* Even Chad seemed turned off. Texas was his home state, and he was the one who had pushed for this meeting, to talk about a possible expansion to Dallas. John personally thought that the Denver office was enough for now. They were busy, but not so busy that things slipped through the cracks.

John was relieved when the meeting finally began to pull to a close. The automatic cringe on Duncan's face and the way he'd shut down when he heard the proposal had said it all. How were they supposed to be effective investigators if their faces were plastered everywhere, as well as their disabilities? That was the part that turned his stomach. Why on earth would he want *more* people to know he was damaged? He could hardly stand the stares now. He had taken the online crimes section and the technology side—the bugs and wires the guys used every day—deliberately so he wouldn't have to deal with the public. To be offered money to flaunt their disability was just crass.

Chad, ever the laid-back Texan, deflected the conversation to a favorite sports team and Duncan told the men they would consider their proposal. John knew by the sound of his voice, though, that they would do no such thing.

The business was doing great, but he couldn't help but be resentful that he was not part of the detectives out on the street. Looking down at his worthless legs, he was once again swamped with anger. As a Marine, it had been standard practice to run for five or ten miles a day. Now he was lucky if he could get his thigh to twitch on command. It was historic if he could get a hard-on.

Although, he thought with a slight smile, it was happening more and more often when Shannon was in the room.

The first time he'd met her, more than six months ago now, she and Mrs. Harrison had been kneeling on the floor going through files. Shannon had straightened and arched her back to work out the kinks. She'd been wearing a cute little pink outfit thing that clung to her lush curves, but she'd kicked off her high heels. The lust that had fired through his veins caught him totally off guard. For the first time in six years, he'd gotten excited looking at woman's ass. Her legs were bare beneath the skirt. He sat stunned, soaking up her subtle beauty and the exhilaration of being turned on.

The women hadn't seen him yet, so he cataloged everything he could about Shannon Murphy. Mrs. Harrison had said Shannon was extremely intelligent and would be a wonderful office manager, but she had not told them how exceedingly beautiful Shannon was, with her petite little shape and curly, dark chocolate-colored hair laying gently on her shoulders. Shannon was a good bit smaller than the older woman beside her, but curvy, and had a husky laugh that gave him chills. His own lips curled up in shared humor, even though he had no idea what she laughed at. Without conscious thought, he pushed his chair forward to get their attention.

Mrs. Harrison noticed him first, and pushed herself to her feet, then urged Shannon to join her. John barely heard the introduction as his eyes took in the details of her face. In honest fact, she was not classically beautiful. Actually, "cute" would more likely be applied to her mobile features and wide-set hazel eyes. Her broad smile started with up-tilted lips on one side, then spread to encompass her whole mouth.

He held out his hand and was entranced as she pumped energetically. Without blinking, he watched for any hint that the chair or his disability bothered her, but she seemed almost oblivious to the fact that he could not stand up to shake her hand. For the first time in longer than he could remember, he had met a person that not by word or deed made him feel like less than a man.

Even her height made him feel manlier. She was tiny. In her bare feet, she was *maybe* an inch over five feet. With heels on, she stood about five-four. Before the accident, he'd been six-three in his stocking feet. Sitting in his modified chair, he was only a bit shorter than she was. And no shorter when she sat in her own office chair, which she seemed to do a lot when he entered the office. She seemed to sense that it put him more at ease, to be on an equal level. John appreciated her thoughtfulness more than she knew. It infuriated him and frustrated him beyond belief to be stuck in this chair, especially when he had to look up at men he could not tolerate.

The Texans stood to make their goodbyes, and John pulled his attention back, glancing at his watch. He was eager to leave Duncan's office and join Shannon for lunch. As often as he could he tried to join her in the break room. Even such casual contact calmed him, and made him appreciate relating to another person. They didn't talk about anything in particular. For the most part, Shannon carried the conversation, and he was content to just sit and listen. And wonder. It sounded like she had an interesting life, with her animals and her family, and the house she'd moved into last year. Totally different than his own boring day-to-day routine. She didn't badger him with questions about what had happened to his legs or try to dance around his disability. The only time she hesitated was when she told him she jogged occasionally. He knew by the reaction on her face that his own must have reflected a crushing desire to feel the hot asphalt beneath his pounding feet. Smiling softly, she had left the table, but not before she rested her hand gently on his shoulder. "Believe me," she told him softly, "you're probably faster in that chair than I'll ever be on my feet. Maybe you can join me sometime."

And, just that easily, she made one of his greatest losses just a bit easier to bear.

He powered out of Duncan's office. He didn't care if he was abrupt. They usually shook their heads at him no matter what he did.

Shannon wasn't at her desk when he rolled by, nor in any of the other offices down the hallway. His heart began to pound as he pulled up to the break room door and looked in the half window. There she was. Laughing and gesturing with her hands to Roger Stottsberry, one of the Night detectives. Roger had been coming in every Friday for Shannon's lunch since she started the practice. And John didn't blame him. When not at the agency, it seemed he just sat at home and stared at the walls. There was only so much brainless TV you could watch before you slowly went insane. It was hard to go out in public, both physically and mentally, and these offices had turned into a haven for the men who worked here. Duncan had let them convert one of the empty offices into a multi-purpose room, with a couple of bunks in one corner in case somebody needed to crash. There was also exercise equipment and a TV and game system on the opposite wall to help them relax. The refrigerator was always stocked with easy, microwaveable foods. John found himself occupying that room more and more. As did a lot of the other guys.

Every week the shift teams—Day, Night and Graveyard— got together for some kind of tournament, be it darts or Jeopardy or anything they could think of to be competitive. It built camaraderie between the teams and was a great way to blow off steam. At first they'd tried to separate into whichever branch of the military they'd been discharged from, but because there were so many more Marines than any other branch, it hadn't always worked out.

He rolled through the break room door and was immediately warmed by Shannon's broad smile. Any aggravation she felt earlier in the day had apparently faded away. The tension in his own body eased.

"I was just telling Roger about my niece naming one of my kittens Boohini. I had called him Houdini because he kept getting out of wherever I put him, and somehow she changed it around to Boohini."

That was kind of cute, and he chuckled along with them, before he wheeled around the table to the large Crockpot on the counter. His mouth watered before he even lifted the lid. Shannon's food was phenomenal. But by the time he got his meatball sandwich made and situated on his lap for the return trip, Shannon had gathered up her things to leave. He almost dropped his plate as she stretched behind herself for a cola, her luscious breasts outlined by the cloth of her peach-colored sweater. Man, she looked nice in that sweater. Dragging his gaze away, he situated himself at the table. She plunked the cola in front of him, threw her stuff away and told the men goodbye.

He watched intently until she disappeared down the hallway, curvy hips swinging.

Roger had his head tilted to one side, and his dark brown eyes were squinted in laughter. "Oh, so it's that way, huh?"

John picked up his sandwich. "I don't know what you're talking about."

The former Marine laughed and slapped his leg with his good hand. The molded right hand rested on the table, currently immobile. John admired Roger, because his amputated arm had been replaced with a state-of-the-art prosthetic that was actually wired into the nerves of his arm. It was truly a wonder to watch, because it was so lifelike. Even the skin tone was incredibly close to Roger's dark walnut color. It was seriously cutting-edge stuff. There were military medical trials going on with paraplegics and quadriplegics using stem cells and spinal implants, but John had chosen not to participate in them. If he'd had a family, maybe it would have been a different story.

Roger had leaned down to try to catch his eye.

"What, damn it?" John shoved his plate away and sat back in his chair, ready to fight. Adrenaline coursed through his veins, disproportionate to the situation.

Roger held up his hands before sitting back in his own chair. "I didn't mean anything by it. I think Shannon is a great girl. Why do you think I get myself out of bed so early every Friday?"

John narrowed his eyes and tried to breathe deeply. Was Roger interested in her like he was? He could understand some women would be attracted to him. The man wasn't bad looking, even with the shrapnel scars covering one side of his face and the prosthetic forearm.

And Roger at least had legs.

"I didn't realize you had a claim on her."

"I don't," John grumbled. That was the whole problem in a nutshell. He had no claim on her. He didn't even know if he wanted to claim her. Yeah, she turned him on, but what could he offer her? Certainly nothing long-term. What would an active, vibrant woman like her want with a broken man like him?

John tried to think of other things as he finished his sandwich, and ignore the ache in his chest.

*****

Shannon hated to leave the break room. She saw John so little, but they were all busier recently. LNF Investigative Services was expanding exponentially as more people learned of their ability and dedication to get a job done. Contracts were rolling in or extending out for the security division. The agency had gone from the three partners when they first started five years ago to almost twenty men now. Shannon knew that Duncan had stacks of résumés from other disabled vets who would love to work here. New ones came in every day.

Just this week they'd hired a brash young Marine that had been a canine officer in Afghanistan. Two weeks before that they'd hired a former helicopter pilot.

Settling into her chair, she began typing up Chad's dictation notes from his surveillance on the Malone divorce case. A couple of weeks ago she'd found him in the spare office hunting and pecking on the keyboard with his good right hand. He admitted that the report writing was difficult, because he did not have the same mobility in his left hand and arm he used to.

The scars that wrapped around his left arm showed that he had been burned terribly, and Shannon's soft heart had gone out to him. All of the men that worked at the agency had been in their prime when they were injured. Most were adapting to their injuries, but a couple still visibly struggled. As the only woman around, she tried to make it a point to bring hominess and comfort to the office. Several of the men had left their families to come to Denver to work for Duncan, because he had been a great Company leader. He'd evoked enough loyalty for several members to move from several states away.

Chad walked into the office and through the reception area to her desk, smiling broadly. Shannon could not help but return his smile as she reached for the candy container in her lower desk drawer. Chad Lowell had a sweet tooth that would not stop and Shannon found that the candy needed to be hidden or it would all mysteriously disappear. In jest, she had tried to hire him to find the missing candy, but he gravely told her it would be a waste of her money, because he did not think the candy was ever coming back. Occasionally, giant bags of his favorites would materialize on her desk. Chad was already turning into a great friend, in addition to a fabulous boss.

"Hey, Chad," she greeted. "What are you up to?"

Chad put on a wounded look that was totally ruined by his twinkling blue eyes. "I don't know what you mean. Why would I be up to something?"

Shannon laughed outright and put the plastic container at the edge of the desk within easy reach. "Right..."

Chad dug a couple of pieces of caramel out of the container. "We have an interview in a while. Boss man wants to talk at us before the kid gets here."

"Jennings?"

"That's the one. Duncan wants to see what we read from him."

Shannon gave a single nod, and kind of hoped that they didn't hire the recently discharged young Marine. There was something that nagged at her about his eyes. Almost as if there was a disconnect there and he seemed to be going through the motions to present himself correctly.

But it wasn't really her place to say anything. If he got hired, she'd do her best to make him as welcome as she did the others.

She saved the work on her computer and printed off the notes she'd just typed up for Chad's case, then attached them with a paper clip and handed them to him.

"Oh, Shannon, you are a doll. That would have taken me two hours." His pretty eyes lost their twinkle.

"It only took me ten minutes. And it was no big deal. I'm trained to do it. You aren't. I do appreciate you using the dictation machine, though."

Chad shifted in front of her and grimaced. "I don't like talking into that thing. Feels weird. Don't be surprised if I'm knocking on your desk again before too long," he told her as he slipped into Duncan's office.

John wheeled in seconds later as she put the lid on the candy container. He chuckled as he pulled alongside her desk, making her shiver convulsively. The man was sex on wheels, literally, and it was all she could do not to jump into his lap. A hint of his deodorant wafted over her. Shannon clenched her teeth in an effort to control her roaring response but it was always the same. And he seemed totally oblivious. Of course.

"Hi, John."

"Shannon. I see Chad's already been here."

She nodded and held the dish out to him, but John declined. His sweet tooth leaned more toward baked goods. Fridays she usually brought in some type of cake or cookies. She'd brought in his favorite today, German chocolate.

"Hey, I wanted to see if you could find a copy of an invoice for me."

Shannon sat back in her chair, fingers ready at her keyboard.

He reeled off the company name and the list of what he'd ordered, and Shannon frowned. "I just put a copy of this on your desk yesterday. You lost it already?"

John glowered, clamped his jaw and scrubbed a broad hand over his short black hair. His heavy chest expanded in a slow breath. He didn't say anything for several long seconds, and when he looked up, his dark brown eyes were calm. "My desk is pretty terrible right now. Maybe it is there. I'll look after I talk to Duncan. Thanks, Shannon."

He turned and powered his chair through Duncan's doorway.

"Lunch was awesome, by the way," he said just before he disappeared.

Shannon could not keep the goofy grin from spreading across her face. John very rarely commented positively on anything. Within thirty seconds she had gotten an "ok, I'll check" and a "lunch was awesome" out of him. That was a new record. Not that he was a grouch or anything. Well, maybe he was a bit on the grumpy side. It seemed like he was genuinely trying to be a little friendlier, though. They'd had to go through some growing pains when she was first hired.

There'd been an incident a couple of months ago when she'd gone off on him. She wasn't even sure what the original conversation had been about, but he had demanded some paper or another that she had already given him. John had said flat out that it was not on his desk. Shannon had to physically walk to his office and pull the paper from his overloaded desk before he believed her.

As she left his cluttered office, she'd snapped at him, "And you could be a little nicer about it, too," before she slammed his office door shut.

Since then, John had tried to temper his snappishness, at least with her. The men were another story entirely. If one of them did something wrong, John let them know immediately. But constructively. She had to give him that; he always yelled with a purpose.

Shannon strongly believed that his paralysis had darkened his already reserved demeanor. And she didn't blame him in the least. If Shannon were in his place, it would have done the same to her.

With his shorn hair, serious eyes and shadowed jaw, John's dour expressions seem to fit his dark coloring naturally. His heavy brows drew down when he was upset, and his olive complexion darkened. More than once, she had compared him in her mind to a swarthy pirate yelling at his crew, or a Bedouin chief directing his desert army. In her daydreams, though, the anger changed easily to lust.

And there was no wheelchair.

Not that being in a chair seemed to have slowed him down at all. He was such a dominant personality, and the chair was such an integral part of him, that she hardly even noticed it after a couple of days. She'd seen him race Chad down the long office hallway and beat him. She'd walked into his office one day and found him rocking backward on two wheels, with the front dangling in the air. It had scared her a little and she'd asked him if he'd ever fallen over that way. She'd snapped her mouth shut, because she hadn't meant to sound so informal with a man who was, technically, one of her three bosses. The twinkle in his dark eyes had brightened, though, and he'd grinned at her. "I have, but not in front of anybody." It was one of the friendliest interactions they'd had at that point, and the beginning of her infatuation.

The outer office door opened, and Cameron Jennings stepped into the reception area. Shannon forced herself to greet him with a smile. "Mr. Jennings. If you'll have a seat, please, I'll let Mr. Wilde know you're here."

He stalked across the office and lowered himself to one of the leather couches directly across from her desk. Shannon called Duncan to let him know his appointment was waiting, then turned back to her computer. She didn't know why the man across from her put her on edge, because he looked decent. Short dark hair, pale eyes. Lean body. In fact, he kind of reminded her of her brother Chris. The entire time she sat there though, she could feel Jennings' gaze resting on her. When she looked up, he would turn his head away. Very disconcerting.

This was his second interview. Duncan put every new hire through the wringer when he considered them. There were criminal background checks, interviews with friends, family and former commanding officers, psychological testing. There was a whole gamut of tests to make sure they were ready for whatever Duncan would throw at them. If they weren't ready, they would be nudged to seek counseling at the VA hospital. Shannon had hoped Jennings wouldn't make it through. The first day he'd come, he'd looked at her as if he'd seen a ghost, and spent most of the time waiting staring at his hands. Shannon glanced up and caught him glaring at her again, but this time his eyes didn't shift away. "Can I help you with something?"

Jennings shook his head. "No, ma'am."

Still, his eyes didn't shift away.

Chad stepped out just then to shake hands with the Marine and guide him into Duncan's office, and the tension eased from her spine. For some reason, Jennings' face took on a vitality that hadn't been present in front of her, and she wondered what was going on with him. For half an hour, the door stayed firmly shut. She heard raised voices once, then Jennings suddenly lurched out of the office and stopped in front of her desk to stare at her for several long seconds. Shannon sat back in her chair as his eyes drifted up to her hair, then back down her face. Her soft heart actually went out to him as desolation swept over his features and he turned to let himself quietly out of the office.

John came out of the office and stopped at her side. "Are you okay?"

She blinked, shook for some unknown reason. "That was very strange. Is he okay?"

John looked at the door, but the young man was already gone. "He will be. He needs to take some time, though."

Shannon made a deliberate effort to calm herself, but things kept replaying in her head. Strange was becoming a way of life recently and she didn't like it. John looked at her for a long moment before she waved him away. He rolled down the hallway to his office and out of sight.

She glanced at the clock and was amazed to see it was almost three already. Her stomach twinged with renewed anxiety at the thought of going home alone, but she pushed it away. Tonight she would put the truck in the garage, like she should have done last night. She just hadn't wanted to chill the kittens in the garage when she pulled in. Tonight, they would have to be cold, and hopefully she'd have full tires tomorrow. It was probably just kids messing with her.

At five o'clock, she cleaned her desk off and dug her purse from the depths of the drawer. She wrapped her muffler around her neck and slipped her dark green coat on, then made sure her gloves and hat were in her pocket. The weatherman had called for more snow tonight, and the temperature had already plunged into the twenties. Although that was nothing new for Denver, it was only the beginning of November. Winter had moved in early.

She ducked her head into Duncan's office. His close-cropped

gray head lifted when she entered. "I'm heading home, boss. Do you need anything before I go?"

Duncan seemed surprised as he looked at the clock on the wall. "Is it five already?"

Nodding her head in amusement, Shannon tucked her hair behind her ear. "A bit after, actually."

"Ugh," he grumbled. "The time just got away from me, I guess."

"Again," she reminded him. "Why don't you do something crazy, like go home early tonight? And do something other than work over the weekend."

Duncan chuckled, but he didn't promise her anything as she headed out the door. She wished he would take her advice. He was a good looking man, with his gray hair and lean face. His brown eyes seemed more tired recently, though. The man worked all hours, keeping abreast of every case they had under contract. Even when the case was complete, he followed up with and maintained contact with previous customers. Shannon was seriously impressed with the work ethic she'd found working there.

Maybe it was a Marine thing.

She'd never had close contact with anybody in the military and it had been an eye-opening experience listening to the repartee and insults that flew between the men. And the cussing. Jeez! But every word was said, or yelled in many cases, with a friendliness that amazed her. They didn't technically have rank in the office, although there was a hierarchy of power. Everybody deferred to Duncan, as was appropriate for the owner of the business. Chad and John had both been sergeants and were next on the list. But even with the rest of the guys, she could definitely tell the leaders from the followers.

She retrieved her Crockpot and cake pan from the break room, and turned to leave, but didn't see John stopped in the doorway. Her toe caught on the edge of his wheel. She flailed, trying to maintain her balance and hang onto the Crockpot and lid, the trailing electrical cord, her purse and cake pan in the opposite arm. She gasped as her purse slipped off her shoulder to land on her forearm, which made the lopsided cake pan tip over.

John snatched the heavy pot out of her left arm, unburdening her. The lack of weight itself was enough to overbalance her in the opposite direction, but she clamped everything to her body and righted herself. Immediately, she could feel her cheeks burn in humiliation. *Good God, you almost landed on your ass with your legs in the air.*

John tried, and failed, not to laugh. She could see it in his eyes. He attempted to pass it off as a cough, but Shannon knew better. In the six months she had been at the agency, she could count on one hand the number of times she had heard him let it all out. It was a very distinctive bass rumble. She allowed herself to sag back against the doorjamb and disintegrate into giggles. John laughed with her, and it was the most amazing thing she'd ever heard.

That was how Chad found them a few moments later, with John shaking his head and Shannon wiping tears from her cheeks.

"What did I miss?"

Shannon giggled, one hand over her mouth. "Chad, did I ever tell you my middle name was Grace?"

John let out a roar of laughter, even as he turned his chair toward the elevator.

"Come on, Grace, let's get you to your car."

Shannon followed obediently, trying not to let the act mean too much to her needy emotions. He was just escorting her to her car, not offering her anything more.

They were both quiet on the long ride down in the elevator, but Shannon knew she was still smiling. It was nice being with him, and having his attention centered on her for a few moments.

"Is your middle name actually Grace?" he asked finally.

Nodding her head, Shannon pulled her hat out of her coat pocket, tugging it over her head one-handed.

"I swear. It was the bane of my existence, because it's so totally opposite of how I actually am."

John shook his dark head, and Shannon was ecstatic for having brought some humor into his day. Walking through the doors in the lobby, she was also pleased she had worn her heavy coat to work that day. The temperature may have been in the twenties, but the wind chill dropped it at least fifteen degrees. She frowned at John.

"I can take it from here," she told him, and reached for the pot.

John wheeled around her and shot toward the parking lot. "C'mon, Shannon."

"John," she warned, "you're only wearing a t-shirt. I'm clear in the back. You'll freeze out here."

"Not if you hurry up, damn it."

Shannon shut her mouth and jogged after him as he dodged vehicles to get to her white Blazer in the back. There was no hesitation on his part, and Shannon shouldn't have been surprised he knew exactly where she parked. John always seemed to know too much.

She dug her keys from her coat pocket and rushed ahead of him to unlock the doors.

"Don't slip on the ice, Grace," she heard him mutter.

Daring fate, she smiled at him over her shoulder, not too flirtatiously, she hoped, as she crossed the last few feet. No calamity befell her, and Shannon mouthed a silent "thank you" to the heavens. She threw her purse in the backseat, tossed the empty cake pan on the passenger side floorboard, and turned to take the crock pot from John's hands. She took a minute to glance at her full tires.

"You have a spare, right?"

She nodded at him, and forced her smile to stay unconcerned.

"Thank you so much for helping me. Now, you better get inside before you catch a cold."

John tipped his beard-shadowed chin towards the vehicle. The man acted as if he wore a parka rather than a thin blue t-shirt. Although if she had a chest like his to show off, she'd probably do the same thing. "Make sure it starts and I'll go."

Shannon slammed the passenger door shut, then scrambled to the driver's side. The hardy little truck started immediately, and Shannon gave John a thumbs-up. With a wave, he turned the wheelchair and started back across the snowy lot. Against her will, her eyes followed him as he wove through cars and finally rolled into the front lobby and disappeared.

What a fascinating man.

Shannon flicked the heat on, sat back in the seat and waited for the vehicle to warm up. Three seconds after he was gone and she was already wondering what he'd be doing this evening. She knew he was single. Most of the guys were.

But prying details out of John Palmer was like pulling teeth. He very rarely told her anything about himself. She knew John had served in Iraq, and she knew he and Duncan had had very similar crush injuries. Duncan's had just been more recoverable. Shannon could not build up the courage to ask John how extensive his injuries were. Wondering whether or not he could operate fully as a man bothered her constantly.

Not that it really made a difference. She had already decided that she would take whatever John was willing to give. Friendship, romance, good sex.

Even if it was just a grumpy "hello" in the hallway.

She slipped the car into gear and turned north, toward home. The roads were not as bad as she first thought. The snow was only blowing right now, making it look worse than it actually was. Later in the week, they were supposed to get the better part of a foot, which was thrilling. It would be the most they'd had since last spring.

Shannon turned left at the intersection of Poindexter and Cherry Creek, smiling. Winter was her favorite time of year in Colorado. The scenery was so pristine and Christmas was her favorite holiday. Yes, sometimes things could be difficult, but those that didn't like the challenge moved away.

Five minutes later, she pulled into the drive of her house. The little ranch blended in with the rest of the neighborhood, and Shannon thanked her stars once again that she had listened to her friend Stacy when she told her about it. Stacy's mother had happened to be good friends of the Johnsons who had lived in the house, and knew they wanted to sell. Mr. Johnson had lung issues, and they wanted to move to Arizona.

Shannon loved the proximity of the house to work, and the interior floor plan, which was wide open with hardwood floors. The kitchen was well equipped, and it was a three-bedroom, which gave her plenty of space to spread out. The garage was just one car, but considering that was all she had at the moment, it worked out fine. The best part about the house was that it had already been modified. Her brother Chris had lived with her several months, and she still looked for him when she entered the house, even though he'd left for his new job in Florida months before.

Shannon pushed the button on the opener and pulled in. She hugged the exterior wall to the left. Pickle and the kittens were in a large box next to the entry door into the kitchen. The four five-week-old kittens watched her curiously as she lugged things from the car to the kitchen, meowing pitifully when they did not get the attention they thought they deserved.

"You guys are noisy," Shannon told them firmly. "What do you want?"

Boohini, the largest black kitten, dug his claws into the cardboard box, trying desperately to get to her. Shannon scooped him up and cuddled him under her chin as she sorted through mail.

Something caught her attention beside her. The trash can was almost full, and right on top was a bright red and blue Pepsi can. Standing upright. Shannon felt goose bumps rise on her skin.

She hadn't had an actual Pepsi in several years. There wasn't even any in the house. She always drank Diet instead. And she had cleaned the kitchen top to bottom yesterday.

The can was not hers.

Dropping her head, she tried to look around the room from under her lashes. Nothing else appeared to be out of place. She tiptoed to the garage door and dropped the kitten back into the box, then crept back through the kitchen and leaned out slightly. She peeked through the living room entryway, but nothing caught her eye there. Pulling a heavy butcher knife out of the drawer beside her, she balanced it in her hand. She wished her gun were closer. Heart pounding heavily in her chest, she crept around the corner into the living room, knife held out in front of her. She tried to feel if anybody was in the house, but she had no sense that anybody was.

As she crept across the living room floor, thoughts of a horror flick she had seen several months ago flitted through her mind. She could only assume it was because of the anxiety she was feeling. Still, she tried to be extra vigilant as she peered behind doors and into closets.

She didn't find anything.

Had she imagined the can? Maybe she drank the cola and just didn't remember. That seemed like a more likely excuse than somebody being in her house.

Certainly, it couldn't be Mike. He was still in jail.

Right?

Shannon had decided that the house was clear when her phone rang, re-energizing her fear. Her heart thudded as she tried to control her breathing, but her voice quivered when she snatched up the handset.

"Hello?"

"Shannon? You okay?"

Unaccountably, her eyes filled with relieved tears when she heard John's clipped voice. She had no idea why he'd called, but she didn't care. His voice was safety to her.

Shannon took a deep breath and cleared her throat. "Hey John. What's up?"

"You were acting a little off at work today. Are you okay?" he repeated, more forcefully.

Shannon swiped her hair off her forehead and tried to gather her thoughts. "Yeah, I'm fine. Just a bit spooked. That's all."

"Why are you spooked?"

"Well, it's going to sound stupid. I, uh, found a Pepsi can in the trash. And I haven't drunk a Pepsi for years. Only Diet. Don't even keep it in the house."

There were several long beats of silence on the other end of the line, and Shannon wondered if John had hung up on her.

"Shannon, are you sure? You didn't buy it for somebody

else?"

She nodded her head emphatically, even though she knew he could not see her. "Absolutely. I wouldn't have said anything if I wasn't sure."

"Okay," he said finally. "I'll be there in five minutes."

"Oh, John, no. That's all right."

But the receiver in her hand was already dead.

Chapter Two

Duncan ran his hand over his face and rubbed at his eyes, trying to clear away the fuzziness. He needed to get this email done while it was still fresh in his mind.

The men from Texas had been polite, but their proposal had left much to be desired. Hell, it had made him grit his teeth most of the time. As much as he wanted to help other vets, he wanted no part of the circus he knew it would turn into down there. Honestly, these guys would leave and probably start their own service, which was fine. They could deal with the mess.

He finished the "Thanks, but no thanks" email and rocked back in his chair, trying to find a kinder position for his hip. His gaze automatically zeroed in across the room. The three foot by four foot whiteboard across from his desk was full of names and colors, identifying where everybody was assigned at the moment, how long they were projected to be on project and every other pertinent detail he might need to remember. It was still a difficult machine to drive.

The whiteboard was one of Shannon's ideas, tossed to him when he'd lost yet another legal pad and had been scrambling for information. But if the company kept growing the way they were, he was going to outgrow this one and have to line the walls.

He looked at the Jennings file on his desk. Until the kid looked for the help he needed, Duncan would not, *could* not, take him on. The men that worked here were damaged. Period. Both physically and mentally. But they were all taking steps to make their lives better, either dealing with the VA or finding alternative counseling.

Cameron wasn't doing either, though he sure needed to be.

Pushing from the desk, Duncan planted his feet and stood, bracing himself against the hardwood. Blood flowed down through his thighs and he winced at the pins and needles. Though it hurt like a bitch, he needed to move around more often. Today he'd been sitting way too long.

Picking up his cane, he stepped to the glass window behind his desk and looked out. Snow streaked across the streets and he shivered. Without even stepping outside he knew the wind would cut like a bitch.

Movement drew his eye down the street. A familiar dark figure shuffled along the sidewalk, head into the wind. He'd seen the man before. Denver had its fair share of homeless downtown, but out here in business area, there weren't as many. Not as many places to curl up at night or get food.

He wondered when the man had last eaten. Or slept.

Leaving his office, he headed to the break room to scrounge through the refrigerator, dropping an apple and bottle of water into a shopping bag. He grabbed two of the pre-packaged sandwiches from the freezer and threw them into the microwave for two minutes. While he was waiting, he went to the multi-purpose room. There were a couple of cotton blankets in the cupboard. He grabbed one and returned to the break room to stuff it into the shopping bag. Then he tossed the sandwiches into the folds of the blanket to stay warm.

Locking the office, he made his way downstairs and through the lobby. His truck was stone cold when he got in, but he didn't give it a chance to warm up before he took off. He didn't want to lose him.

When he turned down the street, the man was still shuffling along. Traffic was minimal, so Duncan pulled along the opposite curb beside the man as he walked. "Excuse me."

The man continued to walk as if he hadn't even heard Duncan.

"Hey, buddy!"

Finally, the man paused and turned toward his truck. Duncan held the bag out, but the man made no move to take it. He wore a hooded sweatshirt that covered his face, and his hands were shoved deep in his pockets. Just as Duncan noticed this, though, the man pulled them free and backed up a step.

"I'm not going to hurt you." Duncan swung the bag in his

fingers and dropped it to the man's feet. "There's a sandwich and a blanket in there. Do you need a ride somewhere?"

The man didn't say anything, and didn't move to pick up the bag. The wind gusted and he shuddered, but he still didn't move.

Duncan waited for a minute, then just pulled away. When he looked in the rear-view mirror, the man's hood followed his departure. It wasn't until Duncan had almost lost him from sight that the man stepped forward and picked up the bag.

*****

John called himself ten kinds of fool as he tapped a finger on the cell screen and slid it into his pocket. He'd known something was up with Shannon. He'd seen the worry in her brittle smile as she tried to reassure him. Reassure *him*. When she was the one unsettled.

John tossed a few items into his chair bag then leaned down into the front closet safe and pulled out his M9 Beretta. The shoulder holster was folded neatly on top of the safe and he slipped it on. It was a struggle to keep his mind clear of memories as he checked the clip and the action of the gun, then shoved it in the holster. Since he was normally in the office, chances to carry his gun were few and far between. He pulled his leather jacket over top of everything.

Adrenaline pounded through his blood as he hurried down the sidewalk. It was so cold outside, the wheels of his chair slipped as he tried to stop, and he scuffed the side fender of his new black F-150. *Fuck!* He waited impatiently for the hydraulic pad to level out, then rolled on. He pressed the button to lift himself inside and seal the door. He set the automatic clamps onto his wheels and twisted the key. The throaty engine cranked immediately. He'd only been at the apartment a few minutes when he had decided to call Shannon. The heater even pumped out lukewarm air when he flicked it on.

Shannon's house was just a few streets over from his apartment building, less than two miles away. John gave little regard to the speed-limit signs as he passed them. He'd sensed that something was wrong by the quiver in her voice when she'd answered the phone. Very little shook Shannon. Even his typical glowing personality hadn't put her off. She was always as cheerful and upbeat as that very first day he'd met her.

The fact that something had shaken her tonight was enough to make him come out in twenty-degree weather to check on her.

Within just a couple of minutes, he pulled onto her block. Automatically, his eyes began to scan the cars on the street, looking for anything out of the ordinary. A dark green Range Rover passed him, but John knew it was the neighbor just a few houses down the street. His observation was confirmed when the vehicle pulled into the drive, then disappeared into the attached garage. No other cars were on the street.

John pulled into Shannon's driveway and turned off the truck. He sat for several long moments and observed what he could of her house and surrounding area. He unlocked his chair and pressed the door release. Shannon's vehicle was apparently in the garage.

John pushed himself up the handicapped access ramp, surprised at the convenience. Why she even had it on her house, he didn't know.

Shannon opened the door before he had a chance to knock. She still wore her office clothes, but she had taken the barrette out of her chocolate-colored hair. It swung freely now to the side of her face, hiding part of her expression.

"You didn't have to come over, John. It's probably nothing."

Rolling inside the entryway, John surveyed what he could see of the living room. It was neat, and picked up. Uncluttered. Easy to see if something was out of place.

"Show me the can."

Her gaze had latched onto the shoulder holster and gun, but she turned and wove her way through the house to the kitchen at the back. The connecting garage door stood open, letting in chilly air, as if she had been interrupted in her routine. Shannon motioned to the white trash can in the corner, near the beginning of the counter. There were miscellaneous items in the can, which filled it about halfway. Placed conspicuously on top of the trash was a Pepsi can, sitting vertically. Almost as if somebody wanted it to be seen.

"Did you touch anything in here? Did you touch the can?"

Shannon shook her head emphatically. "It was exactly like that when I got home."

John pulled the digital camera out of his chair bag and began to take pictures. Then he snapped on a pair of rubber gloves and opened a paper bag. Holding the can very carefully by the rim, he dropped it down into the bag, then sealed it with red evidence tape.

"I'll send this into the lab first thing in the morning," he promised. "But it'll be a while before we hear anything back."

Shannon nodded her head as if she already knew what he said was true. "Tell them to check the Ohio State Penitentiary database, specifically against an inmate by the name of Michael Gerbowski."

John's dark eyes narrowed in on her. "Do you know who did this?" he demanded.

Shannon rubbed her arms up and down, and clasped her elbows. "No, I don't know who it is that put the can here. Years ago, though, I had a problem with a stalker. I just want to make sure he's still where he's supposed to be."

John nodded his head. "Did you check the rest of the house?"

"Yes. Nothing else seems out of place. The doors were all locked when I got home and the windows latched. I wouldn't mind if you checked, though. Maybe I missed something."

John took her at her word and rolled away. Shannon heard him enter the living room, then he was quiet. The rubber wheels on the chair made no sound on the hardwood floors.

She closed her eyes for a moment and felt the tension ease in her shoulders. Just the knowledge that John was in the house eased her mind. She prided herself on not needing anyone for anything, but having a strong man in the house was a nice change.

She turned to the refrigerator to look for something for dinner. Nothing appealed to her. She was too on edge. Maybe John would see something she hadn't on her walkthrough. There were no forced doors or windows. Nothing moved out of place. She was too paranoid to keep a key hidden outside anywhere. She had not the slightest idea how the intruder had gotten in.

Snatching a container of homemade noodles out of the fridge, she tried to think rationally. The only people who had a key to her house were her parents and sister, several hundred miles away, and her brother, a thousand miles away. Lisa had one in case Shannon ran down to her sister's for the weekend or something, but she hadn't asked her to watch the house recently. She also had one taped to the inside of her desk drawer at work, but that was only because she tended to lock herself out of the house.

She thought of the tracks in her driveway and the flat tires. Those had been strange, too.

John rolled silently into the kitchen. Shannon's gaze stalled on his flexing biceps before she dragged it away.

"Did you find anything?" she asked, making her voice firm.

John shook his dark head from side to side. The normal glower was even deeper than usual, and his mouth was tight. "Doesn't mean anything, though. I've never been in your house, so I don't know if anything is out of place or not. And the windows and doors are secure, like you said."

Shannon nodded and stared sightlessly at the door of the white refrigerator. She'd known he wouldn't find anything.

The kittens meowed piteously. Boohini looked up at her reproachfully. She reached down and scratched his head apologetically, then turned back to John.

"I'm sorry I dragged you out in this crappy weather. I probably could have done the same thing if I had been thinking better. It just shook me, is all." She told him about the tracks in her driveway earlier in the week, and his glower deepened.

"And you had a flat tire this morning?"

She shook her head. "No, I had two. My spare was flat as well."

Shannon watched all expression leave his face. It was as if a curtain blanked everything out. For some reason, that worried her more than the glower.

"So that's why you were worried today?" He rolled toward her and stopped fairly close. "I would probably be shaken too, especially if there was a history there. How long ago did Gerbowski get put away?"

Shannon leaned her butt back against the oven door and swallowed heavily. Just on the off chance something did happen, he probably needed to know the details. "About ten years ago now. I was actually in college with him at Ohio State. Business majors. We went on two dates, and things felt really weird, so I told him no when he asked me again. That made him mad, and things got crazy. He would show up at my regular hangouts, and try to put me on the spot, pretending we were boyfriend and girlfriend in front of my friends. He managed to get a credit card issued with my name changed to Shannon Gerbowski, which he hung on the wall we found later. He took pictures of me and lined the ceiling of his bedroom with them. So many things. The stalking finally culminated in an abduction attempt with a gun. He has two years before he can go up in front of a parole board."

She waved a hand at the trash can. "This is the kind of stuff he would do. Leave little mementos to let me know he had been there. And it's the kind of cola he would drink."

When she peered at John's face, she was surprised to see it was contorted by fury. "Why didn't somebody do something about it?" he snapped.

Shannon blinked in surprise. "Well, they did, eventually. But Ohio had very few laws on the books at that time that applied to stalking. They couldn't do much until the gun came into play. Believe me, my family did everything they could."

She dared to reach out and rest her hand on his granite-hard deltoid. All of his muscles were tensed and solid, and he still had a frown on his face. He glanced at her hand on his shoulder, and took a deep breath, visibly trying to relax. He took her hand in his and gave it a gentle squeeze before he turned away.

Shannon was stunned. She'd expected him to shove her hand away in anger or something. John seemed to make it a point never to touch her, even in the most mundane of circumstances, and it hurt sometimes. The squeeze had been sweet, and unless she was mistaken, his fingers had wanted to linger.

Hers definitely had.

She took a deep breath and turned back to the refrigerator. "Since I dragged you out on this crappy night, can I at least make you some dinner?"

John looked intrigued for a minute, then shook his head. "Nah, that's okay, Shannon. I didn't come over here for you to cook for me."

She shrugged, trying to look unconcerned. Inside, she hoped desperately he would stay a little bit longer, and not because she was spooked. "I have to eat too. And it will give me something to do. I was going to warm up some chicken and noodles I made the other night."

For a long moment, he just stared at her, silently. "What kind of chicken?"

Shannon smiled. "Parmesan chicken tenders, no bone, and egg noodles I made last night."

"Okay," he grumbled. "You talked me into it. That sounds good."

And it was good. Everything was warmed up and plated within ten minutes. Shannon defrosted some of her mother's homemade rolls from the freezer, and steamed some peas in a bag. John didn't say a word as he started to eat. Shannon smiled when he cleaned his plate and dished out a second helping of everything. What was it about feeding a man that made a woman feel good?

John sat back in his chair, with a hand across his flat belly. "I can't eat any more. That was wonderful."

"I'm glad you liked it."

"I mean every word of it. It's better than anything I've ever had before."

Shannon felt her brows lower skeptically. "Oh, please. I'm an okay cook, but certainly not fantastic."

"After MREs, hospital food and take-out, believe me, this is ambrosia."

Shannon tipped her head forward. "Well thank you very much

for the compliment, John. It's the least I could do."

She took a piece of chicken over to the box in the corner and broke it into little pieces. One she gave to the mother, and the others to each of the kittens. John rolled over behind her, and peered down into the box. He scowled as he watched them spit and hiss at each other. "Why are they doing that?" he demanded.

Shannon smiled and separated two of the kittens. "Well, they haven't been eating solid food very long, and they're trying to establish a pecking order. They don't usually hurt each other."

She handed a small gray bundle of fur to John. "This is the runt of the litter, and I try to feed her a little more than the others."

John held the kitten awkwardly in front of him. The young cat's paws batted the air, looking for something to claw into.

"No, no, hold her against you, like this."

She settled his hand against his chest and shaped his fingers around the little creature's bottom. Shannon didn't even realize how close she had moved to John until she looked up and found him staring at her. Hard. With those heavy black brows furrowed and his dark eyes full of burning emotion.

"Sorry," she mumbled, and pulled away quickly. She snatched another kitten out of the box and tucked it under her chin.

John's kitten started to purr.

"What's it doing now?" he demanded.

Shannon laughed at the ferocious frown on his face. "Relax," she told him gently, "she's just purring. It means she's comfortable and likes what you're doing."

John eased back in his chair and eyed the cat.

"Haven't you ever had a cat?" she asked him curiously.

John's face lost all expression, and a subtle tension eased into the air. "No, I haven't. Animals weren't allowed at the boy's home where I grew up."

"Oh." Shannon felt like a heel as the revelation about his childhood settled into her. It explained so much of who he was.

"I didn't mean to dig things up," she told him finally.

John shrugged and stroked the kitten on the top of its head with a huge finger. "No big deal. You didn't know."

"So, have you ever had any pets?" she asked finally.

John shook his head. "None. There was a stray dog I used to toss scraps to outside my window at the orphanage, but he wasn't around very long before the pound caught him."

Shannon felt her eyes fill with helpless tears. How very sad. No animals in his life at all, and the one small contact he had destroyed by the dog catcher. She still had three horses at her parent's house in Colorado Springs she needed to decide what to do with. She'd always had animals in her life. From hamsters and hermit crabs as a child to horses and cattle she showed in 4-H in her teenage years. Actually, she couldn't remember ever *not* having an animal in her life.

John fondled the kitten around the ears, and the little animal purred just as loud as she could, her eyes slitted shut in rapture. Shannon knew she would do the same thing if John handled her that way too.

"She really likes you," she told him softly.

John made a non-committal grunt, but he continued to run his big fingers gently over her coat.

"You know," Shannon murmured, "I'm going to have to find homes for these before too long."

John immediately held the kitten out to her. "No, thank you. You'll find a better home for it than with me."

Reluctantly, she took the dangling kitten from his hand. She wouldn't push him on it. They wouldn't be ready to wean for a couple of weeks yet, anyway. Setting the two gently in the box, she turned back to John.

And caught him as he glanced away from her ass.

Shannon felt heat wash across her cheekbones. There was no hiding her curves, but she couldn't help smoothing her hands over her slacks in embarrassment. She turned away from John and went to gather dirty dishes to put in the dishwasher.

John rolled around her and started to hand her things to put in. Shannon appreciated that he put forth the effort. He didn't seem the type to do kitchen chores. Neither said anything about what happened seconds before, but a subtle awareness had crept into the air.

"Thank you, John. You didn't have to help."

He shrugged. "I ate the food. It's only right I help clean up."

Nothing more was said as her kitchen was set right. John went over and, after a last, thorough look at the trash can, lifted the bag from the can. Shannon was thankful that he did that, too. It was one less reminder that something wasn't right in her home. He rolled to the garage door and tossed it into the wheeled refuse can.

"I should probably go, and let you have your evening. Will you be okay?"

Shannon knew he had to leave, but it still made her sad. She liked having John in her house, for whatever reason.

"Yes, I'll be fine," she sighed. "I really appreciate you coming over."

John waved a big hand in dismissal before he powered himself through the dining room. He was almost through the living room by the time she caught up with him. He stopped suddenly and leaned over a picture frame on an end table. Shannon knew it was a group shot of her family.

"This is my dad Charles," she said, pointing to the strapping gray-haired man with his arm around an older woman. "My mom, Elizabeth. My sister Abigail. And my younger brother Chris." Her finger brushed lovingly over the smiling young man in the wheelchair. "I'm five years older than he is. He was kind of a surprise. My parents planned on having just us two girls. Mom was in her forties when she got pregnant again unexpectedly. When they found out they were having a boy, they were so excited. And we were too."

Shannon smiled at John and folded her arms under her breasts. "I owe my brother my life. He was there the night Gerbowski tried to kidnap me, at my parent's house. We used to live outside of Columbus. Mike was holding me hostage when Chris found us. Luckily, my parents were away on a trip, or it could have been so much worse. Chris grabbed my dad's pistol out of the truck when he saw Mike's car in the driveway. And when he realized what was going on, Chris shot at him, but Mike fired back at the same time. Mike's bullet entered Chris's spine, paralyzing him. Chris's bullet went center mass, nicked an artery, deflated a lung. Enough to make Mike let me go. After dealing with months of his obsession, we all hoped he would die before the ambulance got there, but he didn't. We got Chris to the hospital within minutes of the injury, but he was still paralyzed. The bullet is still in his spine. They didn't want to take it out for fear they would damage him more. Mike, on the other hand, is fine. Three square meals a day and all the cable he can watch in prison."

Shannon looked at John. "Isn't that a sad thing to say, wishing death on another person? He terrorized me for months, and if he was here, I would blow him to pieces in a heartbeat."

"You can't help how you feel," John grumbled. "The guy put you through hell. Your whole family. Of course you'd wish him gone. If he is responsible, I promise you, he won't hurt you again. Not with me watching."

Shannon smiled sadly. "Thank you, John. I appreciate that."

She watched as he slipped on the jacket he had discarded on the back of the couch, covering the shoulder holster. "Did you carry a Beretta in the Marines?"

John's sat back in his chair, surprised. "Yes."

Shannon nodded her head. "It's a very good gun."

She laughed at the look on his face. "I have the same gun in my bedroom safe. Though I prefer my little Beretta Bobcat, . 25 caliber. Dad made sure I could protect myself if I ever got into that situation again."

John smiled slightly as he turned away. "Remind me never to piss you off."

She laughed and watched as he rolled down the ramp to his black truck. He pulled a remote from his pocket and pressed a button, and the whole side of the truck seemed to move! He rolled into the contraption and it lifted him up, then slid him inside behind the wheel. Fascinating. She watched until he'd pulled away, then shut and double-locked the door.

As she wandered back through the house, Shannon felt decidedly better since John had gone through it. The violation she had felt was eased, replaced by a warm spot in her heart that he had created. She appreciated that he had come to her house, though he hadn't stayed nearly long enough.

*****

John cursed as he clutched his jacket around himself and rubbed his hands together. If he'd known he was going to stake out her house, he'd have prepared better. Warmer jacket, thermos of coffee. NoDoz pills, maybe. Since he'd been out of the military, he'd gotten used to comfort. And regular schedules. It was 3 a. m. and sleep dragged him down, bad.

Hell, he may be out here for no reason. Shannon could have drunk the Pepsi herself, and just didn't remember doing it. Though he'd only ever seen her drink Diet at work. He sighed as he remembered the call. No, she was positive she hadn't. And he believed her. She couldn't have known he was going to call, and the fear was evident in her voice on the phone. That kind of fear was difficult to duplicate on the spur of the moment. He knew, intimately, the sound of fear.

The pop can had definitely been placed to grab attention. As soon as was decent tomorrow, he would take it over and see what Ralph Jamison could find on it. The ex-FBI forensic criminologist was a boon to the Denver area. Definitely worth his weight in gold. But he wouldn't like being woken on a Saturday.

John thought about the picture he had seen in her living room. It explained so much. From her easy acceptance when he first met Shannon, to her familiarity with the wheelchair, it all made sense now. Her brother had lived with her not too long ago while he was between jobs. She'd told him that during one of their lunches. They were close, obviously. Shannon glowed when she spoke about her little brother. He had a feeling if he spoke with Chris, the feeling would be mutual.

For a long moment, John wondered what it would feel like to be that connected to another person. To have a somebody. His mother had dropped him off at the orphanage when he was five years old. He remembered the day perfectly. It had been bright and sunny, and she had been unusually nice to him that day. Letting him ride in the front seat, getting him a hamburger from McDonald's. And she had been sober. He'd been so surprised and it stuck out in his memory as one of the best times he'd ever had with her.

When she had pulled up to the curb of the big, beautiful church, he hadn't thought anything was out of the ordinary. They often when to church rummage sales and food lines. But when she handed him a paper sack with his clothes in it, he knew something was wrong. There were tears in her eyes as she told him things had changed, and that if he was a good little boy, he would be able to find a family that would love him and be better able to take care of him. John hadn't understood. What had he done to make her mad? Crying had only made her more determined, until she finally snapped at him, "This is why I'm getting rid of you."

She left him standing there on the steps as he cried his eyes out. It was the last time he'd ever seen her.

John contemplated the suburban scene in front of him as he rubbed the bridge of his nose. He'd covered a lot of distance between then and now. Actually, if he thought about it, he was fairly proud of where he was. For an abandoned kid that had barely scraped through school, he did good in the military. Commendations and awards were stacked in a box in his closet, telling him how brave other people thought he was. As a Gunnery Sergeant, he had been well respected by his men. His orders were followed immediately and without question, and his team had had one of the lowest casualty counts in his company.

Well, until that day outside of Kabul. Everything had gone to shit then.

He tipped his head to one side, then the other, cracking the bones in his neck. He scrubbed his hands through his hair and flicked the ignition on without starting the truck. He pressed buttons on the radio until he found an irritating station that would keep him awake.

Shannon was up and moving around by seven o'clock. John

thought it was safe to head back to the apartment. Maybe he could catch a few minutes' sleep in his bed before he had to go in to the office and submit the evidence. Jamison would not appreciate business on a Saturday, but it couldn't be helped.

*****

Through a crack in her bedroom drapes, Shannon watched John pull away from the curb, several yards down the street. Her heart warmed at the thought of him waiting out there in the cold, watching to make sure she was okay. For a man who didn't have any relationships, family or otherwise, she was amazed at how well he took care of her. If she confronted him about it, he would deny it, of course. But she knew the truth. John Palmer had an incredibly warm, caring heart.

And he seemed to have a soft spot for her.

Smiling, she turned and headed for the hot shower. She needed to clean and shop today.

Chapter Three

Chad had called Zeke at three.

"'Lo?"

"Dude, are you still in bed?"

There was silence on the other end of the line, and Chad thought the other man had fallen asleep. "Maybe. What do you want? It's damn…early."

He snorted. "No, it's not. It's after three. What time do you normally get up?"

Zeke yawned on the other end of the line. "Mm, five-ish. Depends on the job the night before."

"Well, whatever. You need to get up. Are you going with me?"

The silence stretched on the other end of the line even longer, and Chad knew Zeke had hoped he'd forgotten.

"I don't know, Chad. I'm not…ch-chomping at the bit for a girlfriend like you…are. I don't need to go out and be looked at like a bug over and over again."

Chad winced at the too-blunt description of their normal nights out. Zeke was all too right. Finding girls was not the problem, it was getting to know them. Between Chad's obviously fucked-up arm and Zeke's long pauses and patchwork face, people tended to give them a wide berth, no matter how friendly they tried to be. And if the women did pause long enough for a drink, they usually fell into two categories: the motherers and the pityers. Neither of which they were in the market for. If he wanted to be mothered or pitied, he could go back home to Texas.

He was hungry for companionship, though. It had been years since he'd been in a serious relationship, and months since his last half-dressed fuck.

The first time he'd been with a woman, she'd said over and over again she'd be fine with his amputation, and that she'd seen injuries like his before. Well, apparently not, because as soon as she caught sight of his stub, she'd paled and shuddered, making an excuse to leave. The second time he'd been with a woman he'd left his jeans and leg on, in spite of her protests, and everything had worked out great, though it had felt shallow. Not as mind-blowing as his first fuck post-injury should have been.

Finding the perfect woman was probably an impossibility for him.

"I tell you what, we won't go looking for girls. We'll just go get a drink, and see if we can get a couple of the other guys to go, too. We'll just hang out and watch the game tonight."

Zeke sighed over the line but agreed. Chad promised to text him where and when once he'd talked to the others.

They settled on a new sports bar in the Flat Irons Mall area, to the north of the city, called Frog Dog. When they walked inside, it was busy. Chad looked at his buddies and saw the same trepidation he felt at being in a group like this, and he would have faded right back out the door if the hostess hadn't arrived just then.

"Four of ya?" She smiled at them all then scanned the wipe-board on the podium. "This way, please."

She started to weave through the noise toward the back of the restaurant. Chad was about to stop her, but she led them to a table along the back wall, a bit detached from the rest of the room. It still had a perfect view of the flat-screens. "Your waitress will be with you in a minute."

He looked at the guys as they sat down. Ortiz took the chair farthest away from the crowd and backed it up against the wall even further, arms crossed over his chest. Chad, Zeke and Terrell took the other three seats, and they all tried to look relaxed, though they were all scoping out the numbers they'd have to take out to get to the exits. Zeke was the only one okay with the crowd at his back, because it was more comfortable than being under scrutiny for his scars.

Chad swallowed heavily and forced himself to sit back. Ortiz was the most newly discharged, and his tension was feeding that of the group. Five years after combat, Chad had learned to tamp down the urge to fight in crowds like this, but the younger soldier had a long road to go.

"Hi, guys! What can I get you?"

The cute little brunette waitress was unaware of the tension she'd just help dissipate. She grinned at Chad with a toothy smile, and her eyes didn't flicker at all, even when she glanced at his hand.

"Ah, beer, please. What do you have on tap?"

"Well, Frog Dog is our in-house brew, but we have just about anything you'd like." She reeled off a list of names but he chose the house stuff. Ortiz asked for a cola, Terrell the same as Chad. All eyes swung to Zeke. The waitress rested her hand on his shoulder, and his eyes widened when they looked up at her. Color leeched from his face.

"And what about you, big guy?"

His mouth worked, but he couldn't articulate what he wanted. The waitress waited, though she had patrons calling her, until he finally wrenched out the name of a domestic brew. She smiled even wider. "I'll get your drinks for you. Menus are there on the table and I'll be back to get your order in a minute."

She turned away and they all watched her cute little backside disappear into the crowd.

"F-fuck! I didn't think I was going to be able to spit it out. She…surprised me."

Chad grinned at Zeke. "But you worked it out, buddy, and she didn't seem to mind at all."

Zeke grinned and nodded.

Chad handed him a menu. "Decide what you want now so you can plan it in your head."

Zeke ducked his head to the menu. Chad knew it would take him a few minutes to work things out, but he'd gotten faster over the past year. In Afghanistan, he'd been standing on the opposite side of a ten-foot cinder-block wall when a mortar exploded. He'd received a traumatic brain injury from the blast, then being buried beneath the rubble, and the bricks themselves had ripped up his face. The docs had patched him up, but he needed a few more surgeries before he would feel confident enough to respond to a woman like their waitress.

If he ever did. Surgery wasn't the answer to everything. And it wouldn't help his stuttering and delayed speech from the concussive injury to his brain. Only time and a lot of therapy would help that.

The waitress returned with their drinks and thumped them down in front of each of them, then pulled a pad from the back pocket of her jeans. "Do you guys know what you'd like?"

They all ordered appetizers and sandwiches. Zeke stumbled over his buffalo chicken sandwich order, but he powered through. It helped that the waitress smiled sweetly at him and didn't seem in any hurry to leave. She nodded to the group when they were done. "I'll get these in to the kitchen now. My name is Ember. If you guys need anything just give me a holler."

Zeke twisted in his chair to watch her walk away. Chad thought it was funny the way he had reacted to her. "She's cute."

Zeke glanced at him and nodded, then picked up his beer and turned enough to watch the screen.

They all had a good night, and Chad was glad they'd gone somewhere different. The crowd was boisterous because the game was on fire, and the enthusiasm was contagious. Even Ortiz relaxed enough to enjoy himself and joke around.

Ember came back several times throughout the night to reload drinks and chitchat, and she made it a point to draw Zeke into the conversation. Although he seemed uncomfortable at first, he appeared to like the attention.

They left that night in much better spirits than when they'd arrived.

*****

At nine o'clock Saturday night, when Shannon peeked out the curtain, John was parked once again several yards down the street. Just barely within sight of the house. Shannon really appreciated that. When she'd returned from running errands, her machine had been blinking with a message. John had given her his house address, and Shannon was surprised at how close they had always been.

Denver was a huge city, so it was a real coincidence that they landed just a few blocks away. In the back of her mind, she had to wonder if his proximity to her was on purpose. He had no other family. The two of them got along well at the office. Definitely better than John and anybody else. He got along well with Duncan and Chad, but they were the exceptions. They acted more like brothers than anything. Everybody else he treated with, well, reserve.

Maybe he just couldn't relate to people without being in charge. He was one of three partners, but Duncan definitely had the authority in the company. Maybe John just couldn't figure out how *not* to be a commanding officer.

She backed away and tried to distract herself by watching some TV, but her eyes were drawn to the window instead. An hour later, she peeked out again. John's truck was still in the same spot, and it had started to flurry. She was too far away to see inside the vehicle, but she hoped he stayed warm.

Guilt ate at her as she got ready to turn in. It didn't seem right that she was in her comfortable bed, and John was out there in the cold. It probably wasn't good for his back either. When he thought nobody was looking, he would often go through a series of stretches forward and back, and twist side to side. Always with a grimace on his face. It was painful to watch, and she always cringed along with him.

Curiously, though, she was not worried about the strange occurrences that had happened. John put her at ease. Well, when he wasn't turning her on. She had given little to no thought to Mike. Certainly, the prison would have notified her if he had been released. Hell, she still had an active restraining order against him. His first parole hearing wouldn't be for several years yet.

An hour later she still tossed and turned in bed. She appreciated John's help too much to leave him out there any longer. Snatching her cell phone off her bedside table, she scrolled through until she found his name.

He answered on the first ring. "Are you all right?"

"I'm fine. Totally fine. You have to be cold, though. Why don't you come in?"

Silence stretched on the other end of the line.

"How long have you known I was here?" he asked finally.

"Since last night."

For a moment, there was just silence, then he snorted. "Fuck. Guess I wasn't as sneaky as I thought I was, huh?"

Laughing outright, she sat up in bed. "Well, normally I'm sure you are, but I'm pretty paranoid recently. I'm, like, hyper-aware of a lot of things right now."

"That's understandable. But you don't have to worry. Until we figure out what's going on, I'll be here every night."

Her heart softened and tears came to her eyes. Her tight throat made it hard to speak. "I know, John. And I can't tell you how much I appreciate that. I would appreciate it a lot more, though, if you were actually in the house and I didn't have to worry about you freezing to death out there on the street. That would not be good for business." Or my heart, she thought. "Come in. I have a spare bedroom, or you can sleep on the couch in the living room. Either one would be fine."

John agreed with a sigh. "Okay. I'll be over in a minute."

Shannon slid off the bed and snatched her robe from the footboard, tossing her phone to the nightstand. She flicked on the lights when she padded into the spare bedroom. The bed already had fresh sheets on it, and the bathroom across the hall had clean towels.

Walking to the front door, she pulled it open just as he rolled up.

"Not very slick, am I? Can't believe you spotted me."

Shannon smiled at him, genuinely tickled that she had needled him. "Nope," she agreed. "I promise I won't tell the guys at work, though."

Shannon thought he was maybe even blushing, but he turned

away before she could confirm it, busying himself taking off his jacket. He tossed it on the bench by the door, and straightened in the chair. Shannon's gaze was immediately drawn to the expanse of his chest, and the way the t-shirt strained against him, outlining his awesome pecs. Shannon felt her nipples react to the sight, and a heaviness settled low in her gut. It had been a long time, years actually, since she'd reacted to anybody with anything other than friendliness.

"Shannon?"

John's voice made her realize she was staring, and she turned away abruptly. Snapping the light on next to the couch, she motioned with her hand. "You can stretch out here, or I have the guest room all made up and ready. It's up to you." Walking to the hearth, she threw a log into the grate, making the coals of the fire flare. It sucked greedily at the fresh wood.

"I think I may just stretch out here, if you don't mind. There's no need for me to mess up a bed."

Shannon nodded her head, trying not to look at him directly. Moving to the hall closet, she pulled down a sheet and a couple of blankets.

"Actually," she told him, "this couch is really comfortable. I slept on it for several nights when I was waiting for my bedroom furniture to get here. You should have plenty of room to stretch out."

When she moved to make up the couch for him, he intercepted her. "I can do it, Shannon. Don't worry about it."

She bit her lip, trying to decide if she had offended him or something. Maybe he just wanted to make his own bed. That was fine.

"Okay. Good night, John. And thank you."

He waved her thanks away and turned toward the couch. Shannon looked at him for a long moment before heading down the hallway. She had a feeling she was going to sleep better with him in the house, for more than one reason.

*****

John released the breath he had been holding until Shannon walked away. She was trying to kill him. She had to be. Telling him she had slept on the same couch. He definitely wouldn't be getting any sleep tonight. Picking up the sheets, he inhaled. Shit. They smelled like her, too. Some kind of fabric softener mixed in with that smell she had, of womanliness and sweetness. John shook his head at himself and snapped the sheet out over the couch.

Hell, he may not even sleep. The whole point of him coming in was to watch her more closely, not stretch out on the couch. At least if something did happen he would be here. Maybe it was a good thing she'd spotted him. Even if it was damn humiliating.

*****

Shannon got up a few minutes early the next morning to start breakfast. She'd slept like a log the whole night through, knowing John was just a hallway away. When she walked out to the living room, she was not surprised to see him sitting in his wheelchair at the living room window. The sheets she had set out were refolded and sitting on the corner of the cushion. Had he slept at all?

She circled until she could see his face clearly. His dark eyes were sharp, but definitely a little heavy lidded. The beard on his jaw was thicker.

"Did you sleep at all?" she demanded.

John shrugged. "I cat-napped a bit. I don't need a lot of sleep."

Shannon frowned at him. She felt secure when he was in the house, but she didn't want his health to suffer for it. Damn Mike for making her crazy like this. Maybe everything was just a coincidence, and nothing was actually going on. Maybe she was putting John through this for nothing. Guilt knotted her stomach.

"I'm sorry, John. Why don't you go home and sleep for a while? I'm not going anywhere today. I don't even know if you need to be here." Running her hand through her hair, she crossed her arms over her tummy. "Maybe I'm just going crazy, and these things are just flukes. I mean, anybody could have turned around in my driveway. And my tires going flat could have been anything."

John regarded her silently, letting her vent. "Did the tire shop find anything in the tires? Any reason for them to go flat?"

"No," she conceded.

"So, why would two brand new tires go flat, unless somebody had deflated them by hand?"

Shannon had no answer to that, and it shut her up. Turning away, she headed in to the kitchen. Crossing the floor to the fridge, she pulled onions, green peppers, ham, cheese and eggs out, assembling an omelet. John rolled in silently behind her and positioned himself at the table in the same spot Chris normally sat at. She plunked a steaming cup of black coffee in front of him, and he curled his hands around it.

"Don't worry about my sleep, Shannon. I'm fine. Until we find out what's going on, I think I should be here." He coughed into his hand before continuing. "This isn't going to cause problems with a boyfriend or anything, is it?"

Shannon looked at him in surprise. Not because of the question itself, but because of the hesitancy she thought she heard in his voice. She turned her concentration back to beating the eggs. "No, no boyfriend."

"Do you date? Any chance this could be another boyfriend doing these things?"

Shaking her head from side to side, she told him, "Nope."

Pouring the onions and other ingredients in the pan, she tried not to let her hands shake. John asking about her dating life was a little strange, because she had been imagining dating *him* for so long.

"You do date, though?"

She nodded her head, still not looking at him. "Of course I date."

"Why don't you have a boyfriend, then?" he asked finally.

Pouring the eggs into the pan, she paused, then turned to look at him directly. Her heart was almost pounding out of her chest as she debated what to tell him. From the first moment she'd seen him, backlit by the sunlight from the office window, she wanted to know more about him. Six freaking months she'd been mooning after an impossible need. *What the hell.*

"I'm pretty picky in who I date, and I'm waiting for the right guy to ask me." She stared at him for several seconds, then turned back to the stove.

*****

Unease curled through John's stomach at her words. Hell, not even her words so much as her actions. Did she mean what he thought she meant? Was she telling him she was waiting on him?

She continued to stir the eggs, and he couldn't see her face clearly any more. Clenching his teeth, he tried to control his galloping heart.

Breakfast, he was sure, was wonderful, but he barely tasted it. He was too busy tossing her words around. As soon as was polite, he made his excuses and headed out the door, promising to be back in a few hours.

John drove to his apartment in a daze. What had she meant, "waiting for the right guy"? He tried to twist things around, but he kept coming back to the same conclusion. With her words and the fact that she was staring at him so hard at the time she said it, only one thing was possible. Shannon was waiting on him to ask her out.

The thought chilled him to the bone.

What on earth did he have to offer a woman like her? She appeared to be his exact opposite. He'd grown up in foster homes and group orphanages with no family to speak of. She had grown up in rural Ohio with parents and siblings that loved her. When he signed up to go to war, she had signed up to go to college. And when he returned a broken man, she was growing into being a professional woman. What could they possibly have in common?

A matching desire to be together?

Snorting out loud, he turned into the parking lot of his apartment complex, automatically winding his way through the generic boxes to his own. He pulled past the spot assigned to him, with its very own bright blue handicapped sign, and slid into one further down, not marked. That fucking sign pissed him off to no end. He knew the anger was irrational. But he couldn't help it.

Hell, he should thank them for having the spot at all. Not every business did.

John's mood was sour, to say the least, when he finally let himself into his apartment.

He knew what the problem was. It was Shannon.

What the hell was he going to do with her?

Reclining on his couch hours later, the question still nagged at him. What if he did make a move on her? And she laughed her ass off?

What if he made a move on her, and she *didn't* laugh her ass off?

That was even scarier.

*****

Shannon had not intended to make John uncomfortable with that statement at the table. Just wanted to…open his eyes a bit. For months she had hoped he would look at her as something other than an employee. Even though it was wrong, she had not looked at John as an employer for a long time, rather as a potential mate. He had every characteristic she had always wanted in a man. Humor, strength, level-headedness. The physical characteristics came in a distant second to his quiet personality and sardonic humor. *They* were what had drawn her most at the beginning. As well as his unrelenting loneliness. Shannon felt special in that he seemed to relate to her on a level that he didn't with anybody else, so he opened up much more with her than anybody. Granted, she was the only female in the office, but Shannon had a feeling it was more than that. Possibly much more.

While he was gone, Shannon spot-cleaned and went from window to window putting little tiny pieces of blue tape over the crack where the window met the sill. She had heard once that you could tell if somebody had opened a window that way. If the tape was loose, there was a high probability that somebody had been in the house.

She felt neurotic doing it, and a little stupid, but it made her feel better. Every piece of tape was hidden out of sight from the exterior. It didn't make sense to do it at the garage door, because she used it so much. The French doors at the kitchen she put two pieces on.

At noon, she sat down to watch the news. It wasn't good. A cold front was sweeping down from the north. When it hit the warmer air over Colorado, it was expected to dump a boatload of snow. The mountain passes were already closed, and were expected to be closed for several days, if not weeks.

Shannon took stock of her pantry and set candles and gas lamps out, in case she lost power. What little laundry there was she finished, then ran several buckets of fresh water, and filled several large soup pots as well, leaving them sitting on the back burners. She emailed her family, telling them she would probably be without power for a couple days. Courtney, her sister, lived about four hundred miles south, and would probably get the same, if not worse, weather. Shannon debated telling her family about the Pepsi can and the fears that had been nagging her, but changed her mind. It wouldn't be fair to scare them without concrete information yet.

John arrived shortly after four, laden down with several bags of groceries.

"Oh, wow. You didn't have to do that, John." Shannon struggled to relieve him of them, and even the small contact of his fingers on hers transferring the bags sent a thrill through her. He had on the standard leather, but this coat was longer than the bomber jacket he normally wore, with a wool collar around his neck. The dark brown complemented the color of his skin perfectly, and the beard stubble growing in made him look dangerous. *More* dangerous, actually. There was an army-green duffel hanging off the back of his wheelchair.

"If you take the groceries, I'll get my bag."

Nodding, she carried what she could into the kitchen, then returned for a second load. He must have bought two of everything. Two packages of steaks, two containers of potato salad, two bags of chips. Ten cans of miscellaneous veggies and fruit. There were also several bags of the frozen steamer bags of vegetables she preferred. And chocolate. Lots of chocolate. Her heart warmed as she found her favorite dark chocolate treat. Times four.

Tears actually came to her eyes. Why would he do that for her?

Heading back out, she found him in the guest room, pulling clothes from the bag.

"I hope you don't think I'm too presumptuous. I claimed the closet." With a big hand, he motioned to the closet to the right of the door. "I think I'll probably sleep out on the couch, more central, but I'll keep my things in here."

Shannon nodded, trying not to let the sight of his clothing hanging in the closet mean too much. "That's fine. I'm sorry you have to go to so much trouble, but I really appreciate you being here, John. I slept better last night than I have in several days."

He nodded. "I checked on you once, and you were totally out. You looked exhausted."

Shannon felt color creep up her neck at the thought of being watched in her sleep, especially by John. "Was I snoring?" she asked with a laugh.

John shook his head firmly. "Nah, you were just deep asleep. Hey, uh, I talked to Jamison. He called a friend of a friend, and Michael J. Gerbowski is still behind bars in the state penitentiary."

Shannon plopped down on the end of the couch, her legs suddenly boneless. What a relief that was. She had logged onto the prison website to try to find out if he was still there, but the computer kept locking up on her. After several attempts she had stopped looking.

John rolled in front of her, looking her directly in the eye. Knee to knee, he stopped, and Shannon knew more was coming. "Shannon. The prints on the can matched Gerbowski's intake prints."

"What?" Shaking her head, Shannon tried to understand what he just told her. "You said he was still in prison."

John nodded. "I know. He is. I called my own contact and confirmed it as well. Michael Gerbowski is still in prison, but somehow his prints are on that can."

Shaking her head, mouth open in disbelief, she just sat there. "How the hell is that possible?"

John's face had hardened into a glower. "I don't know. But we will find out. Consider Lost 'N' Found officially on the case. I already talked to Duncan about it."

Shannon nodded. How had everything blown up this way? God, in had been almost ten years exactly since all this crap had gone down. Why was somebody resurrecting it now?

John touched her knee with his hand. "Don't worry. I'll be here. I'll be everywhere you are. If I'm not, one of the other guys will be."

Shannon was more heartened that he touched her than by his words. It was one of the few times she remembered him actually doing that. Hell, John didn't touch anybody if he could avoid it.

Nodding her head firmly, Shannon straightened. "I'm fine. Just a little shaken. I'm not worried, though." She patted his hand in return, and he pulled away. "So, logically, if he is still in prison, how can his prints be on that can?"

Shrugging, he rolled back a bit, readjusting in the chair, cocking an arm over the back. "Well, somebody may have smuggled it out of the prison. Most have scanners going in, but I'm not sure if they make visitors pass through one going out. It may be a can from several years ago. The logo looks a little dated. It may be a fingerprint transfer somebody lifted and placed on the can. It's hard to tell. There are a lot of different options."

Shannon stood and started to pace. What craziness. The man was in prison, but he still caused problems.

Her brother Chris was going to be devastated.

Thanksgiving was a few weeks away, and she would have to see him then.

Emotion swamped her, and she walked to the window, fighting tears. She felt more than heard John roll up behind her. "Shannon, I know this is hard. I'm sorry."

She turned to him with a smile and pushed away the tears. "John, that sounded very comforting. You better be careful, or you'll turn into a nice guy. I'm all right." Smoothing her face, she turned to him fully. "Did you get any sleep at all?"

Rubbing a hand over the stubble of his face, he avoided her eyes. "I got enough."

In other words, no.

Cursing stubborn men in general, she gave him a reproachful look. "What good are you going to do me if you can't keep your eyes open?"

"Don't worry about me, I'm fine. Believe me, my body knows what it can take and what it can't. I'm nowhere near my breaking point."

*****

Overall, Shannon believed him, but she watched him a lot. This was not a chore, of course. She just didn't want him to overwork himself. For the most part, he stayed busy. He had stopped at the office and gathered some "toys", as he called them. To her it looked like a jumbled box of wires, but to John they were security. When she asked what they were, he explained they were door wires, window sensors and cameras. Shannon found herself recruited for mounting in places she could reach but he couldn't. By the way he gritted his teeth and was short with her, Shannon knew he hated having her do anything like that. He wouldn't let her get on the ladder to mount the higher cameras, though. Roger, he told her, was on his way over to do the job.

No sooner had he said that than the front door bell rang. Automatically, Shannon headed for the front of the house.

"Shannon! I'll get it."

Rolling past her, John gave her a scathing look. Shannon bit her lip, because he'd warned her that she was not to open door for anyone unless she knew exactly who it was, and even then with caution. He positioned himself beside the doorway and she was hit with exactly how much danger they could possibly be in. John in particular. Fear tightened her scalp as he pulled the gun from the holster he wore constantly now. Michael had already proven he was willing to kill for her. The shot that hit Chris *should* have killed him. And as forceful and masculine as John was, it was a fact he was still in a wheelchair, and definitely would not have the same advantages of an able-bodied man in a fight.

She hoped they caught whoever tormented her before it came to that.

Roger called out a greeting from the other side of the door, and John opened it cautiously, before sliding back to let him in. The gun disappeared into the holster.

The men nodded to each other, and talked briefly about a stakeout Roger was assigned. He held out his arms, and she had no problem taking a firm hug from him.

"You okay, girly? John filled us in on what's going on."

"I'm fine," she told him honestly. "John's here. Nothing's getting through him."

Roger gave her that knowing look, and she gave him a reassuring smile back, telling him without words she really was okay. Roger knew how she felt about John. She had admitted it a month ago during one of their lunches. Actually, Roger was the *only* one that knew.

"And when John's not here, one of us will be," he promised. "We'll get these cameras up and catch this guy."

The living room turned into security headquarters, cluttered with wires and closed-circuit monitors. There were now seven cameras mounted in and around the exterior of her house.

Shannon felt like she was living in a goldfish bowl. They even put one in her bedroom. When she objected, John overruled her. "It's your most vulnerable place," he told her simply.

Which didn't make her feel any better.

He called her over to the table and motioned for her to sit down in the chair beside him.

"I want to give you something."

Her heart slammed in her chest when he stretched a glittering tennis bracelet between his hands. Shock held her immobile for several long seconds before she held out her wrist. She felt blood rush into her cheeks and she struggled for something to say. "John, I—"

"You need to keep this on twenty-four seven, even in the shower. It has a short-range transmitter in it that feeds to this GPS"—he pointed to one of the black boxes on the table—"but it only has a range of about five miles."

Shannon blinked at him, knowing she had "stupid" written all over her face. "Oh, okay."

"And I want you to start carrying your gun. Do you have a holster for it?"

She nodded. "An ankle one."

"Good. Later we'll get it out and go over its action."

John turned back to the monitors and she was left sitting in the chair with her arm still held out. She pulled it back and lurched to her feet, humiliated tears burning her eyes. Roger stepped forward to say something, but she waved him away and escaped to the kitchen.

How stupid could she be? John would never have actually given her a piece of jewelry. They weren't dating. They were barely even friends. She'd just let herself react before her brain had a chance to compute.

At loose ends, she started to bake. In little time, she had a corn cake in the oven, and Mexican food simmered on the stove. The men entered the kitchen just as she removed everything from the burners.

"Damn, girl, whatcha cookin'? Smells too good in here."

Shannon laughed at Roger. "Mexican food. Hungry?"

"Even if I wasn't I'd eat, just to have your cooking." Eagerly, he grabbed a plate and began building a burrito.

John was still in the doorway, brows furrowed, watching the banter between she and Roger.

"You okay?" she asked.

He nodded and rolled forward. "Fine."

Dinner was a fun escape for her. Roger made sure she didn't linger on the heavy stuff, and instead steered the conversation to lighter topics. Shannon was a little uncomfortable with how John acted. He didn't talk. He glowered. At Roger specifically.

Roger didn't seem to mind, he just kept talking. She couldn't help but laugh at some of the stories he told her. And it seemed every time she laughed, John frowned all the harder. It was actually a relief when Roger said he needed to head out. It was after nine and he had work in a few hours, covering a shift for a buddy.

Roger promised to see her the next day and pressed a kiss to her cheek. Snow fell heavily outside. "Maybe. Maybe not. Look at it."

"Aw, Shannon, it's just a few snowflakes."

Roger pulled the hood up on his coat, and was gone. Shannon closed the door after him and leaned back against it as she glared at John.

"Why were you mad at him?"

John's lip curled before he turned away. "I wasn't mad at him."

She followed him to the fireplace, where he tossed another log on the already roaring blaze. "Why were you scowling at him like that then? You looked like you were going to rip his head off."

John stared into the fire and didn't respond right away. "It was nothing. Just stuff. Don't worry about it."

Shannon turned away angrily. She hated feeling like she was not seeing something right in front of her, but everybody else was. And nobody was telling her what she wasn't seeing.

She stomped to the kitchen and cleaned up the leftover food, then started the dishwasher. The kittens cried piteously, so she sat down on the floor to play with them. Within seconds, she could feel the anger fade away. How could she stay mad holding such beautiful little creatures?

John rolled in and stopped a few feet away. Shannon knew he was too hardheaded to ask, so she reached into the box and fished out a kitten. It was one of the black ones with orange markings that looked like Pickle. Silently, she handed it up to him and watched as he folded it into his chest. He chuckled quietly as the little animal started to purr.

"Not very discriminatory, are they?"

"Nope," she agreed. "They love all grumps the same."

"Well, that's good."

Shannon noticed he didn't disagree with the "grump" assessment.

For a good fifteen minutes, they just sat there petting the kittens. John seemed to prefer the gray female she had given him the first day, and the love seemed reciprocal. Pickle preened over her babies and licked each one as they were handed back to her care.

John seemed more relaxed after he held the babies too, but she didn't say anything. Tiredness deepened the brackets around his mouth, though, and Shannon knew he had to be dragging. His eyes were getting heavy lidded, too. He had probably only gotten a few hours sleep, at most, in the last twenty-four hours. Well, if she couldn't make him go to bed, she would at least relieve him of watching her.

"I think I'm going to head to bed. I'm tired."

"Before you do that, why don't you go get your pistol. I'd like to look at it."

John seemed impressed with the little gun's action, and commended her on keeping it clean. He made her go through the motions of loading a magazine and chambering a round, which she did easily. She even held it up and sighted down the barrel.

"I think you should carry it from now on."

She frowned. "I'll think about it."

"Okay. Good night, Shannon."

"Night, John."

She pulled the stack of blankets down from the hallway closet shelf, along with a sheet, and placed them on the corner of the couch. If he wanted to sleep on the couch, he could make it up.

*****

John watched Shannon leave regretfully. It made him uncomfortable to know she was irritated with him and not do anything to explain. But there was nothing he could say to exonerate himself. Roger had stoked his jealousy, plain and simple. Stoked it to where it was a roaring blaze of anger. But the anger was at himself, not Shannon or Roger.

He should have approached her with the bracelet differently, so that she understood it was work and not personal. Roger had punched him in the arm as soon as she was out of earshot. "You dumb shit. You just made that girl think she meant something to you, then ripped her down. You need to get your head out of your ass before somebody steps in with a real offer."

As much as he hated to admit it, the other man was right. Shannon was a fantastic woman. And she reacted to Roger as if he were her best friend in the world. He didn't blame Shannon for responding that way. The man was likeable. He blamed himself for not making an effort to even try to be personable.

Shannon had to think he was a total ass. And it was his own damn fault.

It wasn't as if she would seriously consider you for an option, but damn, dude. Show some sense. Don't alienate her for no reason.

As he rolled up to the monitors, his gaze zeroed in on her form lying in the bed. The blue satin comforter was pulled up and tucked beneath her arms. She was crazy hot, in a simple white flannel nightgown. And she looked to be already asleep. What he wouldn't give to be in that bed with her.

His mind flashed back to her handling the gun, and the feelings that it had brought up. He was impressed that she knew what to do. More disturbingly, though, he was turned on.

Fuck.

Chapter Four

Duncan stared out his apartment window at the swirling snow and tried not to worry about the homeless man. But it was fifteen degrees outside and colder than a witch's tit. The concrete alleys around the office offered little escape from the weather, and it was only supposed to get worse overnight.

Once again, he bundled up and limped for his truck. It was worth going out in the weather if it would ease his mind. Although he hadn't seen the man's face or heard his voice, there'd been something about him that said "military".

He started at the office, where'd he'd seen him before, and began searching outward in a grid pattern. There was very little traffic this late, so he idled back and forth on the streets. At times the snow got so heavy he wouldn't have been able to see the man if he'd been standing right in front of him.

When it got too blinding to drive, he pulled to the curb and waited for it to ease up. He'd just pulled over for a third time when he spied an odd lump wedged against a dumpster. What caught his attention was a flag of light blue cotton flapping in the wind, the same color as the blanket he'd given the man the day before.

Duncan shoved the truck into park and turned the heater on high. Tugging his hat down over his ears, he stepped out of the cab and circled the hood. He was glad he'd thought to bring his cane, because the footing was treacherous.

The man seemed to be curled into a ball, with that blanket wrapped over top of him. Snow had accumulated on top of the blanket. Duncan called out a hello, but the ball didn't move. He reached forward with his cane and poked at the lump.

In a blinding swirl of snow, the man lurched to his feet and fell into a defensive stance, with his fists up. Duncan backed away and held his hands palm out to show the man he wasn't armed, but his own adrenaline spiked as well.

"I'm sorry for poking you, but I didn't know how else to get your attention." He motioned to the idling truck. "Can we sit inside for a minute where it's warm?"

The man didn't move from his defensive position. By the light of the headlights, Duncan could see he was still only wearing the black hooded sweatshirt, not nearly enough in a Colorado snowstorm. His hood was down and Duncan could see light brown hair blowing in the wind, and a stubbled, haggard face.

"My name is Duncan Wilde, former Marine MP, Combat Logistics Battalion 26. I'm not going to hurt you, I just want to help you out. Please, come sit in the truck where it's warm."

Duncan backed away through the headlights, went to the driver's side and climbed behind the wheel. Then he waited. The man stood just outside the beam of light, but there was enough illumination to see when he finally moved. He walked to the passenger side, opened the door and slowly climbed in, staring at Duncan the entire time.

Duncan made sure to leave his hands on the wheel, though he had a weapon within reach. As much as he wanted to help this guy out, he wasn't going to get hurt doing it.

The man blinked and looked away, toward the dash. He raised his hands and cupped them around one of the heater vents, then leaned his face into the air. With a shudder, he basked in the warmth.

Duncan slowly reached down to the seat and moved a couple of granola bars beside the man. It had been the only thing he'd had in the apartment. Most of the time he ate at work or just ordered drive-thru.

The man's eyes flickered to the food, then Duncan, then back to the heater. He wasn't in any hurry to move away from the warmth.

"What's your name, soldier?"

"Willingham. Aiden Willingham."

"Nice to meet you, Aiden. Do you have someplace I can take you so you can get out of the cold tonight? Family, or a friend's house?"

Aiden shook his head, still wrapped around the vent. He did take a minute to grab one of the bars, rip it open and shove it in his mouth. He chewed slowly, obviously savoring the granola. Duncan wished he'd brought something else for him.

"I know of a shelter downtown. Can I take you there?"

Anger flashed in the man's eyes before he looked away. "No, thank you."

Duncan frowned at him. "Is there any reason why not? You'd have a warm place to sleep and food in your belly."

"And be disgusted with myself. I don't go to those places. I do fine out here on my own."

Duncan couldn't help but raise his eyebrows at the statement. "Why don't you go to those places? They're there for a reason."

Aiden shook his head. "I just don't. There are people that need it worse than me around here."

"Probably not very many. Dude, you're going to die of exposure if you don't get out of the weather."

Aiden looked out the windshield and seemed to realize how nasty it actually was. Or maybe he realized how cold it was going to be when he left the heater.

Duncan let him stew on it a few minutes. "So, can I take you to the shelter? It's only going to get colder tonight."

With a weary glance outside, Aiden nodded his head. "Let me get my stuff, though."

Cold swirled into the cab as he stepped out to gather his belongings. He snapped the snow off his blanket and bundled it into his arms. He dug a pack from beneath the dumpster he'd been leaning against and swung it over his shoulder, then came back to the truck.

As Duncan shifted into gear, he felt the tension increase on the other side of the cab. "You okay?"

Nodding, Aiden turned to look out the window.

Catholic Samaritan House was usually the only one with empty beds when it got this cold, so Duncan turned the truck in that direction. But the closer he got, the more tense Aiden became. Duncan pulled over and parked between two cars.

"What's wrong?"

Aiden shook his head. "I don't know if I can be in there. It's going to be crowded and people are going to want to talk to me."

"Well, it probably will be because of the weather, but I think if you let them know you need to be alone, they'll respect that."

But the anxiety didn't leave his face. By the time he pulled up in front of the building, Aiden looked ready to leap out of the truck.

Duncan shifted into park and leaned back in the seat, deliberately trying to look relaxed. "Let's just sit here a bit, okay?"

The younger man nodded and seemed relieved not to be pushed.

"Is this how you ended up on the streets? Anxiety? PTSD?"

Aiden shrugged, looking out the window. The snow continued to come down steadily, highlighted orange from the vapor lights on the street. But the heater continued to pump out hot air.

"Answer me one question. Were you in Iraq or Afghanistan?"

"Iraq."

As much as twenty percent of returning veterans from Iraq had post-traumatic stress, some thought even more. Aiden's anxiety was par for the course. Duncan wondered why he hadn't gotten therapy at the VA.

"Well, how about I go in and talk to the manager here and see what we can do for you? Maybe they have a secluded area where you can stay away from the crowds or something."

Aiden glanced at him and nodded.

"Can I trust you if I leave the truck running?"

"Yes, sir!"

Duncan fastened his coat and slipped out of the truck, being sure to plant his feet and cane before he moved. It was slow going across the snowy walk. He glanced back at one point and Aiden was watching him. Duncan's mind blanked out for a moment, and he had the thought that he would not see young Aiden again, but he brushed it away, hurrying into the building.

The manager on duty was harried and kind, but she shook her head regretfully when he told her what Aiden needed. "We separate the men from the women and families, but I'm almost at capacity now. I have room for him but he would have to go into the group."

Duncan nodded and headed back out to the truck. Once on the sidewalk, he could see Aiden was no longer inside.

Glancing up and down the street, Duncan looked for his form, but he didn't see him anywhere. He debated driving around looking for him, but he had a feeling Aiden would be hiding now. Not wanting to be found. He'd gotten spooked, and Duncan honestly couldn't blame him. With a regretful look around, he climbed into the idling truck and pulled away.

*****

Shannon woke up at three having to use the bathroom, just like every other night. As she padded her way back to bed, she heard something bump out in the living room. She peered out the crack of her door, but couldn't see anything. Stepping out quietly, she tugged her nightgown down her thighs as far as it would go before heading down the hallway.

The glow from the fire had died down, but she could still see John's outline. One long arm rested across his forehead while the other twitched beside him on the couch. Shannon could see now that one of the backrest cushions had been knocked off and into an unlit candle on the coffee table, and bumped it askew. It wasn't hurting anything where it was, so she just left it alone, rather than risk waking John up.

Shannon bent to put a fresh log on the fire. The hot coals felt good, warming her front as they began consuming the log. She rubbed the gooseflesh away from her arms.

"Did I wake you?"

Shannon jumped as the deep voice came out of the darkness. She spun and sought John's eyes in the weak light.

"Jeez, you scared me! I thought you were sleeping."

"I was. A dream woke me up."

After she put one more log on the fire, Shannon crossed the

room and sat on the corner of the coffee table. "I think you knocked a cushion down and into the candle. That's what I heard."

He rubbed a rough hand over his face and turned his head toward her. "I looked up and saw you in front of the fire, and thought it was a different kind of dream."

Shannon sat back as his words sank in, then she felt her face burn. With the fire behind her, her nightgown had probably been transparent. She gasped, placing her palms over her cheeks to try to cool them. "Oh, my gosh. I'm sorry you had to see that."

"I'm not," he told her firmly. "It's the best thing I've woken up to in years."

Her heart pounded heavily as she savored his words. Was it just the darkness that was creating this...intimacy? "Well, thank you, then."

"No, thank you," he returned firmly. "I'm sorry I was an ass earlier. I just...Roger makes you laugh."

Surprise straightened on the corner of the table, confused. "And that's bad?"

"No," he grumbled. "Just..." He hesitated, running a hand over his face. "Frustrating. Never mind."

Not sure what to do, she tried to redirect the conversation. "Do your dreams wake you up every night?" she asked softly.

John folded his arms under his head. "No, not all the time. It seems like when I'm especially tired they get worse. Tonight I've been restless."

"I'm sorry. Is the couch not comfortable?"

"No, no, nothing like that," he told her. He briefly rested a hand on her bare knee before drawing away quickly. "I've actually been very comfortable in your home, Shannon. It's just...other things."

"Oh, well, if there's anything I can do to help you out, just let me know."

For the longest time, he didn't say anything, and Shannon thought he had gone back to sleep. She couldn't see his eyes very well, because she blocked the light from the fire.

"Would you mind..." he started quietly, before he stopped to clear his throat. "Ah, don't worry about it."

"No, what?" Shannon leaned forward, fighting to keep her hands to herself.

After a long silence, he finally asked her, "Would you mind just sitting and talking for a while?"

"Absolutely," she told him with no hesitation. "I like talking to you, John. You're a hard-ass, but you're interesting."

"A hard-ass?" he asked in affront, obviously teasing her. "I don't know what you're talking about."

Shannon laughed at his expression, outrage mixed with twinkling devilment in his dark eyes. This side of John appealed to her desperately and Shannon was beginning to see it more and more. Was it just because he was getting used to her in the office, or was it something a little more personal? Did he see her as a woman he had an interest in? She had no clue.

"So, what do you want to talk about?" she asked him.

"Hell, I don't know," he told her as he propped himself up on one elbow. "You're the talker, you come up with something."

For the first time, she noticed that his shoulders were bare. The quilt was over his chest, but his heavy arms were exposed. Her eyes traced over the line of his biceps, highlighted by the firelight. Did he work out, like, all the time? Only heavy-duty weightlifters usually had those kinds of arms. Or was all that bulk from being in the chair? An intricate Marine insignia tattoo wrapped around the deltoid of his right shoulder. The quilt covered most of his chest, but Shannon knew it had to be just as impressive. The tight cotton t-shirts he wore left little to the imagination. Shannon's mouth watered at the thought of tugging the quilt down just a bit to explore.

She forced her eyes away, and struggled for something to talk about.

"Where did you get your tattoo?"

John's dark brows raised in the weak firelight."Uh, some little tattoo shop off base. Working on service personnel was pretty much all the guy did."

"What base were you at?"

"Camp Lejeune, North Carolina. 24th Marine Expeditionary Unit."

Shannon her satisfaction lacing his rough voice.

"Sounds like you liked it there."

He looked down at the couch for a moment before meeting her gaze. "Very much so. More than any other place I'd been in my life."

Smiling at her slightly, he shrugged his shoulders, which dislodged the quilt a bit more. Shannon forced her gaze away again, and swallowed heavily as she rubbed her hands over her goose bumped flesh. The man could probably turn on any woman from eighteen to eighty, so she didn't castigate herself too much. He just had too much natural testosterone.

John apparently noticed her goose bumps, and assumed it was because she was cold. He sat up and tugged the quilt toward her. "Here, I didn't mean for you to get chilled out here."

Shannon waved a hand and lurched to her feet. "No, no, don't worry about it. Keep-keep yourself, uh, covered. I'll get another blanket."

Quickly, she moved to the hall closet and tugged down another blanket, this one fuzzy with a horse running across the width of it. She wrapped it around her like a robe, then settled on the floor in front of the couch. Shannon felt like a coward, because now she didn't have to look at John directly, but she was still close enough to feel his body heat behind her. She worked one elbow out enough to prop it on the edge of the couch in front of him, and rested her head on it. John shifted back to his side, and mirrored her position.

"Sorry," she told him. "I had to move. That corner was getting a bit sharp."

"That's fine. I don't want to put you out."

Shannon frowned at him. "You're not putting me out at all. I owe you for helping me out."

John frowned, then changed the subject. "What is your brother doing in Florida?"

Shannon laughed lightly, pulling the fuzzy blanket closer

around her. "Who knows? It seems like he's had ten different jobs since he's graduated school. He's spreading his wings. He's only twenty-seven, so I guess it's okay. It's just kind of hard, because he was living here not too long ago. He wanted to get away from Mom and Dad after the shooting, and I was the farthest away. But not far enough away that they didn't come to visit. A lot. I think he just poked his finger on a map one day to find a job far enough away that our parents wouldn't check up on him day and night."

"Are your parents hard to get along with?" he asked finally.

"No, no, not at all," she told him quickly. "They just love us and want to see us do well. And with Chris's injury, it just seems to be a bit harder for them to let him go. They've taken care of everything for him. He was just seventeen when he got shot. I think they're kind of lost as to what to do now, without him nearby. Dad still works, but Mom always stayed home with us kids, and it's hardest for her."

John stared off into the fire, and Shannon wondered if this was painful for him to talk about. "What happened to your parents?" she asked quietly.

Tension leapt into the air, and John tensed. Although he hadn't physically moved, Shannon could feel his withdrawal.

"I never knew my dad. My mother left me at a church when I was five. I remember her saying she didn't have the money to keep me."

"Wow," she said softly. It took all the strength she had to not let him see how much his history hurt her. "Did you have any brothers or sisters?"

His dark brow furrowed. "You know, I think I did. A younger brother, maybe. Though I may just be confusing one of the other orphanage kids. I don't know for sure. It was a long time ago."

Shannon turned to face him fully. "Aren't you curious? Why don't you look him up? You're in a perfect position to do some snooping. It would kill me to think I had a relative out there I had never met."

John shook his head. "I'm sure he doesn't even remember me. Why should I stir stuff up?"

"John, what if he does remember you, though? What if *he*'s been looking for *you*?"

There was a fierce frown on his face, like he was actually thinking about what she said, but he shook off her words.

"It doesn't matter. It's not pertinent to what's going on now. Besides, he probably couldn't care less."

Shannon sighed at the hardness she heard in his voice. Obviously his mother had cared less, so of course the brother wouldn't care either. That kind of stance was difficult to reverse. Honestly, she would probably feel the same way.

"So, how long were you in the orphanage? Did you have friends?"

"Friends?" he asked her with a snort. "No, no friends. What was the sense in making friends if they were just going to be gone in a day, or a week, or a year? I was in the home for most of my childhood, give or take a few months here and there when somebody would take me in and try to mold me into what they wanted. I was eventually sent to a boy's halfway house and strongly encouraged to join the military when I was old enough. I didn't have anything better to do at the time, so I joined. It's turned out to be the best thing I've ever done."

"Were you in the Marines with Duncan and Chad?"

He rocked his head on his hand. "Nah, I didn't meet them until I was injured in combat almost six years ago. I met Chad first and the damn kid wouldn't leave me alone. Duncan came along a few months later. We were roomies at Walter Reed."

Shannon smiled. "I thought you guys had known each other longer. You seem like brothers."

John laughed lightly. "Well, I wouldn't know about that, but they've gotten me through a lot of crap. I'd give my life for either one of them."

Shannon blinked at his vehemence, but she shouldn't have been surprised. When he decided to do something, he did it whole-heartedly.

"Can I ask you a question?"

He just looked at her for a moment. "You can, but I may not

answer it."

She took a deep breath. "How were you injured?"

His brows quirked and one side of his mouth tipped up in a sardonic smirk. "Well, we were on patrol and we came across this vehicle that was broken down in the road. We knew something was up, so we parked about thirty yards away and approached it cautiously. It ended up being exactly as it appeared. A broken-down vehicle. When we headed back to the Hummer, though, we were attacked. The Hummer was blown into the air and came down in pieces. A door landed on me, shattered a couple of vertebra."

Shannon swallowed heavily. His words were flat, as if he had told the story many times, although she had a feeling quite the opposite was true. Her heart ached at the thought of his being injured in a foreign land and coming home to no one. That was so wrong.

They were both quiet for a long time, lost in their own thoughts. The fire spat and crackled merrily, in counterpoint to the heavy overtones in the room. She wondered if John realized how much anger he carried around inside him. It was obvious to her, and she wondered why he even told her about it. Another attempt to connect in some way?

She felt a tug on her scalp, and looked back to find John running a thick curl through his fingertips.

"Can I ask you a question?"

"You can," she told him with a smile, "but I may not answer it."

John grinned at her as she parroted back to him. "Is this your natural color?"

"Muddy brown, you mean? Yes, it is."

"It's not muddy," he told her firmly. "In the firelight it looks about ten different colors. None of them mud-colored."

"Thank you," she said finally. He tugged the loose curl out straight and let it fall, then pulled it out again. Finally, he tunneled his fingers in against her scalp, and Shannon could not help but groan. Nerve endings on her head leapt to attention. "That feels really good," she told him, and tipped her head to rest completely against the couch.

For several long minutes, he ran his fingers over and under and through her hair. "I have to warn you," she told him finally, "that if you don't quit, I'll be asleep in no time."

*****

John chuckled quietly, and continued to tug and massage her scalp. True to her word, within minutes, she was asleep, her head lolling with his movements.

John sighed and let his head rest on the pillow while he continued to run his hands through her hair. It was soft as silk, and smelled like some kind of fruity confection. Actually, *she* smelled like some kind of confection. It was a distinctive mix of sugar cookie and ocean. He could tell hours later when she had been in a room, and he always found himself inhaling more deeply, trying to track her down.

Hell, he'd known the minute she entered the living room, but he had feigned sleep for a moment, to watch her. And what a show he had gotten. The thin cotton gown she wore was nearly transparent, and he had seen every delicious curve of her body. The sight had turned him on unbearably, and he had spoken out so she wouldn't leave. Shannon's attention was becoming something he required, rather than just wanted.

His background was not something he ever talked about, but he had felt as if Shannon would understand and not pass judgment. It had been a long time since he thought about that period of his personal life, and he'd almost forgotten about his brother until she asked. What had his name been? Jason, James? J-A something. The only clear memory he had of him was when he was playing on the floor. John had had one of those wiggly-eyed rotary phones, and he remembered specifically giving that to the little guy before he was dropped off. They had been in an old blue station wagon, and the kid had been crying in the back. John had handed it over the seat, and gotten out of the car. There had been no goodbye kiss from his mother. She barely even looked at him as she drove away, leaving him on the steps of the orphanage.

What had happened to…was it Jake? No, that didn't sound right. James, Jamie. That was it. Jamie! What had happened to him when he disappeared? Had his mother eventually gotten tired of him as well, and dropped him off somewhere too? The thought nagged at him for a long time.

Shannon was beginning to slump forward. He sat up and debated what to do. Could he lift her up onto the couch? Did he have the leverage? There was plenty of room for her if he could. John reached down as far as he could, scooped underneath her legs and back, and lifted. Her weight overbalanced him a bit, but once he got her past a certain point, everything straightened out. She hardly weighed anything at all. Hell, the gear he used to carry weighed more than she did. He held his breath and waited for her to waken, but her eyes remained closed. She mumbled a bit in her sleep, but John whispered to her that everything was fine, and she quieted.

John lowered them both down to the couch cushion, Shannon's head on his shoulder. She was quiet as a mouse, and John felt a little bad about taking advantage of her this way, but he couldn't help himself. His heart pounded so loud he was afraid the sound would wake her. It had been so very long since he had held somebody against him in sleep. He tried to remember when it had been, but his brain was beginning to slow down. At least six years. There'd been nobody since he'd been in the chair. He wrapped his arms around her belly and pulled her against him. She sighed and melted into him, and his blood headed south. He tried to think generic thoughts to tamp down his desire. If she woke up, he didn't want her to run from the room in disgust.

Taking a deep breath, he buried his nose in her hair. Just the smell of her turned him on even more. God, what was he going to do with her?

*****

Shannon woke up slowly. She was incredibly warm and content. Somebody had bumped up the heat. With a sigh, she tucked her chin into the quilt and snuggled down.

She woke again a little later.

Eyes squinted, she looked for the alarm clock at the side of the bed, and was totally confused when she saw the fireplace. The fireplace? She was in the living room? Consciousness was returning quickly, and she realized the burning heat behind her was not the cat. It was a hard, masculine chest branding itself to her back. How on earth had she gotten here? John had been rubbing her hair. But she had been on the floor, not on the couch. Trying to move slowly, she turned her head to look behind her.

John's somber dark eyes regarded her quietly. "Good morning," he rumbled.

Damn, Shannon thought, his voice was even sexier with that rasp in it. She tried to summon up a smile. "Good morning. Uh, how did I get here?"

"You fell asleep, and rather than let you crumple on the floor, I brought you up here with me."

Blood crept into her cheeks. "Oh. Sorry 'bout that." Shannon started to peel back the blanket to sit up, but John tugged her back down.

"Don't leave just yet. You're very warm. And don't be sorry. I enjoyed every minute of it. I actually slept very good with you, which is surprising."

Shannon eased back down onto his shoulder and pulled the blanket up to her chin. A heavy hand resettled at her waist.

"You don't normally sleep well?"

"No. Dreams wake me up a lot, like last night."

"Oh," she said, inanely. Duh. Shannon felt so out of her depth as she lay here and tried not to breathe. Last night John Palmer was her somewhat friendly boss she had a crush on, but this morning they had stepped over some line. They were teetering, she felt, on the cusp of slipping into a relationship. Which was what she wanted, right? Her heart pounded so loud she knew he felt it.

Looking at the front window, she saw it was still dark out, so it had to be early.

"Can you fall back asleep after the dreams wake you?"

He was silent for a long time, and Shannon relaxed as she listened and felt his deep breaths. The burning heat from his body tempted her back to sleep as well, and she felt her eyelids drift down.

"Sometimes," he said finally.

John's right arm tightened over her belly, pulling her back snug against his front. Suddenly, she was not tired anymore. Shannon's skin tingled where it made contact with his, and her breath caught as she realized her nightgown had worked up around her hips and she couldn't feel any clothing on his legs. Bristly hair tickled the back of her knees, and she was hit with a wave of need. How bad was it that a man's legs turned her on? Instinctively, she arched her back and pressed her bottom into his groin.

John gasped and clenched a heavy hand on her hip. He also could not seem to prevent the involuntary grind, and Shannon was so extremely relieved to feel him swell into her bottom. They had not gotten to the point where they talked in depth about his injuries, so she had had no idea whether or not he could participate in a physical relationship. Even while her body readied itself for him, a corner of her mind cheered that this intrinsic part of being a man had not been taken from him.

And oh, if what she felt could be trusted, it would have been an incredible loss to womankind.

Shannon realized his hand on her hip trembled, just slightly. She peered over her shoulder at him.

"Are you okay?" she asked softly.

Heavy black lashes rested on his cheeks, and his skin looked ruddy in the dim glow from the coals. He inhaled deeply through his nose, lifted his lids and gave her a slow, sexy smile. All the angst of the week, and the worry, faded away at the sight of the most beautiful expression she'd ever seen on his face.

"I'm totally fine. Better than fine. Just relishing the feeling."

"I'm very happy for you too." Shannon could feel a heavy blush work up her neck and into her cheeks. "I worried that you…couldn't, ahh, do that."

In mortification, she turned her face away, back to the fireplace. John chuckled softly behind her, and squeezed her even tighter.

"Shannon, you're adorable. Thank you for worrying about me."

"I worry about all you guys," she told him firmly.

"I know."

With a last glance behind her, Shannon reluctantly slid off the couch. The chill of the room raised goose bumps on her arms. She retrieved the spare blanket from the floor and wrapped it around her. Outside the frosty windows, the sky was beginning to lighten, so she knew it had to be almost six. Time to start the day.

Turning to look at John, she saw he was once again on his back, with his arms folded behind his head. The homespun quilt rested below his pectorals, and Shannon had a difficult time making eye contact, with all the visual candy screaming at her. John's twinkling dark eyes told her he was not unaware of her problem, and he almost seemed to be…preening. Her eyes flicked south, and she moaned at the erection she could see even under the heavy quilt. It took a monumental effort to drag her eyes back up to his chest.

Clenching her teeth, Shannon spun away.

"I'm going to take a shower. Breakfast will be ready in half an hour."

*****

John chuckled outright as Shannon swept down the hallway, blanket corner trailing behind on the floor. The happiness he felt inside seemed almost out of proportion to the situation. What had actually happened? They had talked, then slept together on the couch for a few hours before he got a hard-on and scared her away.

So what?

So, big what.

For the first time in six years, he had slept with a woman.

Kind of.

And she had responded. That one small arch of her spine had made him feel ten feet tall.

Kind of.

It had made him forget, for one infinitesimal moment, that he wasn't even six feet tall anymore.

So, where did they go from here? It was obvious there was desire on both their parts, but was it enough? What if he couldn't perform once he got it up? And if he did get it up, would she expect a relationship? Gratification for the moment was all well and good, but what if the relationship did not survive? The two of them had to work together every day. What would happen if they fell through? Hell, even thinking the word "relationship" gave him cold chills.

The questions chased each other around in his mind for several minutes. Finally, he devoted a small sliver of time to imagining the best-case scenario. But with his limited relationship experience, he had no real idea where exactly it could go. It was not as if he had great role models, either. The only somewhat working marriage he had seen had been Duncan's parents, Meredith and Joe. They had been together for almost forty years. They still got along fine, and seemed to genuinely care about one another. It was a fact they both loved Duncan. That was very apparent. But John had never really paid much attention to their relationship dynamic.

He reached for his clothes on the floor under the end table and dragged them up beside him as he sat up. Pushing his legs to the floor, John dressed and transferred himself to his chair, then rolled into the bathroom to relieve himself and clean up. By the time he returned, he heard Shannon in the kitchen rattling pans. After checking the security cameras again, he took a deep breath. There was a chance she'd be pissed or aggravated at him for taking advantage.

John rolled into the kitchen and parked himself at the open spot at the table.

Shannon glanced at him as she moved about the kitchen. Within a few seconds she brought over a cutting board with two big potatoes on it.

"Would you slice those for me?"

John stared in bemusement as she retreated. Nothing made him angrier than people who wanted to do everything for him. Women who looked at him in pity as they held a door open for him really pissed him off. Or men who smirked as he rolled into the handicapped stall of public restrooms. Why couldn't they keep their noses to themselves?

Shannon, on the other hand, had never treated him as if he were disabled. Not once. Several times, *he* had held the door open for *her*, not the other way around. Although, he did concede, she had held doors for him on occasion.

It surprised him that he only just now thought of that. She *had* opened doors for him. Why did it bother him when other people did it, but not Shannon?

Maybe because she treats you as an equal, not as someone who has to have the door opened for them.

"Come on, John. I need those potatoes."

With a wave of his knife, John quit daydreaming and started peeling.

*****

They didn't get as much snow as was predicted, though there was some to shovel Monday morning. The storm had moved slower than expected and would arrive later in the day. Shannon scraped the ramp and walkway clean while John watched. Actually, he glowered from the front porch.

At the driveway, she used a broom to clean a path to the driver's side of his pick-up. She assumed she would just ride with him today. She stomped her way to John, trying to knock as much snow from her boots as possible before she went inside.

John looked thoroughly pissed when she stopped in front of him. "What's wrong?" she asked, winded from her exertions.

He didn't say a word, just turned and rolled into the house. Confused, Shannon followed him. "What?"

"Nothing Shannon. Just…nothing."

Shannon pulled off her snow boots and shoved them in the closet. Obviously he was pissed that she was the one shoveling snow. Well, he'd just have to suck it up, otherwise they wouldn't be able to go anywhere.

Shannon didn't say anything, just walked to the bedroom to change into her work clothes. She needed to get into a different frame of mind.

Chapter Five

Work was different that day. All the guys on shift came to her to tell her they had her back, and if she needed anything to let them know. It made Shannon's heart warm with gratitude that they would tell her that.

Then Duncan told her there would be no charge for any of the services rendered.

"You're part of the family," he told her. "I wouldn't charge my little brother for anything."

Shannon almost cried. Instead, she just hugged him.

"Don't get too excited," he warned her. "We need to have a meeting, and we're going to have to dig into what happened years ago."

Shannon nodded that she understood. Whatever it took to be done with this mess.

John disappeared as soon as they came in the door, and she didn't see him for several hours. Which was fine. By the time this was all over, they would probably be sick of each other. But she couldn't help but glance up every time she heard a sound in the hallway or office.

Lunch was a mediocre affair in the break room. Chad came in and sat with her to eat his own sandwich, but they avoided talking about Michael or anything that had gone on. He did tell her about the group of them going to the bar, and Zeke talking to a girl.

"Did he really?" Shannon was impressed.

Chad nodded and told her they planned to go again next Saturday.

"Good, you all need to get out and be social."

When two o'clock finally rolled around, she was nervous and anxious to be done with the meeting. Then she was angry at herself. There were just trying to help her.

Duncan had papers spread across his desk when she walked in, and his computer had several different screens up and running. He hung up the phone when he saw her.

"Hey, Shannon. Have a seat. I just called the other two in. They'll be here in a minute."

Chad came in first, with John bringing up the rear. Shannon tried really hard not to stare at him too long, but it was obvious he noticed. His eyes flared with something hot before he looked away and guided his chair to the other side of Duncan's desk. Chad handed Duncan a file folder, then sat down in the chair beside Shannon. Patting her knee, he smiled his charming smile.

"Don't worry, babe. We'll be done with this in no time."

Shannon didn't know if he meant the meeting or the situation they were in, but she smiled anyway.

"Okay, Shannon," Duncan leaned forward and steepled his hands together in front of his face, "I know this is difficult, and John has filled us in a bit on what happened, but in your own words, could you tell us about Michael Gerbowski? What you did, how you met, all that. And take your time. We're not going anywhere."

Shannon nodded, reassured. Taking a deep breath, she launched into her tale. Most of the things she had already told John, but she filled in what she knew of the police and psychiatric reports gathered in the investigation. She told them about the whispers she had heard about her not being the first one he had done this to, but nobody being able to substantiate the rumors. Duncan took notes, and asked questions here and there, but mostly stayed quiet. John rolled over to the window to watch outside.

"So, nobody has a key to your house?" Duncan asked finally.

"My parents do, but they're several hundred miles away. I have a spare here, taped to the inside drawer of my desk if I need it, and yes, I checked, it's still there. Hasn't been moved. Tape hasn't been broken. And my neighbor Lisa has one, because I have a tendency to lock myself out."

Duncan nodded his silver head, appreciative she seemed to know what he was going to ask. Shannon could tell him she'd been through these interviews before, but most of the other times nobody could help her. She clasped her arms under her breasts and rubbed at her cool skin. She really hoped it didn't get to the same point this time.

"Well," Duncan said finally, "you've told us about everything we've already discovered. The only bit I have to add is that I talked to the Warden at the Ohio State Pen. He says Gerbowski has very few visitors, and is generally a good inmate." He turned to John. "He said that they do have metal detectors going in and out."

John turned his chair with one hand. "So, the can didn't come from the prison, then?"

Duncan shook his head. "If it did, I don't know how."

John scowled and crossed his arms over his expansive chest.

Shannon could tell by the look on his face he had hoped for a lead. A visitor they could investigate. Something.

"Well, we'll keep the investigation going on the can. They did find something else of interest. There was a rose petal inside the can."

Shannon actually felt her face pale. "A rose petal?"

"Yes."

John pivoted until he could reach a hand out to her knee. "Does it mean something to you, Shannon?"

"Well, kind of. Mike used to leave roses in places he knew I was going to be."

John's mouth tightened and his gaze shot to Duncan's across the desk. But Duncan didn't appear ruffled. "For now I suggest you file a police report, just to get these strange occurrences down on record." He winked at her. "Just in case somebody breaks into your home and gets shot trespassing."

Shannon's gaze shot to John. He had the most threatening grin on his face she had ever seen, and she had to laugh out loud.

"Bloodthirsty?"

He winked at her, out of sight of the other men. Warmth coursed through her. It was the most intimate thing he had ever done in the company of others, and it warmed her heart.

The meeting broke up, and Shannon did as she was instructed

and called the police to file a report. The officer arrived within just a few minutes. He was polite and oozed charm, and he noted everything down diligently. John stayed in the meeting room with her, to explain that the evidence had already been turned in and to fill the officer in on the steps LNF had taken in the investigation.

Shannon did not miss the look of pity the officer cast at John when he first walked in and saw John sitting at the end of the table in a wheelchair. Unfortunately, John didn't miss the look either, and Shannon recognized the signs of an impending blow-up. His square jaw was clenched, and his eyes were squinted.

To make things worse, Officer Wilkins flirted with her, just a bit. Shannon tried to respond unemotionally to his questions, and did not acknowledge in any way his flirting. Maybe if she ignored the advances, he would get the hint. Actually, she was getting angry on John's behalf. The officer completely ignored him, even going so far as to step into her line of sight to block her view of him. Shannon shifted just a bit to the opposite leg, where she could watch her boss out of the corner of her eye.

But the officer didn't get the hint. As the interview drew to a close, Officer Wilkins removed a business card from his breast pocket. He scrawled another number on the back of the crisp white card.

"Ms. Murphy, here are my work numbers and email. And I put my personal cell number on the back, you know, just in case something comes up and you need to talk."

If Shannon had been any other woman, she probably would have taken him up on his advances, because the officer wasn't bad looking. Dark hair and kind eyes, but he *knew* he was cute, and that was very off-putting. Her eyes drifted to John. He looked ready to blow up. Shannon actually felt a shiver of fear for the officer.

She smiled and thanked the man for his time, then walked him to the door. The report would be done within a couple of days and she could pick up a copy at her convenience.

John was still in the conference room when she returned.

"Well," she said, "that was interesting."

John glowered at her from beneath his brows. She took the chair beside him.

"Don't they teach tact in police academies?" she asked curiously.

Incredibly, John's face closed down even more. "You mean when they deal with cripples?" he snapped.

"What?"

John glared at her. "You heard me."

Hurt ripped through her. Is that what he thought she was talking about?

"Actually, I meant him hitting on me in the middle of an investigation." Gathering her dignity, she carefully stood and pushed the office chair under the table. "Thank you for sitting in on the meeting, John."

With as much dignity as she could muster, she walked out.

*****

"Fuck!"

John called himself ten kinds of idiot asshole as he watched her walk out the door, head high. She didn't look back at him, and he couldn't blame her. He'd behaved like a child. Pouting and belligerent. That guy, standing tall and strong in his uniform, had pushed every one of his buttons. Attractive, cocky. Hell, he'd been just like him not too many years ago. Maybe that was why he had such a problem with him—because he saw so much of himself in the officer.

Shannon hadn't reacted the way he'd expected, though. Instead of being flattered, she'd been uncomfortable and angry because of the way the officer had acted.

And he thought it was all about him. *I'm such an ass.*

Shannon avoided him all afternoon, and John felt nauseous to his stomach, which just pissed him off. He felt like he was in trouble. Hell, he *knew* he was in trouble. And he didn't like being in the wrong. He watched until the minutes dwindled to five o'clock. Trapped in the car, she had to talk to him.

At five after five she was dressed and waiting for him in the reception area. They didn't say anything as he followed her onto the elevator, went down the four floors to the lobby and out the front door of the building. Outside, snowflakes swirled, but John didn't even notice. He scanned the street left and right. His gaze was caught by a man diagonal from them. In the swirling snow, John couldn't make out many details, but his senses went on edge. Tall. Wearing a dark hooded coat and leaning against the corner of a building. A red, white and blue RTD bus gasped to a stop, and when it pulled away, the man was gone. He'd just been waiting for the bus. He noted the number of the route to check later, and continued to scan.

A car idled at the curb with tinted windows, exhaust fumes curling lazily into the air. He maneuvered himself between Shannon and the car, and also memorized the plate number to check later. A smartly dressed woman in heels walked out of the building behind them and climbed into the car.

John stayed alert all the way to the truck. He unlocked the doors but he waved her back so he could check the vehicle. Nothing looked tampered with. He pressed the button on the remote to lower the lift. Once inside and with the truck started, he looked at her through the windshield.

Shannon waited patiently, arms crossed, at the front of the vehicle. A cream-colored hat covered her chocolate-colored curls, and matched the thigh-length coat she wore. The cold had brought out color in her cheeks, and John was distracted for a moment by how beautiful she was. It was no wonder the cop had hit on her. Even as she stared at him mulishly, he couldn't help but smile.

That just seemed to make her madder. "Are you done?"

He nodded and she climbed into the passenger side of the truck, setting her lunchbox and purse on the floorboard.

Shannon rubbed her hands together as she settled in. She flicked the heat on. John stopped her hand as she started to pull away.

"Just a minute, please. I need to talk to you."

Shannon's gaze turned wary as she sat back in the chair. "Did you hear something?"

"About the case? No. I wanted to tell you I was sorry for the way I acted earlier."

"Oh. That's okay. No big deal."

John watched her out of the corner of his eye. He didn't like the offhand way she said that.

"It is a big deal. I overreacted, and I apologize. I just"—he turned his head to look at her—"got defensive, because he was hitting on you. Honestly, if I were you, I'd take him up on it. I mean, he was good looking, and healthy. Seemed charming. Your age."

Shannon held up a hand to cut him off. "Did you check his teeth?"

John frowned at her. "What?"

"If you're buying a horse, the first thing you check is his teeth."

John knew he stared, but he had no idea what she was talking about.

Shannon waved a hand in frustration. "You've already decided we'd be a perfect couple. You're trying to sell me a horse I don't want."

John reared his head back in realization. "Ah. Okay. Sorry." Man, could he screw this up anymore than he already had? His relationship inexperience was really showing. "I didn't mean to sound like that. I just…" He took a deep breath. "I don't want to hold you back."

Shannon's face scrunched up in confusion. "Why would you think you hold me back?"

John clamped his jaw and looked away.

"Ah," she said softly.

John hated that one small sound, and the wealth of meaning that went with it. Something popped in his jaw.

"Let me tell you something, John." She leaned back in the chair and took a deep breath.

He didn't dare look at her, but the breath stalled in his lungs as he waited. He kept his face deliberately turned to the window.

"I want you to listen to what I say, and actually hear. Your disability is more of a hurdle to you than me, and I don't mean physically. I've lived with a paraplegic, so I'm probably a little more cognizant of what you go through every day than anybody else here. As well as the kind of care you may eventually need."

He caught a glimpse of her hand in the air, and he assumed she had waved at the building. John had to admit, she was probably right. Other than Duncan, none of the other operatives were wheelchair-bound. Several had been in the chair during recovery, but only he and his partner had spent any length of time in one.

She was silent, but she leaned toward him enough to catch his gaze with her own. John couldn't look away from her gentle smile. "I like you. A lot. I wasn't flirting with that cop because he didn't do anything for me. You're the one that makes my heart race."

Fear and exhilaration flashed through him, heady in their force. On the one hand, he was man enough to admit he was scared to death that she was interested him. Because interest led to other things, and he didn't know if he could fulfill her expectations. On the other hand, the fact that she admitted out loud that she was attracted in him floored him and humbled him. What did he have that that cop didn't? What did she see in him that nobody else ever had?

Unable to help himself, John cupped her head in his hands and brought his mouth to hers. She was surprised for a moment, then her luscious lips softened and she pressed back, clutching at his shirt and jacket with her gloved hands. He teased her lips with his tongue, requesting entrance. With a moan, her mouth opened, and John found himself lost in the sweetness inside. It had been so long since he'd been intimate with anybody, but his body remembered what it was supposed to do, and responded with enthusiasm, which thrilled him even more. The rush of blood heading south made him lightheaded.

Nibbling his way down her neck, John tried to absorb her intoxicating scent into his body. Even when he'd gone home the previous morning, he could still smell her in his clothes.

Shannon pulled away enough to look in his eyes. One hand brushed at the beard growing on his jaw, and he moved away, concerned. "Is my beard too rough?" He rubbed one of his own hands over the hair, but it was too calloused from the chair to feel how rough it was. He scanned her skin for redness, but didn't see any.

Shannon smiled at him and shook her head gently. "No, it's fine. I was just looking at you. I've never had a kiss like that."

Immediately, his defenses came up. "Like what?" Maybe he'd been out of the dating game too long and had done something wrong. Some faux pas he knew nothing about.

"I've never had a kiss that gentle. It was very nice."

With one last brush of her hand against his cheek, she faced forward and gripped her hands in her lap. Eventually, she connected the seat belt and sat back.

John gripped the steering wheel, shook. That kiss had knocked him on his ass, and she called it nice. Fuck! He turned to scan their surroundings as they headed for her house.

*****

It was everything she could do to keep her hands to herself as John drove them home. John had kissed her. Not some peck on the cheek, but a rockin', wet kiss that made her melt all over. She shifted subtly in the seat and tried to ease the pressure from her pants. Deliberately she kept her eyes facing forward. What she really wanted to do was look at him to see if he was as affected as she was. There had been a slight tremble in his hands, but maybe it had just been her trembling. She certainly was now. Her stomach quivered with nerves and her mind repeated those few seconds over and over. As hard and forbidding as he was, his lips were as soft as down, and gentle as a whisper. Totally the opposite of how he presented himself.

She wanted to taste him again. And more. She could feel how wet she was. Her body wanted to go all the way, and her brain was heading that way as well.

They didn't speak as she drove them home, which was okay. They were each lost in their own thoughts. When he pulled in the drive, John had her sit in the truck for a few minutes while he observed the surroundings. Then he lowered himself in the chair to the driveway, pushed the button for the door to retract and powered himself up the ramp. Shannon watched, heart pounding, as he let himself into the house and disengaged the alarm. She counted the seconds as she waited for him to reappear and wave her in.

Minutes ticked away, and her tension mounted painfully. She was just about to call Duncan on her cell phone when John appeared at the doorway with Boohini in his lap. Shannon climbed out of the truck, snatched up her purse and lunchbox and jogged up the ramp.

"You scared me," she told him as she crossed the threshold. "I thought something had happened to you."

John's eyes narrowed into a squint, as if he didn't know what to make of her words. He took her lunchbox from her hand and motioned to the cat on his lap. "I heard something, and the motion detectors had gone off, so I had to sweep the house. This guy was in your bedroom, as far underneath the bed as he could go. He was a pain in my ass to get."

The tension in Shannon's stomach eased. She'd left the cat box inside the kitchen this morning. The little cat was an explorer, and she had found him under her bed once herself. But the lingering taste of fear in her mouth was not pleasant. She had really been worried about John. Was the entire ordeal going to be like this?

She turned to the closet and removed her coat and hat and hung them on one of the hangers. John still wore his, so she wiggled her fingers at him to take it off, then hung it beside her own. Her hand dragged down the sleeve slowly, savoring the warmth.

John was looking at her oddly when she turned from the closet. "You okay?"

Shannon nodded and walked around him. "Yes. I'm going to

go change."

Without waiting for a response, she headed for her bedroom. Heels went into the closet with a thump and the outfit went onto a hanger for the dry-cleaner. She tossed a set of soft pink sweats on the bed and crossed to the bathroom to brush out her hair. If she were home alone, she would strip off the constricting bra too, but she didn't think that was wise with John in the house. She needed all the support she could get around him. It seemed like her nipples waited for him to notice them, pressing as hard as they could against the cup of the bra. It drove her nuts constantly being aroused.

And certainly tonight would be harder, considering the kiss they'd just shared. He hadn't said anything about it, of course, but she had felt the weight of his gaze on her face several times on the short trip home, and her lips had tingled every time. Desire beat at her almost constantly now.

What would he do if she made the first move? Would he respond, as she thought maybe he would? Or would he try to be a stand-up kind of guy and keep the situation on an even keel? Things could get difficult if they entered into a relationship that didn't work out. There would be no escaping each other at the office. Shannon knew in her heart that if a relationship with John didn't work out, she would leave to find a job elsewhere.

As she looked at herself in the mirror, and saw the dazed, fuzzy look in her eyes from that kiss, she vowed to herself that she would try to make the relationship work. John would have to be the one to take it in that direction, though. He needed to have enough faith in them to try.

Pulling her hair back into a ponytail, she went to the bedroom to slip on her sweat suit. It wasn't until she padded down the hallway that she remembered the cameras. There was one in the corner of her ceiling sighted directly at her bed.

Exactly where she had stood to pull on her clothes.

John could not hide the guilt in his face as he turned away from the monitors in the living room. "I, uh, was going over the recorded footage. Just so you know, the cameras don't come on until there's movement in the field of view. You may want to remember that when you change. And stuff."

Color flushed his lean cheeks, and Shannon forgot her own embarrassment. He had watched her. Damn, how long had she stood beside the bed in just her bra? Several minutes, anyway. Her gaze dropped to the remote control that rested on his lap. It was no shield for the erection she could see behind the zipper of his jeans. Glancing up, she was surprised to see him glowering at her. "Quit it," he growled.

With a grin, she turned for the kitchen. Maybe it would be fun to tease the lion in her den, so to speak.

*****

Dinner was a plain affair of hamburgers topped with mushrooms and French fries done in the oven. John ate quickly, then retreated to the living room to keep an eye on the monitors. Shannon didn't think they needed to be watched so closely, but she kept her mouth shut. If he wanted to avoid her, that was his prerogative.

Heading out to the front closet, she retrieved the officer's card from her pocket and stuck it to the fridge with a magnet. Aggravation ate at her, and she wondered if she should report him to his superiors. How many other women had he hit on that way, she wondered? She was loath to bring it up to John because of the reaction he had, but maybe she could say something to Duncan.

The kittens were more than happy to occupy her for a while, and Shannon laughed at some of their antics. They were almost six weeks old now, and she would need to find homes for them soon. The neighbor's child down the street wanted one of the kittens, and had already chosen one of the black ones with white feet. Actually, the little girl wanted Pickle too, but Shannon just couldn't part with her.

And even though John denied it, she thought he wanted one too. Having a little cat to come home to would probably do him good.

With a sigh, she wished she knew how to get close to him. She walked out into the living room.

"I'm not really tired," she told him finally. "Want to watch some TV?"

"Sure."

Shannon pulled the remotes to her and plopped down onto the couch, legs stretched out along the length, before she started to flip through channels. What would John want to watch? The cooking show with the yelling chef? No. The travel channel going to New York? Probably not.

"If you see something you want to watch, let me know."

Nodding his head, he turned his chair and rolled a little closer to the couch.

"There. That's good."

Jeopardy was on the screen. "Jeopardy? Really?"

Dark brows lowered over his dark eyes. "What's wrong with that?" he demanded.

Shannon held up her hands with a smile. "Not a thing. It's one of my favorites too. You just surprised me."

The show was, of course, a re-run on the Game Show Network. Shannon was surprised when John started to blurt out answers. He did not seem the type to be like that. Shannon tossed out her own responses, although most of them were incredibly wrong.

They were both laughing when the show went to commercial before Double Jeopardy. Shannon went to the kitchen for popcorn and drinks, and when she came back, John had positioned himself on the opposite end of the couch, and had just pushed his chair behind. Shannon's heart began to pound as she sat in the couch corner and tucked one leg underneath her. It would be so hard not to touch him when he was this close. She placed the bowl on the cushion between them, and tried not to choke each time John's hand bumped hers.

After a while, Shannon did begin to relax and enjoy herself again. John grumbled when his answers were wrong, and pumped the air with his fist and an "oorah!" when he got one right that the contestants did not. Watching him was vastly more entertaining than the show.

Somehow or another, his big left hand ended up wrapped around her foot. Shannon did not even notice it at first, because she was laughing at him, but when he started to massage, all the nerve endings in her foot started to scream. John himself did not seem to know he was even doing it, and it made Shannon's heart pound when she realized he had reached out to her, not vice versa.

The show finally drew to a close, and Shannon muted the sound.

"You impress me, John," she told him honestly. "I guess you're not just a jarhead."

John tipped back his head and laughed, and Shannon could not help but laugh with him.

"When we were in the hospital," he murmured, "we would have competitions for all the game shows. Helped to break up the time."

"I'm sure."

He suddenly realized his hand was wrapped around her foot, and his laughter subsided. With narrowed eyes, he wrapped both hands around her narrow foot, measuring it against the length of his hand, from heel to toe. Shaking his head, he wrapped his fingers around her anklebone. Long, calloused fingers overlapped.

"You are so small," he said finally.

"I know, I know. Don't bother with the short jokes. I've heard them all."

It was meant to be funny, but he didn't laugh the way he was supposed to. Instead, he ran his fingers inside the edge of her sock and circled gently. Shannon was intrigued by the thoughtful look on his face. She didn't believe he was actually thinking about how small she was.

"You okay?" she asked softly.

Deep brown eyes flicked to hers, then latched on. Shannon was curious about the tension she felt in the air.

"You know I'll never walk again, right?"

She cocked her head to the side and regarded him carefully. Why was he asking her this?

"I know that as of right now," she said carefully, "you are not able to walk."

"No, not as of right now. As of *never*. My spine was crushed, Shannon. That's not going to change. I have feeling occasionally in one or both of my legs, but I was told that it didn't necessarily mean anything."

Anger vibrated in his tone, but Shannon could not tell if he was angry with her or the fact that his spine was crushed. Six years after the injury, the anger should have at least started to ease. But maybe not. Treading lightly, she agreed with him.

"No, your injury isn't going to change, but every day there are new advances in the medical world. You never know when a crush injury like yours may have a chance of being repaired. Is it a complete or incomplete injury?"

John shook his head at her stubbornness, but continued to rub her ankle. Finally, he looked up at her with troubled eyes. "Incomplete. I still have some feeling in my legs, but it doesn't mean anything. I like you Shannon. I don't want to…hurt you. Or lead you on thinking you might have a future with me."

Her heart warmed at the timbre of his voice, and the thought that he had considered a future with her. "I don't want to be hurt either. I can't help but be hopeful, though."

He looked away, back toward the fire. He still rubbed her foot, though. Shannon tried to remember when the last time was she had seen him voluntarily touch anybody, and no instance came to mind. Usually she was the touchy one, but he had reached out to her a lot recently. It was hard not to put some kind of stock in his actions. John was not the wasteful type. If he touched her, it was for a reason.

Shannon's breath stalled in her throat as his hand began to glide up her leg underneath the soft cotton of her pant, all the way to her kneecap, then back down. Several times he repeated the action. Instinctively, her muscles tightened when he reached her knee, waiting to see if he would go any farther up or not. Honestly, Shannon had no idea what she would do if he did. The cotton was getting too tight for him to go much farther anyway.

His troubled eyes followed his hand now, as if he were trying to reconcile in his mind what his hand was feeling. "Your skin is so soft," he whispered.

Shannon turned her leg slightly to give him access to the even softer skin on the inside of her knee.

"Damn," he whispered. "It's like butter."

Shannon fought the shivers that coursed through her. The tentative, gentle motion of his fingers turned her on. She had never felt anything so exquisitely pleasurable. She loved touch. She loved anything with texture. And, right now, John's rough hands on her skin felt sublime.

He motioned for her to turn around and back up against him. Holding her breath in anticipation, Shannon nestled into the crook of his shoulder. He shifted her a little bit and rested his arm over her shoulder, folding her into him.

Shannon was in heaven. The man smelled so good! She couldn't even identify exactly what he smelled like, just "spicy man". And he was so warm. His skin burned like a furnace. She found herself nestling in closer to him just for his warmth. He dragged a blanket up over the both of them, and snagged the remotes from her side of the couch.

"Ah, I see now," she told him laughing. "You wanted me distracted while you stole the remote. Okay, buddy, you can have it for now."

John chuckled and un-muted the screen. He squeezed her and began flipping through channels. He stopped on Animal Planet at a popular law-enforcement show. Shannon settled back happily.

"I love this show."

John's chest jerked underneath her in a laugh. "I figured you would."

They watched TV for a couple more hours. She eventually slid down until her head rested on John's thigh. He kept his heavy hand on her arm, or her shoulder or hip. She didn't care what they watched, as long as he held her the way he was. Her eyes drifted shut.

She woke when John prodded her gently. "I'm going to have

to shift. I've been in one position too long."

Shannon sat up immediately, blinking heavily. "Oh, John. I'm sorry. I was just so comfortable."

John smiled slightly. "I was too, actually." He reached around the arm of the couch and pulled out his chair. Shannon began to gather the dirty dishes, and watched as he shifted himself over to the sleek silver-wheeled chair and tucked his feet against the bar. He made it look easy. After so many years, it probably was easy for him, or at least not as hard. Her eyes lingered on his upper body, honed by time to perfection. The deep hills and valleys of his abdomen tightened and released, and it was a struggle to remember what she was doing.

John made a round of the house, ending in the bathroom. Shannon felt on edge, and didn't understand why. She slipped down the hall and into her own bedroom to change into nightclothes, then went back out to tell him good night.

John was at the wide bay window in the living room, peering out the tiniest slit between the closed drapes. Beyond him, she could see snow swirling.

He shoved himself away from the window, and fiddled with one of the dials on the little closed-circuit TVs.

"What's wrong?"

He glanced up at her. "The snow is swirling too hard for the cameras to see anything. It's white out."

Shannon wasn't too worried. The delayed storm had finally rolled in. It happened all the time in Colorado. As long as John was in here with her, she was sure she'd be fine.

There was a fierce frown on his face, and Shannon felt her own tension creep up. "What else?"

He didn't respond for several seconds. Finally, he shrugged. "Not sure exactly. Something just feels off."

"I feel it too," she admitted, and crossed her arms over her breasts.

John stopped what he was doing and looked at her hard. "Like something's creeping up your spine?"

She nodded. "Or watching us."

The warrior in front of her grinned fiercely, and she had a flash of what he must have been like before the war changed him: brash and bold and playful, daring life to hand him its best. Or worst.

The lights suddenly flickered and went out.

Shannon gasped and moved to the wall closest to her, then slid down into a crouch. "John?"

The glide of his chair wheels on the hardwood floor barely made a sound, but she could feel his warmth as he drew closer. He leaned down and cupped her face to whisper in her ear. "Stay right here, no matter what, so I know where you are."

She nodded firmly. Her eyes strained in the darkness as he rolled away. The fire had died down to coals. She should have stoked it by now. Then she'd have light.

Time dragged unmercifully as she sat hunched on the floor. The wind from the storm howled outside, and she thought she heard it get louder at one point, as if somebody had opened a door. A swirl of cold air swept across the floor, and she shuddered, praying that John wasn't going to try to go outside. She counted her heartbeats as she waited for him to return. A crash in the garage set her heart racing, but she forced herself to stay still.

The lights flashed back on, blinding her. Nothing moved in the house, but she stayed crouched where she was. John had told her to stay right here, so she would.

Shannon clamped her jaw to keep from calling out. She didn't want to endanger him if he responded. When he rounded the corner from the kitchen, though, she couldn't keep in a small gasp. She bolted across the room and stopped just short of slamming into him. She reached one hand out to touch him. "I was worried."

*****

John froze for a moment, stunned that she would even care. He folded her hand into his own and tugged, and she wrapped her arms around his neck. Slipping one arm under her knees, he swung her into his lap. She curled into him as if she belonged there.

He fought to maintain some kind of emotional distance. There was a bad guy out there messing with her, and he needed to keep his cool. The problem was, he'd never meant anything to anybody. He'd been a buddy and friend to the guys, but he'd never been involved with a woman the same way.

As she tightened her arms around his neck, emotion clutched at his throat.

"I thought you were in trouble. I heard the door open and I thought somebody had come in."

John cleared his throat and stroked a hand over her loose curls. "No, no, I just checked the power box in the garage. It's fine. Must have been a tree branch falling on the power line or something to make it black out."

She pulled back enough to look up at him. "I didn't want you to get hurt."

Those big hazel eyes looked at him as if he were the most important thing in her world. John leaned forward and covered·her lips with his own, desperate to maintain that connection.

After so long without, he should have been rusty at kissing, but everything was so natural with Shannon, it was no effort at all to just let himself drown in her. She tasted so good. Freshness, and mint, and something more abstract too. She tasted of hope, and fear, and desire.

John didn't dare look for anything other than what she offered right that second. As much as he enjoyed her company, he didn't think he was built for relationships. He didn't want to hurt her when she wanted more than he could give.

That sober thought made him pull away in regret. He wished he could go back five years and tell Hanity to drive on past that vehicle. Hell, he wished he could just go back and talk to Hanity, who'd stayed in the vehicle. The kid hadn't deserved to die over there.

John cringed at the confused look on Shannon's face. She'd been enjoying a kiss, and he'd been replaying traumas in his head. "Sorry, Shannon. I just don't know that right now is the best time to do this."

It was like he'd kicked a puppy. The aroused, slumberous look faded away to be replaced with reserve, and she slid off his lap.

"Yes, of course. Okay. I'm going to bed. Do you need anything?"

He shook his head and she turned and padded down the hallway. He watched her hips sway for a minute before he dragged his gaze away.

Stupid asshole. She was right there on your lap, kissing you better than you've ever been kissed, and you shut her down.

The erection strained his zipper, but he tried to ignore the distraction. Somebody was after Shannon, and he needed to figure out whom.

Chapter Six

After a restless sleep that night, Shannon rose and dressed in the bathroom, then headed to the kitchen. John was already up and in his chair, and she had to wonder yet again if he had even gone to bed. The blankets were folded the same way she'd left them, although his clothes were different. His short hair was slicked down and glossy, so he must have managed a shower.

"Good morning." She was determined to play it cool.

"Morning," he rumbled.

Shannon fought not to react to his rusty voice, even though it sent chills racing down her spine and made her nipples tighten. The man was too sexy for her peace of mind.

She threw something together for breakfast, then escaped to finish getting ready. When she glanced out the bedroom window, she had second thoughts. The snow had really accumulated last night. The boughs of the pines dragged the ground, and she couldn't see anything moving on the street.

"Hey, John," she called.

"Yeah."

"Have you looked outside?"

"Yeah. Don't think we're going anywhere today."

That was what she thought too, but she just wanted to hear him confirm it. She pulled a favorite sweatshirt over top of the long-sleeved t-shirt she already had on and slipped her feet into her slippers to pad down the hallway. John was on his cell phone, obviously talking to Duncan. Shannon picked up the receiver of the house phone. Dead.

She wasn't surprised. Colorado was notorious for bad weather, and if a person got upset by minor things like dead phone lines and car batteries, it wasn't the place for them. At least they still had power. She had a generator in the garage if they needed it.

Difficult to start, but a necessity, nonetheless. Crossing to the fireplace, she stoked the coals, and within minutes had a wonderful blaze going. The stack of wood beside the grate had dwindled quickly. John was still talking, so she grabbed a jacket from her closet and stepped out onto the back porch.

And screamed.

A bloody, mangled, furry mess lay on the concrete porch lightly covered in snow, and Shannon stumbled back into the house, slamming the door shut. John was right there when she turned, and she clutched his shirt in her hands, gasping. He shushed her and set her gently aside, then opened the door and scanned outside. His gun was already in his hand. Shannon backed farther into the kitchen as he rolled out the door. She didn't know what the thing lying on the concrete had been, but it had died a horrible death.

John came back in a few minutes later. Shannon had gotten hold of her emotions, somewhat, but she felt brittle.

"It's just a dog, Shannon." He pulled her hands into his and stared into her eyes. "It looks like it was hit somewhere else and dragged here. There's no fresh blood. Whoever brought it here dropped it on the concrete and left over the back fence, dragging a branch or something behind them to cover up their tracks. The snowstorm then covered that track, so that we wouldn't see anything unless you looked specifically. I need to get a crew out here, to catalog the evidence and get photographs as soon as possible. Okay?"

Shannon nodded, and crossed to the sink to scrub her hands. She hadn't actually touched the poor thing, but she still felt dirty.

"You shouldn't have gone out there alone."

She could tell John was angry at her, and it made her defensive. "You were on the phone, and I didn't want to bother you. It was just the back porch."

"What if the guy had been standing out there waiting for you to come out?" John actually growled, and smacked the cupboard beside her. Shannon jumped in surprise and winced at the sound. Tears came to her eyes. She didn't want John to be mad at her.

It *had* been irresponsible. Hell, she hadn't even looked through the vertical blinds before she walked out. Taking a deep breath, she forced the tears away. "You're right, and I'm sorry. I didn't think, I just went along like I normally do." She looked him in the eye. "I won't do it again, I promise."

John was still angry, but he accepted her apology. He turned away to the living room, and within a few seconds she heard him on the phone, calling people in.

For two hours, her house turned into a circus. The police came to file another report and take pictures. The detectives arrived to ask questions, and the crime scene people stomped through her house and outside as they gathered evidence. Duncan stopped to look things over and talk to John. He gave her a big hug when he walked in the door. "Don't worry, Shannon. We'll get him."

She nodded and hugged the older man back. He'd become a dear friend to her over the months and she had a lot of faith in his abilities. She retreated to her bedroom and curled up in the soft little chair beside the window. Here she could watch the cars pull in and leave her driveway, but she didn't need to talk to anybody else.

Duncan was the last to leave, and the house finally quieted. At some point she drifted off into a weary doze. When she woke John sat beside her in his chair. The light had dimmed outside, fading into afternoon. A snowplow lumbered past, spitting salt.

Shannon adjusted and stretched her arms above her head. When she looked at John, he was just shifting his eyes away from her breasts. Shannon smiled inwardly, even as she girded herself for him to say whatever it was that had the frown on his face. He started to say something, then looked like he changed his mind and went in a different direction.

"I, uh, shouldn't have snapped at you." The words were quiet, and sounded like they were forced out.

She shrugged. "I think I needed it. Walking out the door was irresponsible. I'll remember next time."

He blinked at her as if he were surprised at how easy the apology had been. He ran his palms down his jean-clad thighs.

"It'll be a while before we hear anything from forensics, but on preliminary examination, it looks like the dog was just road kill. There were bald patches where the hair had been scraped off, and a couple of minor marks that looked like tire prints. If I had to guess, the prick saw the dog and thought it would be funny to throw on your back porch to spook you."

She ran a hand through her tangled hair. "Well, it worked."

John didn't look so chipper himself. Deep lines bracketed his mouth, and the black stubble on his jaw was longer than normal. Shannon knew it had to frustrate him, because the weather wasn't cooperating. He hadn't seen the intruder on the monitors because of the swirling snow, and she had a feeling the crime scene people didn't get anything either, for the same reason.

"Duncan and I talked, and we're going to bring in another guy."

Surprise lifted her brows. "Really?"

John's expression completely closed down, and he crossed his heavy arms over his chest. "Really. I can't protect you properly with just me. I need backup. Legs, basically."

Shannon wished things could have been different. John had probably been a force to be reckoned with a few years ago, big and robust. Bitterness rolled off him now, and his mouth twisted when he said the words. It was the biggest humiliation in the world for a man to admit he needed help.

"Who's coming in?"

"Harper."

She nodded. The former SEAL was one of the few men actually not on assignment right now. He worked graveyard shift, so she didn't know him as well as the others, but he seemed like a very dangerous individual. Even more so than John. He set her on edge, actually. Almost as bad as the Jennings kid had.

"He'll be here within the hour."

John turned his chair to go, but Shannon reached out and brushed her hand against his arm. She wanted to acknowledge how hard it must have been for him to request backup, but if she said anything it would only make him feel worse. "Thanks for letting me know, John."

He stared at her for a long moment. "Whatever we need to do to get this guy, we'll do. I promise." He tipped his head and rolled away.

Shannon felt her heart melt as she watched him maneuver out the door. John Palmer was a good guy, whether he wanted to admit it or not.

When the sky started to ease into evening, she headed to the kitchen to make dinner. John sat, elbows propped, at the table. Harper Preston leaned against her counter. Shannon was a little spooked, because she hadn't even heard him enter the house. She certainly hadn't seen him. He had an open blade in his hand, and was scraping the edge against his black jeans, back and forth, back and forth. His pale silver eyes pinned her to the doorway, and it was all Shannon could do to contain a shiver. He had the eyes of a killer, cold and merciless. His head was shaved so close, only the barest hint of dark stubble remained.

Those eerie eyes settled on her, and he folded the knife away. "Ms. Murphy."

"Hello, Mr. Preston. I'm sorry you got dragged into my mess here."

Extra-wide shoulders jerked in a shrug. "It's all work."

John's expression was guarded as he watched them. Shannon didn't like feeling he examined her movements. She crossed to the refrigerator. Preston moved as far away from her as he could, then turned to lean against the wall, looking out the sliding glass doors. The space in the room was stifling.

Shannon ducked her head back into the fridge. "Is there anything you'd like for dinner, guys?"

Preston didn't say anything, but she didn't really expect him to.

"Anything is fine, Shannon. The easier the better."

She pulled pork chops and a bag of vegetables from the shelves. A can of fruit got dumped into a bowl, and she warmed up the few remaining noodles from a few nights ago. Within minutes, she had set the table and was passing around food.

Preston filled his plate, then moved to stand back where he had been, leaning against the jamb. Shannon had to clamp her mouth shut not to say anything about his behavior. John smiled slightly and winked at her.

The agency wouldn't hire anybody not suitable for the job, she knew that. And Duncan certainly wouldn't put a man in her house that he didn't trust. More importantly to her, John didn't seem to mind him either. Maybe it was just a military thing.

Dinner was tense and quiet. Shannon ate quickly just so she could get away from the menace in the air. She offered seconds, which the new guard promptly accepted, and put the food away.

"I'll get the dishes."

The thought of the muscle-bound hulk with tattoos on his arms filling her dishwasher almost made her smile. "Thank you." Hell, she wasn't going to argue with the man.

Shannon didn't give him time to change his mind. She grabbed the box of kittens and walked them down the hallway, with Pickle trailing behind. She heard the whisper of John's rubber wheels on the floor as he brought up the rear.

He stopped inside the doorway and closed the door behind him.

Shannon's heart began to accelerate. The door had been open before. Closed, it suddenly ratcheted up the intimacy.

"Don't worry about Preston. As long as he has focus, he's good. Just try to stay out of his way, and for God's sake don't come up behind him." His full lips spread in a grim smile.

Shivering, she crossed to the bed and reached the kittens out of the box, setting them on the comforter. John rolled to the opposite side of her bed to keep one from falling off. Boohini clawed into her pant leg and climbed into her lap. Shannon stroked him, and he set up a little rumble in his throat.

"I'll remember. Is he really that dangerous?"

John sighed. "Let's just leave him alone, okay? Don't try to butter him up with your cooking or anything." He dropped his head when he said the last, and she had to strain to hear.

Shannon laughed. "Oh, please. He doesn't look like the

German chocolate cake type."

John raised a dark eyebrow. "That's my cake. You better not make him that."

Shannon knew he was trying to tease her out of the funk she was in, but she wasn't sure if she was ready for that. "I won't make that cake for anybody but you," she promised.

The laughter in his face faded away as he heard the sincerity in her voice. He cleared his throat sharply. "Maybe, you uh, should. You know, just in case somebody likes it better, or appreciates it more. Or something."

He avoided her eyes until she moved off the bed to stand in front of him.

"John."

He dragged his gaze up to her face, but he wasn't happy about it. "I just don't want you to settle."

"How the heck am I settling? That's not the way I see it at all. Move your hands."

He held his arms at his sides, and she settled crossways onto his lap. Automatically, his hands settled at her hips, and he leaned to the side to look in her face.

Shannon didn't give him a chance to complain; she just wrapped her arms around his shoulders and nuzzled her nose into his neck. She sighed and melted into him. "I'll cook anything you want if you just let me rest here for a little minute."

*****

Well, fuck.

Here he was, trying to do what was best for her, and she was having none of it. Instead she curled up against him and destroyed all reasoning. How the hell was he supposed to do the right thing with all this softness nestled on his lap? And, God, what was she doing to his neck?

John fought to keep things even, but his body welcomed her presence like a desert begging for rain, finally being granted just a few precious drops. She smelled so good he wanted to lick her, just to see if she tasted like he thought.

Awareness coursed through him, and heat began to build in his groin. *Oh, yeah.*

Desperate curiosity ate at him. He was getting erections more often, but would he be able to follow through? He'd masturbated this morning before she got up, and it had definitely been easier than normal. All he had to do was remember her bent over the first day he had met her to get hard. That didn't mean he'd actually be able to have sex, though.

Doubts crowded into his mind.

"Why did you tense up?" she whispered. "Oh." She stiffened and pulled away, sliding her legs off his lap. "Sorry, I forgot."

Against his better judgment, his hands tightened on her. "Don't leave."

She looked at him warily, and John was hit with a fresh surge of guilt. She didn't know what he wanted. *He* had put that uncertainty in her eyes.

"Shannon, I like being close to you, and you didn't put me out by sitting on my lap. I just…I'm not sure what I want."

That was a total lie, of course. He knew exactly what he wanted, and she sat on his useless legs waiting for him to make up his mind.

"Well," she said softly, "maybe I can give you something to think about."

John knew the kiss was coming, and he froze. He willed himself not to move. Shannon's plump lips brushed his once, twice and nibbled at the corner of his mouth. John forced himself to rein in his frantic excitement. Shifting to the side a bit, she nibbled down the hardness of his throat. It was all he could do not to grab her and devour her. Deliberately being gentle, he burrowed a hand into her thick hair and dragged her mouth back to his to taste again.

Shannon moaned in her throat, making his excitement spike, and his erection fill. John knew the moment Shannon felt his excitement. She stilled, then pulled back to look at him.

Instead of the condescending pity he expected to see, her face was drowsy with her own need. For him. In spite of all the obstacles.

"I'm willing to go as far as you'll let me."

John felt his throat tighten with emotion at her words. She was prepared to give herself over to whatever he wanted, with no promise as to what might be in it for her. Nobody had ever offered themselves to him like that. One nagging part of his mind had to wonder *why* she offered herself to him. Was she curious if he could get it up? Or keep it up? Did she think he'd be grateful for any attention he got?

No. Shannon wasn't like that. He knew that, in spite of what his brain was trying to tell him. She wasn't the type to play with a person's emotions. If she offered herself to him, she had to have a strong motivation.

Was it possible she did actually care about him?

Unable to even comprehend the possibility, his mind veered away from the question.

Shannon waited for him to make a move, but John honestly didn't know if he could. He cleared his throat and looked toward the door. "I don't know if this is the time. I need to finish briefing Preston."

She stared at him for several long seconds, and he felt like a damn schmuck, always making excuses to get away from her. Finally, she slid off his lap and turned to the bed. "Okay, John. I'm going to read for a while, then I'm going to bed. I think for now I'll keep the kittens in here with me."

The tightness in his throat didn't allow him to respond, so he just rolled out the door.

Preston was in the living room, at the bank of security monitors. John felt a moment of embarrassment that the soldier had probably seen Shannon on his lap, but he brushed it away. Shannon was a beautiful woman. He would be proud to be seen with her anywhere. *Should* be proud.

The burly soldier looked up with a smirk from the monitors. "Personal protection, huh?"

John clamped his jaw shut and stared the man down. "Yes,

and if you have problems with that, let me know now. I'll have somebody else assigned."

Preston shook his bald head and backed down immediately. "No, Gunny. No problem. Just collecting intel."

John nodded, and briefed the man on the particulars of the case. Duncan called about halfway through, and informed John that they'd gotten a tiny break. Carpet fibers had been found in the hair of the dead dog. They were running them now, and assumed they came from the vehicle the dog had been transported in. He said he'd call as soon as they had more information. Clayton Williams, another investigator, was also being sent out to Ohio to interview Gerbowski. He would arrive in the morning, and hopefully by tomorrow afternoon they would have some insight into the stalker.

John told Preston about the find, but the ex-sniper didn't seem impressed. "Even if you figure out what kind of vehicle it came from, it probably won't help you until you pinpoint a suspect."

He was right, but John couldn't help but be encouraged. This was the first tiny break they had. And Williams was a professional interrogator. They would have answers, soon.

Preston waved him away when John started to go over the camera angles again. "Dude, you're half asleep. You need to catch some Zs. I'll be fine here. Nothing will get past me."

John knew he was probably right. He nodded and pushed his chair backwards, away from the table. "I'll be in the guestroom."

Preston thumped his fist on one of the monitors. "We've got something wrong with camera three. You better check it out."

John snorted. "Camera three, huh?" Shannon's room.

Preston nodded. "Yep. It's all snow. Maybe you should just camp out in there."

John tipped his head, unwilling to argue. His estimation of the man had just gone up. "Will do."

Trying not to look too eager, he shoved away from the table and down the hallway. Shannon's door was firmly closed, but a light still glowed beneath the crack. When he tapped, she opened it a mere inch. "Yes?"

"Preston says there's a problem with the camera, and maybe I should just camp out in here to make sure everything stays secure."

She raised her brows in disbelief, even as her eyes flared with heat. "Really? Well, maybe you should."

She stepped back from the door, and eased it open.

John's heart pounded as he rolled across the threshold. He wasn't sure exactly what would happen tonight, but he was tired of worrying about it. He'd just let the dice fall as they would.

Then he caught sight of what she wore. Though she wasn't tall, her legs looked a mile long. The hem of a threadbare t-shirt just brushed the top of her thighs. It used to be red, but it had softened to a multi-hued pink, and the lettering had faded to illegibility. The elastic had relaxed too. The cloth clung to her curves, outlining her breasts and ass. As he watched, her nipples hardened, and it was all he could do to drag his eyes back to her face.

She crossed her arms over her chest and nodded to the bed. "I was just turning in. Since we, um, slept together the other night, I don't see why we can't again."

John fought to keep the stupid grin off his face. Now that he'd decided to give in, he felt lighter in his skin. Hell, maybe nothing would happen, but at least his options were open.

His eager dick demanded otherwise.

He escaped to the bathroom for a moment to catch his breath. He'd been in firefights, had a gun held to his head, jumped out of airplanes in the dark, but the thought of baring himself to Shannon eclipsed all of those things. Everything else had been work. Shannon meant something to him.

You need to get your fucking ass out there!

He used the bathroom and washed his hands and brushed his teeth. When he had nothing else to do, he rolled out into the bedroom.

Shannon had turned off the lights, and only the soft glow from the bedroom window illuminated the room.

The bed presented a bit of a problem. It was taller than his at the apartment, and would be a struggle to get into it from the chair. Surveying the problem, he moved to the bottom and used the short corner foot post as leverage. Straining, he got himself onto the mattress, but his face burned with humiliation. He wasn't graceful at the best of times, let alone when he was at a disadvantage in a new environment.

The embarrassment was for naught, though. Shannon was curled up on her side, facing away from him. John's throat swelled with emotion at her sensitivity. She knew there was no way in hell he'd ever ask for help, so she left him to his own devices.

John dragged himself up the bed and under the covers. He left his jeans and t-shirt on, simply because he didn't want to look like he expected more. The only thing he removed was the Beretta and harness, which he placed within reach on the bedside table. His heart pounded his chest in expectation as he settled back against the bed. All thought of danger outside the house slipped away as her scent overwhelmed him.

Shannon peeked at him over her shoulder, then rolled over. As if she'd been doing it for years, she laid her arm over his belly and nestled her head on the cup of his shoulder. John allowed himself to cradle her closer. He pressed a quick kiss to her head. "You're really something, Shannon."

Her arm tightened around his middle. "You're pretty awesome yourself."

He didn't know about that. Sure, he'd gotten attention for doing his job in the Marines, but he'd never had anyone tell him that in his personal life. Relationships had been few and far between, and superficial at the very best. The way Shannon affected him was outside his scope of knowledge.

But he enjoyed learning. Even when she was pissed at him it allowed him to know more about her. It was fascinating.

She ran her hand over his chest now and outlined his pectoral muscles. Her fingers pressed against the creases between the muscles of his stomach, and it felt so good. Lying down beside her was supposed to give him a chance to catch a breath, but it only aroused him further. Her fingers teased along his waistband, and the tension between them suddenly skyrocketed.

He grabbed her hand. "Shannon, I don't want you to be...disappointed." He could feel his face burn with humiliation, and was thankful it was fairly dark in the bedroom. "Things don't always happen the way I expect them to, if they happen at all."

She sighed beside him, and propped herself up on her elbow. There was just enough illumination from the outside street light he could see the curve of her cheek as she smiled. "John, like I told you before, we can do as much or as little as you want. There's no pressure, other than what you're putting on yourself. I love being with you. If lying beside me is what you're comfortable with, that's what we'll do."

Squeezing him with her arm again, she rested her head back against his shoulder and hummed contentedly.

John appreciated her willingness to go slow, but it aggravated him too. He wished she *would* push, because the curiosity was slowly killing him. Doubts battered at his mind, but one thought ripped through more clearly than any other.

Could he actually perform?

His stomach twisted in knots as he debated how to proceed. His hard-on ached, and demanded attention.

Twisting, he reversed their positions until he loomed over top of her. His dick rested against her lush hip, and it was all he could do not to grind into her. "I can't promise you anything beyond this, Shannon. Hell, maybe nothing will happen. My body isn't like it used to be. But I can make sure you're taken care of."

She gave him the sweetest, sexiest smile and looped her arms up around his neck. "John, I'm sure you'll take care of me. I have no doubt. And don't worry about promises. I'm here, number one, because I am your friend. I want the best for you. If I can help you over this hurdle, so to speak, I will."

His throat tightened with emotion, and his eyes burned. He buried his face in her hair to keep her from seeing. He had to clear his throat several times before he could talk though. "Thank you, Shannon. We're friends with benefits, now, huh?"

She giggled beneath him, and nipped his neck. "I guess so."

He couldn't help it. Dragging her hips against him, he pressed his erection into her side.

"Oh, damn," she sighed.

John found her mouth with his own, and sank into her. For months he'd moped after her, watched her, fantasized about her. She had tormented him with her sweetness and sexiness. But nothing could have prepared him for the absolute enjoyment he felt as he explored her mouth. Shannon let him have everything she had, and gave him more than he'd ever hoped. She pulled away and lifted the ragged t-shirt over her head, baring her full, unbound breasts. John's vision actually darkened. He thought he was going to pass out as all of his blood headed south, to his already rock-hard cock. The tingle in his balls told him orgasm was not very far away, and he couldn't believe how aroused he was.

Dark, cinnamon-colored nipples pouted up at him and he wrapped his mouth around the one closest to him. Shannon moaned as he drew the nipple deep and teased it with his tongue. He shifted to the other side and drew that one in as well. He lifted his head enough to blow a gentle breath across both tips.

Shannon tugged him against her. John levered himself up onto his arms and shifted his lower body over hers. She bent her knees to cradle him against her pelvis, and John couldn't restrain himself any more. Tightening his stomach for all he was worth, he curled his stomach and pressed his cock against the hardness of her pubic bone. The movement felt freaking sensational, so he did it again. Shannon moaned in his ear, and her tiny hands slid beneath his waistband to clench his ass.

John ground himself against her again, then again, unable to help himself. Shannon pressed kisses against his chest and neck, whatever her lips could reach, and rocked him against her. Her hands left his ass and circled his waist. John felt a tug at his zipper, and the gentle brush of her soft hands on his naked cock was his undoing. He felt the orgasm rush at him, and couldn't get his mouth to move quick enough to tell her to stop. "Wait, I can't...oh, fuck!"

For the first time in years, he had an orgasm with a woman. Kind of. John let his body play out the movements, but humiliation burnt the edge off quickly. He wanted to burrow into her neck and disappear. Furious with himself, he rolled to the side and sat up. One glance at her lower body confirmed that he'd come all over her, and her hand. He couldn't force his eyes to her face, because he knew he would see the same things he felt. Disgust, embarrassment. Ripping his shirt over his head, he turned it inside out and used it to clean every bit from her body. "Shannon, I am so incredibly sorry."

He reached for her hand, but she pulled it away. John watched, fascinated, as she lifted the hand to her mouth, and slipped one wet finger between her lips. Electricity shot through him as her eyes fluttered shut as she licked herself clean.

Even though it had been mere seconds since he'd come, his cock tingled.

Her languorous eyes opened, and she smiled. "I think that's the hottest thing I've been a part of in, well, ever."

Exhilaration slammed through him, and he closed his eyes for a second. She wasn't disgusted. He swallowed thickly, unable to believe his good fortune in finding a woman like her.

Shannon looked at him with one brow raised in question.

"I thought, you uh…" He had to stop to clear his throat. "I thought you'd be disgusted I came all over you."

She looked down at her still moist belly. The cotton of her pink panties was dark with wetness, and she undulated on the bed. "Not hardly. That was the hottest thing I've ever felt. Although I'm kind of. . ." She shifted on the bed again, and reached both hands up to tweak her hard nipples.

John cursed when he got her meaning. Of course she was still hungry. She hadn't come yet. "Take your panties off."

She scrambled to do as he said, but looked at him out of the corner of her eye. "You're overdressed too."

John couldn't agree more. He maneuvered his legs around, and stripped the clothing off. And was attacked by self-consciousness again. His heavy thighs had withered away with disuse, and it was difficult to sit beside her and not compare. Her body was heavenly, lush and firm with health. And he was pale. He had Italian in him from his mother's side of the family, so that left him with some natural color, but the dark, sun-baked tan he used to have had faded long ago.

When he met her eyes, she smiled gently. "Whatever it is bothering you, get over it."

John laughed outright, and leaned down on his right elbow beside her. Her expression was clear and eager, and she turned to face him so she could run her hands over his chest. Her fingers traced over the tattoo on his arm, outlined the anchor, the eagle, and the globe. "Did this hurt?"

"No."

She raised her eyebrows at him, and he shrugged his high shoulder. "Okay, maybe a bit. But it was worth it."

She smiled in agreement. "I think so. It's very sexy."

Resting her hand behind his neck, she leaned up to kiss him, and he met her halfway. The ease with which he accepted the intimacy scared him. He'd never been this easy, or relaxed, or turned on with another human being.

Flat out, he was humbled by her acceptance.

Kissing her with everything he had, he glided his hand down to pluck at her nipples. She moaned into his mouth, and it was all he could do to go slow. The patch of dark brown curls at the juncture of her thighs taunted him. He wanted to spread her wide and explore her. And taste her. God. His mouth watered.

His almost-erection flexed at the thought, drawing her attention.

*****

Shannon tried not to pant as she looked down at John's body. Yes, the paralysis had had an effect on him, but it wasn't nearly as bad as she expected. His legs were crisscrossed with pale silver scars. It certainly wasn't as bad as what his own mind probably concocted. And the working parts more than made up for the nonworking ones.

His cock flexed and hardened. The thought of having that lurid purple head in her mouth, or body, made her shudder. Her clit pulsed with the need to come. Daring to reach out again, she squeezed the tip of him with her fingertips.

John surged into her hand, his cock filling quickly and impressively. Shannon didn't know he'd be so big, and it actually worried her.

With a groan, he pulled her hand away. He kissed her palm and rested it on her own breast. "Your hands are dangerous. Leave it there."

Shannon grinned in spite of herself, but it slipped away as he lifted her thigh up over his hip. His cock was only a couple inches away now, and her heart thumped painfully against her chest. She wanted to nestle him between her legs more than she'd ever wanted anything before. Her pussy clenched in expectation, and her eyes fluttered shut.

He didn't do what she expected, though. She felt a tickle at her pussy lips, and looked down to find him swirling her short, damp hair with his fingers. Even that felt wonderful. Then he slipped his thick middle finger between her folds, and just held it there.

Shannon moaned, and pressed a kiss to his mouth. It was a struggle not to grind against his hand, and he seemed to understand that. The tip of his finger danced up around her clit, then swept down around her opening. He paused there, building her anticipation, before gently sliding his finger inside.

Shannon panted, willing him to move. "Please," she moaned. "Please."

John plunged his finger deeper, grinding the palm of his hand against her clit. She gasped as pleasure slammed through her. "Harder," she whispered.

In and out, he set up a steady rhythm designed to build. "You are soaked," he grumbled.

Then he lowered his head to her nipple, and started to suck. Shannon cried out, and her hips worked against his hand.

Frantic heat built deep in her body, and she didn't try to fight it. She'd lusted after John for months, and now that she was finally with him, she wasn't going to waste the opportunity to enjoy him. She gripped his cock in her hand and pumped lightly.

John pulled away from her touch and pushed her flat on her back. Then, more gracefully than she would have thought possible, he rolled over and pushed himself down the bed. His moist breath suddenly teased her wet folds and his hands pressed her knees wide. A split-second later, his tongue laved her cleft from top to bottom. Shannon cried out, and tried to cover her mouth with her hand to keep the sound in, but she had no control over her body. That frantic heat grew and became too big to contain. John shoved his finger deep as he flicked at her clit with his tongue, driving her over the edge. Shannon whipped her hands out to clutch the blanket, and let the scream go that had been building for so long.

But he didn't let up. Her body quaked and shuddered through one of the hottest orgasms she'd ever had, and just as her body began to calm, he flicked his tongue again to prolong her pleasure. Shannon moaned and clutched his short hair, not sure if she was shoving him away or holding him to her. Finally, though, she did push him away, gently. "Oh, my God."

John looked up the length of her body, mouth glistening with her release, and gave her the sexiest, most self-satisfied, manly grin she ever seen on his face. "I'm glad I still remember what to do."

Did he ever. Her heart contracted in her chest, and tears actually came to her eyes. *Friends with benefits, my ass. He's mine.*

He elbowed his way up beside her, and gently fondled her breast as she recovered her breath. Shannon knew he was hard, and the need to take the night further pushed her. John covered her mouth with his own and nibbled softly. Shannon tasted her own saltiness, and it made her clit contract.

She pulled away and pushed against his massive shoulders, guiding him flat. Then levered herself up and over his hips. She held her body high, away from his, and plumped her breasts for him. John's face darkened as he watched her, and his strong hands clamped onto her hips. She brought one knee up, centered herself over the tip of his cock and lowered.

The work they did before was good, because the moisture from her release eased the way for his size. Even then, it still took several movements to seat him in her body. Shannon had never felt so full.

"Oh, fuck," John whispered. "Just hold right there for a minute."

His hands trembled on her hips, and his strong jaw clenched. "I never thought I'd feel this again."

Shannon leaned forward and pressed a kiss to his pursed lips. John moaned and clasped her head in his palms, guiding her mouth. Wrapping an arm around her waist, he held her to him and flexed his stomach, shoving into her. She gasped as the fullness intensified. Originally, she'd planned to ride John, but he plunged well enough beneath her that she didn't want to move.

That expectation began to build again, and she panted, making minute adjustments to what he was doing to heighten the sensation. His excitement began to build as well, and he guided her to sit up, then held her hips in his hands.

Shannon gasped at the position change. It was too much. Her body struggled to accept him. Her thighs quivered as she lifted high, bouncing lightly before sinking down again. Within seconds, though, she wasn't doing enough. She seated herself harder, panting, as that tantalizing flame grew brighter. It suddenly flared out of control as John rested a thumb just above her clit.

When she rocked down, her clit bumped against his finger, and that tiny touch was enough to swing her over the edge. As she orgasmed around his body, crying, John tightened his hands on her hips and slammed her down against him. It was good he was as strong as he was, because she had gone beyond coherence. Within just a few seconds, though, he stalled out beneath her, quivering, shaking, and roared out his own release. Shannon rocked against him, and felt the spread of scalding heat as he released into her body.

She collapsed against him, boneless, crying, rocked to her

very foundations. John wrapped both arms around her and held her to him. He seemed just as affected as he wiped her tears away with the pad of his thumb. When his body relaxed out of hers, Shannon forced herself to get up and go to the bathroom to clean up, even though she didn't want to leave. John seemed just as reluctant to let her go, and eager to have her back in his arms when she returned. Shannon snuggled in against his chest, more content than she could remember being in a very long time.

John cleared his throat and tilted his head to meet her eyes. "Are you okay?"

She smiled, and raised a brow. "You mean after my ravishing? I can't walk straight yet, but I think I'll be okay."

Even in the dim light, she could see his face turn ruddy, but he grinned. "I don't think I can do much right now either, but I feel fantastic. Actually, I feel like I did when I was fifteen and lost my virginity with Ellen Nichols."

She grinned with him, proud to be a part of his reawakening. "I'm happy for you. I didn't know what to expect, but I have to say, I've never been so thoroughly sexed. You've blown me away."

He relaxed back and closed his eyes, looking more content than she'd ever seen him, his mouth open as he breathed. Now that the excitement was over, her body was pulling her into sleep. Tugging the comforter up over them, she adjusted a bit and settled into sleep.

Chapter Seven

John pulled away from Shannon, careful not to wake her. She slept deeply, her mouth curved in a slight smile. He hoped she was dreaming of their loving earlier, but he didn't want to bet much on it.

He adjusted the chair beside the bed and locked the brake. It held steady as he fell down into it. He glanced back at Shannon, but she was still asleep. Shifting his ass center, he pulled his feet up on the bar and rolled out of the bedroom. The hallway bath was his first stop, and he took the time for a quick wipe-down with a wet washcloth. Shannon's fragrance was suddenly all around him, and it made his heart clench. She'd been freaking phenomenal last night, no judgment, no impatience. More than he could have ever hoped for.

Had he been enough for her, though?

If her reaction had been any indication, then hopefully yes. She'd come several times, and that kind of response was hard to fake. At least, he thought it was. *Hell, I don't know.*

Rolling down the hallway gave him a chance to distance himself, physically and mentally. There were other things to worry about than his sex life. He stopped in the guestroom long enough to grab a fresh t-shirt, then headed to the living room.

Preston watched one of the security monitors intently, and the attention was enough to alarm John.

"What's going on?"

The big man shook his head and shifted on the chair. "I'm not sure. Something." He stood up abruptly. "Are you going to stay up? I might run outside."

John nodded once. "I will." The clock on the mantle ticked just past three o'clock. He reached into a box beside the table and pulled out a headset. "Put this on."

Preston didn't argue, just fitted it to his big head and pulled a black skullcap over top. John liked the headsets because they were so similar to what they used to use in combat.

"If I'm not back in twenty, call for backup."

John nodded, and checked the Beretta. "Will do."

Preston faded out the back.

John scanned the cameras, but nothing stood out to him as being out of place. He flicked the monitor on for Shannon's bedroom. She was still curled up in the center of the bed.

As the minutes ticked away, and Preston didn't break radio silence, John's anxiety level increased. He didn't know what Preston had seen, but the man was not known for dramatizing a situation. Calm, cool, deadly described him better, exactly what a sniper needed to be. If something was important enough for him to leave tracks in the fresh snow, John would have to trust his judgment.

Nineteen and a half minutes later, the big man padded silently back into the room.

"What did you find?"

Preston stripped off the cap and mic, as well as his black fleece jacket, and tossed them onto a chair. "Nothing. Not a goddamn thing."

"What did you think you saw?"

Preston shifted his shoulders. Something cagey slid through his eyes. "I just had a feeling."

John didn't laugh. He'd been with guys who "just had a feeling" and lived to tell about the experience. Hell, he'd had a feeling like that just last night before the power had gone out. Gut instinct was the most important thing a soldier could have. "Well, if you get another feeling, let me know."

Preston gave him a nod and settled back into the chair, glancing at John. "Looks like you had a good night."

John fought not to grin like a motherfucker, but he didn't think he was very successful. "It was all right."

Snorting, the other man rocked back in the chair. "Just all right, huh?"

He couldn't hold Preston's too-knowing gaze. "Yep."

186

The other man didn't say anything, just turned back to the monitors.

"I can relieve you, now."

Preston waved a hand. "Nah, I won't be able to sleep tonight anyway. Too tense."

John understood. Your body just wouldn't allow you to relax after a false alarm like they just had.

At loose ends, he rolled into the kitchen to find something to drink. In spite of the situation they were in, he felt very light inside, like a weight had been lifted. The feeling made him uncomfortable, because he wasn't normally that way. He wanted to go in and wake Shannon up, and look at her, and touch her. Some imaginary barrier had been broken inside him, some reserve, and he wanted intimacy. He wanted to be with her.

Snatching a Diet Sprite from the fridge, he chugged it in a few heavy swallows, and tossed the can. The he paced the house, going from window to window, peering out between the cracks of the curtains. The street was quiet, and the roads were once again covered in snow. A couple of heavy pines bordered her driveway, their limbs hanging heavy with snow. His eyes zeroed in on something out of place.

"Preston!"

Preston joined him at the big picture window where he was parked.

"Did you walk to the end of the driveway?"

"No."

John pointed. "I need you to go check that out. Those limbs have no snow, like somebody brushed against them."

The ex-sniper didn't even question, just gathered the headset and went out the back.

There was no way to be stealthy working under the glow of a streetlight, but Preston managed. He was a shadow, working along the line of trees until he got to the last one. The radio crackled. "Definite sign. Male boot, size ten and a half. Looks like a Bates imprint. Definitely military or police type. Looks like he rested against the tree for a while. Tracks go over the snowdrift and onto the road, but I lose them there. I'll track down the street a bit."

There was click over the air, and Preston was gone out of John's sight.

John was relieved, though, that something had been found. This cat-and-mouse game was getting old.

Preston returned ten minutes later, shaking his head. "Didn't pick up the sign anywhere within a three-block radius. He had to have gotten into a vehicle."

John nodded, and sent Duncan a text message on what they'd found. Duncan called back almost immediately.

"What do you have?"

John related what Preston had found, and his "feeling" from earlier.

"Sounds like we have military or cop. You sure it wasn't one of the uniforms patrolling?"

John repeated the message to Preston, but the man shook his head.

"Preston does not believe so."

"Hmm…well, the problem is, if it is a Bates shoe, they sell to everybody. Hell, cops, guards, food service people, sanitation. Anybody can buy them, so I don't know that that really limits our suspect pool."

John grimaced, because he knew Duncan was right. They even offered them to their guys if they wanted them. The faint glimmer of excitement died.

"I'll send somebody out to get a plaster cast," Duncan continued, "but I wouldn't expect anything from it."

John appreciated the call so late at night, even though the news was not promising. "Thanks Duncan. Why are you up, actually? It's almost four in the morning."

There was a long silence on the other end of the line. "Same old, same old. Why are you up?"

John was suddenly uncomfortable with the conversation. He didn't know if he wanted everybody to know what he and Shannon had done together. Especially right now, with what was going on with Gerbowski. "Ah, same thing. I better go. I'll watch for the tech."

Zipping his finger across the touch screen, he released a sigh. Later, he'd tell his partner what was going on. Face to face. Losing his "cherry" wasn't something to be mentioned in passing. If anybody would understand how momentous it was, Duncan would be the man. When he'd returned from Iraq, he'd been in a wheelchair as well. Through therapy and multiple surgeries, he'd recovered enough to walk with a cane. He still had a heavy limp, but he was at least mobile.

Turning his chair back to Preston, he related what Duncan had said.

"I heard. I'll watch for him. Why don't you head back to bed." A slight smile eased the hardness of his face. "You have a warm woman waiting for you. Take advantage of that."

John didn't need to be told twice. Trying to control his excitement, he powered down the hallway.

*****

Shannon felt a warm weight ease in behind her. She hummed in happiness, and snuggled her bottom into John's lap. "You're warm," she whispered.

John slid one arm underneath her head, and wrapped his other around her hips. Shannon thought he felt better than any bed she'd ever laid on.

She was still comfortable when the alarm on her phone woke her several hours later. She tapped the screen, but was too blurry-eyed to actually turn it off. When it woke her five minutes later, she roused enough to focus. She tapped the button to turn the noise off, and noticed she had several text messages in her inbox. Who would be texting her in the middle of the night?

She gasped as she scrolled through them.

John leaned over her shoulder, immediately alert. "What?"

Shannon handed him the phone. "Read them."

Nausea turned her stomach, and she rolled out of bed. John's jaw was clenched in anger when he read them, and he sat up, flinging the blankets. "Has he texted you before?"

"No, never."

This was a new invasion. She wrapped her arms around her waist and fought a shudder. If this was Gerbowski somehow, he had hit a new level. Granted, cell phones weren't as prevalent years ago, but he'd never sent her messages like this. There were four text messages in the space of about two hours, and they escalated. The first "who's the guy?"wasn't bad, but the last one had been something about killing her "gimp lover" in front of her.

"He has to have been watching us," she whispered. "We only made love a few hours ago."

John shifted to his chair, and he looked livid. "Preston's spidey senses went off earlier tonight, and we found an area where somebody stood out by the road. He must have a telephoto lense."*Or a fucking rifle scope.* He set the phone on the bed and jerked his t-shirt over his head. "We need to go in to work today."

Shannon nodded. "I had already planned to go. The roads are clear and I can't hide out here forever."

She hustled into the shower and scrubbed the night away. Even with the worry and fear dogging her, she still paused when she came to her tender breasts. Their first night together had been wonderful, more than she'd ever expected. She'd worried that John's sexuality had been compromised from the injuries, but she'd never been so satisfied in her life. Hell, just thinking about it made her puss tingle.

Breakfast was a quick pan of scrambled eggs and microwave bacon. Again, Preston stood against the wall, peering out the blinds as he shoveled food into his mouth.

John was quiet, but he did touch her arm lightly as she set a plate in front of him. Shannon knew that was probably all the PDA she was going to get today, so she leaned down and pressed a quick kiss to the top of his head.

"I need you to put your phone on the charger, but do not erase those messages."

Shannon nodded and hooked it up to the charger on the counter. The message icon was blinking again, but she didn't want to read any more. She disappeared into the bathroom to finish getting ready.

Preston slipped out the door a few minutes before they were ready to leave—to retrieve his truck, he said. John nodded and planted himself in front of the cameras until the other man came back in. The men nodded to each other and told her to get her stuff together.

Grabbing her phone and purse, she was guided out to a huge black Humvee outfitted with spotlights and a black matte grill. it almost looked like a military vehicle. While she climbed into the back seat, John hoisted himself up into the truck using the "oh-shit" handles in front. He managed to make it look easy, even though he had to really reach. Preston folded the sport chair and placed it in the back beside Shannon.

She caught his eye in the rearview mirror when he climbed behind the steering wheel. "This is a truck?"

The forbidding former SEAL sent her an audacious wink, and backed out of the drive.

It was difficult to believe that all the extra hoopla was needed, until she remembered Chris. He was in a chair for the rest of his life because of that crazed maniac. A cold chill shook her. She didn't know what she would do if anything happened to John. Or any of the guys that worked at the agency. They'd all come to mean a great deal to her.

Walking into the office building was almost surreal. So much had happened in the few days she'd been gone. She felt older, and wiser. More scared. Yet hopeful of what could happen with John.

John had put himself between the street and her body as they entered, squeezing her hand as they rode up in the elevator.

Shannon unloaded her crap on her desk and sat in the chair. Memos and notes were stacked on her blotter, waiting for attention she wasn't sure she could pay them. She switched her computer on and listened to the hum as it booted up. John disappeared down the hallway with her cell phone on his lap, and Duncan headed that way as well. If anybody could track the caller down she honestly believed it was the men who worked here. She'd seen them do amazing things.

The computer beeped for her password, and Shannon grabbed a stack of papers. She had work to do. She shoved the worry about Gerbowski to the side.

*****

"I don't like it. It's too easy."

Duncan shrugged. "I know. But Quillen confirmed it." He had the phone to his ear, and was on hold. He shifted his stance as he leaned against the corner of John's heavy desk.

John gritted his teeth in frustration. The phone number had traced back to a criminal by the name of Reginald Barnes, currently incarcerated in the Colorado State Penitentiary in Canon City, a hundred miles away.

Mr. Barnes was enjoying prison life for twenty-five years, after he'd raped and murdered a woman in Colorado Springs. Patrick Quillen, the Denver PD police chief, had tracked the information down for them. They had called the number to see if anybody would pick up. A confused intake clerk in Denver PD booking had answered.

Duncan explained who they were, and requested to be hooked up to a supervisor. They had eventually been connected to Quillen, who was just as confused as they were.

Duncan's gaze focused as somebody obviously came on the line. He fumbled the phone a bit, and found a speaker button.

"Can you say that again Chief? I have somebody in the room that needs to hear that."

"Mr. Barnes left our facility two weeks ago. All his belongings went with him. I'm looking at the sheet now. The phone is listed and he signed off on it."

Duncan was quiet for several long seconds. "When was he originally arrested?"

The other man sighed. "He's been in and out all his life, but the rape he was convicted of happened about two years ago. He was arrested in June of oh-nine. Been incarcerated ever since."

John motioned to the phone, and Duncan turned it toward him. "Who was the arresting officer?"

"Mmm, it's listed as Detective Angela Halloway, but I know SWAT actually apprehended him."

Frustration tightened his fists on the wheels of his chair. "Can you do us a big favor, and confirm that Barnes is still in prison? Have a guard confirm by sight."

"Can do. Give me a call-back number."

It took the better part of half an hour, but Quillen called back and confirmed that the warden herself had verified his body was still in her prison. Quillen promised that he would submit the found cell phone to evidence and dust for prints, and he'd call no matter what they found.

John slammed his fist into a box on the desk, knocking it to the floor and scattering packing peanuts all over the floor. "Fuck!"

Duncan watched him shrewdly, as if he knew there was a reason for John's reaction. "You okay there, buddy?"

"I'm fine," John snarled.

Duncan chuckled and knocked a peanut away from his foot with the tip of his cane.

John felt ridiculous. It wasn't like him to act this way. He was known as Mr. Cool, unflappable, nothing bothered him. But the thought of Shannon being in danger set his teeth on edge. The thought of not being able to do anything about it was even more infuriating. His hands clenched around the wheels of his chair and took a deep breath. This anger shit wasn't getting them anywhere.

"I think I've lost my objectivity," he admitted. "Shannon and I are involved."

Duncan didn't even blink. "About time. Maybe you'll quit moping around now."

John sat back in his chair, offended. "I don't mope."

Duncan chuckled, which made John all the more frustrated. "I don't," he snapped.

His best friend squeezed his shoulder as he headed toward the door. "You're right John, you don't mope. You just get...moody. I'm glad for you, though. Shannon is really a great girl. I think she'll be good for you. If you let her."

John watched Duncan limp out the door. "If you let her." What the hell?

He'd be incredibly lucky if she would take a chance on him.

He couldn't help but worry that he wouldn't be enough for her, though.

*****

The work that had accumulated while Shannon had been off for the day kept her from thinking about anything. The Malone case was dragging on and Chad's notes indicated as much. He was getting frustrated because there was very little to investigate. the woman they'd been contracted to watch wasn't doing anything suspicious.

Roger was working undercover in a warehouse, trying to cut back on a company's theft problem, which was a little more interesting reading. Grafton Parks, another agent, had just been dispatched to Vail for a security detail with a Hollywood starlet. Shannon was impressed with that assignment. It showed that they were branching out and making a name for themselves.

John joined her for lunch in the break room and filled her in on the details about the phone.

"So this dude is in prison, but for some reason his phone didn't go with him?"

John dug into his delivery Chinese. "The Captain sent over a booking photo. Do you recognize this guy?"

He pushed a paper across the table with a headshot of a man in front of a blue background. The guy looked like an insurance salesman, balding on top, beady dark eyes, but he wasn't familiar to her. She told John her thoughts.

"I didn't think you would."

"So who sent the messages, then?"

He wound his fork into a pile of noodles. "Well, the texts stopped as soon as the phone was found, so the Captain is going over booking footage to try to figure out who put the phone there."

Shannon felt deflated. She had hoped John would suddenly be able to work magic and be able to tell her all the answers. Now they had to wait some more.

"Eat, Shannon. The asshole's trying to knock you off balance. Don't let him do that."

John was right, she knew that, but she couldn't not worry. She'd seen what this man was capable of, and it disturbed her to know she was the target of his fascination.

Stabbing a piece of chicken, she forced herself to eat. John would take care of her. She needed to be as strong as he was being. He pushed away from the table and circled around to her side. Clasping her hands in his own, he looked at her, dark eyes gleaming with determination. "I won't let anything happen to you, Shannon."

Tears came to her eyes, and she rubbed them away on her shoulder so that she didn't have to let go of his hands. "I know. It's just frustrating. I wish I had a normal life, you know? There must be something about me that attracts psychos. You're the first regular guy I've hooked up with."

He snorted, and scrunched his face. "Normal? Not even close."

Shannon smiled, like he meant her to do. "Yes, normal."

She leaned her head against his shoulder, and he rubbed her back. It was the most comforting thing he'd ever done for her, and it actually made her tear up more.

She pulled away and wiped her eyes. "Thanks, John. I know you'll catch this guy."

*****

Shannon was surprised when Lisa called her later that day.

"Hey, Shannon. Just wanted to catch up with you a bit and see what all the commotion was at your house the other morning?"

Shannon stalled. It probably wouldn't be wise to let everybody know yet what was going on. But Lisa may have seen something. "Uh, well, I think those flat tires were from my ex." Not exactly a lie. "And he left me a couple of nasty presents, too. Stuff like that."

"No way! Your ex did that? Some guys just don't get it though, you know? This ex I've got just shows up out of nowhere too, and he's been coming around more often recently. Sweet talks his way back in. I think he just doesn't want me with anybody but him, you know?"

"I know. You haven't seen anybody hanging around my house, have you?"

"No. Well..." Her voice lowered. "No one other than that hunky guy in the wheelchair I saw you with yesterday. Who's he? And does he have a brother?"

Shannon laughed. "That's actually one of my bosses. He's helping me out with the ex."

Lisa hummed over the phone. "He looks yummy. When he's done helping you out, send him my way."

Jealously spiked, and Shannon clamped her mouth on the automatic denial. "Well, we'll see. I may need help for a while."

"Yeah, okay." Lisa laughed softly. "I hear your warning. I'll leave him alone. If you need anything just let me know."

"I will. Hey, if you see anybody let me know, would you?"

"Sure thing. Later, chickie!"

"Bye, Lisa."

Shannon shook her head as she replaced the receiver. Lisa seemed like she had a good heart, but she needed to ease back on the loser. If he wasn't into her by now, he never would be.

She took a few minutes to call her parents and tell them she was getting a new phone number, and if they needed anything to call her at work. They were immediately suspicious, clamoring on the speakerphone, but when she told them she was switching carriers and would be issued a new number, they seemed to accept the excuse. Shannon felt guilty lying to them, but she didn't want them to worry. If they knew she was having problems, there was a good chance they'd drive out to check on her too. And that couldn't happen.

They chitchatted for a while and caught up on news. As subtly as she could, she sprinkled queries into the conversation. Everything seemed normal. She promised to call them when she got her new number and she hung up.

Turning back to the computer, she stared at the screen as she tried to work out who could be after her. She debated pulling up a blank Word doc, but she knew there was no way she could fill it up. Mike had been the only aberration in a fairly mundane life. She pulled a yellow pad to her and started to doodle. Frustration ate at her. Why had she been chosen to put up with this crap?

John rolled into sight, and she smiled. She couldn't help but smile when she saw him. When his gaze connected to hers, and he grinned, all the angst and frustration of the morning melted away.

He stopped beside her desk and just looked at her. "Are you okay?"

Nodding, she ripped the paper off the tablet and crumpled it, then sent it sailing into the trashcan across the way. He raised his dark brows in surprise.

"Yes, I am. I've been racking my brain for suspects, but it has to be Mike, or somebody connected directly to him. My life is boring, and I don't have weird things happen to me. Mike is the only aberration."

John scanned her face. "We'll concentrate on him, then."

Shannon felt tears start in her eyes at his easy confidence in her, and she nodded her head.

"We've already got somebody investigating the family. Maybe they'll turn something up."

Shannon tried to remember who had been in the courtroom during the trial. "I think he had a couple of brothers, and a sister, but I don't think either of his parents were alive."

"Did you interact with any of them?"

She nodded, and tears filled her eyes. "I walked by a couple of them during the trial, and I could tell they thought I had led him on. It was the story he spouted all through court. You have to understand, Mike looks like this nice, normal guy. Not bad looking. In general, people liked him. Intelligent. He had scholarships for college. We were hooked up by a mutual friend, but within just a couple of hours I could tell something was off. He was too…interested in everything I did. He wanted to know every detail of my day."

John frowned fiercely. Shannon didn't think he liked hearing about her ex-stalker. She shrugged uncomfortably. "It went downhill from there."

Shannon folded her arms, cold at the thought of what might be ahead. John motioned her up from her office chair and guided her into his lap. She cuddled into him and inhaled the scent of his skin. This was her new favorite place in the world. He wrapped his arms around her, and she relaxed into him gratefully. Nothing could go wrong when John held her like this.

He seemed to take comfort from her as well. He pressed a kiss to her head, and worked down to her ear."We'll get him," he whispered. "Whoever it is, we'll get him."

*****

Shannon was getting used to the security measures, but she still didn't have to like them. As they walked out of the LNF offices and onto the cold street later that day, Preston led the way, hand hanging to his side and ready to grab his exposed sidearm. Shannon walked behind him, and John pulled up the rear. The tank idled at the curb, and he guided her into the back. John hoisted himself into the passenger seat as quickly as he could, and Preston folded his chair and slipped it in beside her.

As they drove toward her house, she found herself scanning every vehicle they passed, trying to spot something incriminating. But the traffic was random. Nobody followed them, or pulled out in front of them. She doubted anybody would chance doing anything with this huge vehicle.

Her house was a welcome sight, and she began to relax.

"Turn away, turn away!"

John's yell startled her enough that she yelped. Preston had been about to turn into the driveway, but he jerked the wheel at the last minute and kept the truck on the street.

"Park in front," John told him, twisting in his seat to try to see behind them. "There's something in the snow on her driveway."

Preston left the truck idling as he slipped out the door and looked around. Shannon couldn't see his eyes behind the reflective wraparound sunglasses he wore, but she had a feeling he had immediately cataloged every car on the street. He walked to her driveway and knelt then brushed at the snow with his hand. Curling his fist, he stood and looked around, but the street was quiet.

John's yell had made her heart pound, but it settled when there was no immediate danger.

Preston returned and handed John a strangely shaped piece of metal.

"What the heck is that?" she asked.

John frowned, then turned the piece over in his hand. "It's called a caltrop, or tire spike. They're designed to deflate tires and incapacitate a vehicle. The Iraqis used them on our vehicles occasionally, though this is just a small one. I don't know that it would have done anything to this truck, but I'm more concerned as to why they put them there."

"To get us out of the truck," Preston rumbled.

John's jaw tightened. "If you hadn't been driving us, it would have been Shannon getting out and me getting these in my wheels."

Preston shifted into drive and floored the accelerator, making the vehicle's heavy tires bark on the asphalt. He zigzagged his way back to the office. Shannon felt sick to her stomach. This was getting out of hand.

Her phone buzzed with a text message, and she pulled up the screen.

Damn, I missed.

Growling, she handed the phone to John.

"Fuck this." He began tapping keys on her keypad.

"John, what are you doing?"

He glanced at her, then continued to type, jaw clenched. "If he wants to play games, we'll let him. He'll screw up one of these times." He held up the screen for her to see. *Puhleaze. Not even close.* Shannon grinned in spite of herself, and shook her head at him.

The phone buzzed almost immediately with another message and John read it. Shannon knew it wasn't good, because his face turned red in fury. She leaned over his shoulder.

I'm going to hurt you Shannon. And enjoy it.

She sat back in the seat, all the laughter gone. John pressed a button on the phone to shut it down, and slipped it into his pocket. "The asshole's not going to touch you Shannon. I won't let him."

She nodded her head, even though she knew he couldn't actually promise that. They could only protect her for so long.

Preston parked the truck in front of the agency, and the earlier process reversed. He grabbed John's chair out of the back seat, positioned it, then helped Shannon down and escorted her into the building, this time walking behind her. The lobby doors weren't locked yet, so she pushed straight through.

And ran straight into Cameron Jennings.

The young man grabbed her arms above the elbows, and stared down at her. He seemed not so surprised to see her, as if he had been waiting for her. Purple smudged the skin beneath his manic eyes, and he was unshaven. It looked as if he had been sleeping on the street. He opened his mouth to say something, but Shannon was suddenly ripped away from him and shoved aside.

Preston was a lion. The huge former sniper spun the young man and shoved him into the nearest wall face first. He cranked Jennings' arms high up behind his shoulder blades, and the man cried out. The old security guard behind the desk lurched toward them, but it was obvious he would be more of a hindrance than a help, and Preston snapped at the man to stay back.

"Preston, wait." Shannon didn't know what to do. John blasted in behind her, surveyed the situation in a split-second and tried to herd her to the elevator. "John, that's the Jennings kid that came in to the interview yesterday."

John slowed for the briefest second to confirm what she said, then continued to goose her forward. When she didn't move quickly enough, he tripped her down to his lap and shoved them both onto the elevator, slamming his hand against the buttons.

Shannon didn't know what had just happened, but she was shaken. Her arms were aching where the kid had grabbed her, and her heart was thudding in fear. She began to wonder if Jennings had been the one following her. His behavior was strange at best, and had escalated each time she saw him.

John rolled off the elevator and into her reception area.

Her blood chilled at the thought that somebody would come after them in daylight. And if they wanted to hurt her, they would hurt John. Yes, he was a smaller target in the chair, but he was definitely more vulnerable, having to deal with vehicles and handling doors as he entered and exited buildings. It would kill her if something happened to him.

Rubbing her back with his broad hand, John whispered that everything was going to be okay. Shannon appreciated the contact. Her emotions were at a boil.

Duncan stepped out of his office to see who was there. The looks on their faces must have been pretty grim.

"What happened?"

They filled him in on what had occurred. John tossed him the spike and urged her off his lap, then motioned her down for a kiss. "I'll be back. I want to talk to the kid."

Duncan wrapped an arm around her shoulders and gave her a squeeze. "Are you okay?"

Shannon nodded and pushed him toward the elevator after John. "I'm fine. You probably need to be down there when they talk to him."

Her boss watched her for a second, as if to reassure himself she was indeed good.

"Go! Preston is down there alone with that guy."

With a final nod, the elevator doors closed behind them and they disappeared.

Shannon sank down into her office chair with a shudder. Hopefully they wouldn't be gone long. She was as curious as anybody about why the kid kept showing up, but she knew her presence down there would probably not be conducive to him talking.

At loose ends, she walked into Duncan's office to look out the window at the dark night. Preston's Humvee was parked directly below the office, but the snowy street was quiet. Lights twinkled across the city, but she wished desperately she could see what was going on directly below her. Within ten minutes, a Denver PD squad car pulled up behind Preston's truck, and the officer got out and headed for the front of the building.

Shannon stood watching the street as long as her tired feet could hold her, then she sank down into Duncan's chair. She tucked her feet beneath her and shut her eyes, just for a moment.

Chapter Eight

John fought to calm the rage inside him. The kid, Jennings, wouldn't say a word about why he was so into Shannon. Everything else he was very forthcoming with, but not about her. John had enough information in his head, though, that he should be able to track down the reason within a few hours. The cop had stepped in when John got too aggressive, and it had pissed him off to no end. The only thing Duncan could do was file trespassing charges against Jennings, and he hesitated to do that. Technically, the kid hadn't done anything wrong, just waited to talk to Shannon. When that hadn't gotten him anywhere, he'd changed the story to say he'd wanted to speak to Duncan about the progress with his therapy.

Jennings and Duncan had spoken for several minutes, then Jennings had been free to go, with a warning not to return to the LNF office building unless he'd made an appointment ahead of time. Something in his gaze, as it slid away, told John he would see Jennings again.

Without waiting for anybody else, he shoved toward the elevator. Shannon was upstairs alone, and that made him worry. The elevator doors opened immediately, and he rolled inside. Preston slipped in behind him and left Duncan to finish up with the cop. John was glad he didn't have to deal with all the public relations bullshit. They'd be out of business in a minute if it were left up to him. There was one thing he did need to do, though.

"Thanks for getting to her as quick as you did."

"No problem, Gunny."

Shannon wasn't in the outer office, and she didn't respond when he called her name. Preston jogged down the hallway to the restrooms and John rolled for the break room. When he didn't find her there, and Preston walked up the hallway shaking his head, John's heart began to thud painfully and his throat began to ache.

Had Jennings been a decoy while somebody else snuck in the back way and snatched her?

He found her curled up in the big office chair behind Duncan's desk, her tiny feet tucked beneath her. Every muscle in John's body quivered with tension he had no release for. She was safe, but he was having a reaction as if something had happened to her. As quietly as he could, he backed out of the office and pulled the door shut. Then he sat staring at the door as his body calmed.

"Did you find her?"

He nodded but didn't turn around. "She's asleep."

Preston chuckled, and it was the first time John had ever heard the man do that. The sound was curious enough to make him turn around and look up at him in surprise.

"Gunny, you better let that poor girl sleep at night. She's got a lot going on right now."

John snorted, then chuckled, and it was exactly the release he needed. Preston had managed to hone in on the most lighthearted aspect of the night and spotlight it. "Hey, it's been a while. What can I say? I've got catching up to do."

He reached out and clasped hands with the big man. "You're all right, Preston."

Shannon stepped out of the office then, rumpled and bleary eyed. "What's going on?"

"Nothing, Shannon." John reached out, and as naturally as breathing brought her down onto his lap. She pressed her lips to his, and wrapped her arms around him. She had to be the sweetest weight he'd ever carried. He rubbed her back up and down.

Shannon let him cuddle her for a minute, then pulled back to look him in the face. "So, what's going on with Jennings?"

John shrugged lightly, trying to keep the anger off his face. "Nothing right now. He got a warning to stay away from the building unless he has an appointment."

Pursing her lips, Shannon nodded once. "Did he say anything about me? Why he looks at me like I broke his toy? Any hints?"

"No."

John wished he could wipe the dismay from her expression,

but he didn't know how. He continued to rub her back and just let her know he was there.

The elevator dinged and Duncan stepped off, just as grim faced. He forced a smile for Shannon, though. "Don't worry, Shannon. Old Frank knows not to let him in the building now unless I let him know he's coming ahead of time."

"Thanks, Duncan." She smiled at him and winked. "Maybe I'll get some overtime into pay for all this security."

John chuckled and let her slip off his lap. Duncan glared at her. "No, you won't be working. Go into the lounge and chill out, both of you. We'll order take-out while we decide what to do."

They settled on Chinese. Again. John headed to his office to work on something. Shannon ordered while Preston flipped channels on the big flat-screen mounted to the wall. He settled on a show about sharks and the Great Barrier Reef. Shannon thought it was appropriate for the big ex-soldier, and sat on the couch catty-corner from his chair. "Have you ever been there?"

"No."

Guess that was the end of that conversation. Restless, she rose and headed to John's office.

Hunched over the computer, he didn't even look up when she entered. Shannon thought he seemed excited. "What do you see?"

His dark eyes flicked to hers. "For shits and giggles, I had Preston mount a camera with an attached transmitter to the tree where we noticed the snow was brushed off the other day."

"Did it record something?" She leaned over his shoulder to peer at the screen. Excitement sped up her heart as she followed the line of his finger. The video was in black and white, but it captured a lean figure as he knelt at the end of her driveway. Even her sharp eyes couldn't see anything distinguishing about the person, although something seemed vaguely familiar. The camera was too far away to see their face, just a lean shape as they hunched over, packing the barbs in the snow. John tapped a couple of keys, and the camera zoomed in, but the image degraded too much to be visible.

"It's not Mike. I actually had doubt about the prison keeping track of him. But it's definitely not him. Too skinny."

"Okay. Does the person look familiar at all?"

Shannon racked her brain trying to figure out who it was, but the video was too far away. "Not really."

She must have sounded frustrated, because he turned enough to catch her gaze. "Don't worry about it. We'll figure it out. With any luck the camera will pick up a license plate or something."

But it didn't. The person stood and stepped out of view and the camera stopped recording. The next image was of Preston's truck tire just before it pulled into the driveway.

John stopped the recording and pivoted to face her. "Obviously they didn't see the camera, so we'll leave it there for the time being and hope the guy slips up."

Shannon ran her hand across her brow, so incredibly tired.

"Why don't you go lie down on the bunk for a while. We're probably going to be here for at least an hour or so."

Too tired to argue, Shannon pressed a kiss to his forehead and turned away, but John stopped her with his hand on hers. He tilted his head up, and Shannon gladly rested her lips on his. She needed this closeness that was growing between them, and it make her incredibly happy that John seemed to need it too. "I just wish this was all done so we could concentrate on us."

He squeezed her hand, then let her go. "I know."

Surprisingly, she slept like a log for two hours on the lumpy futon. And when she woke, famished, Duncan microwaved the Chinese for her and sat with her while she ate it. She must have looked like she was searching for John. "He's still on the computer."

Shannon nodded. She'd assumed as much.

"We had a call back from Quillen at Denver PD."

Shannon didn't like the way Duncan was looking at her. "What did he find?"

"He sent over a clip of the footage, and it looks like the phone was placed in the booking room by a nurse. Reddish-blond hair, five-six. She was a PRN nurse by the name of Lisa Dixon."

No. "Lisa Dixon? Are you sure of that?"

Duncan nodded regretfully. "John says he recognized her, but you ought to go in and confirm it."

She didn't even realize she was running until she slammed through John's office doorway. "Can I see the clip, please?"

John typed a couple of things and double-clicked on a file. The back of Lisa's head flashed onto the screen. The strawberry blond was brightly distinctive in the dingy gray of the booking area. The view was obstructed, but it looked like she reached into her left pocket, pulled something out and placed it at the back of the booking counter, under a shelf.

Shannon was heartsick. She'd known Lisa for a year now, and thought she was a friend. They'd shopped together and grilled together, and they'd comforted each other over men. "There has to be some other explanation. She can't be the one that did all those things."

"No," John agreed, "but she's a lead we need to check out. I don't think she did everything either, but we need to know more about her. Who is she involved with? What about her family?"

Shannon sank down to the chair across from his desk, and tried to get her mind in order. "The guy she dates is kind of off and on. I've never met him. I think they've been dating for almost a year."

Disbelief still had her shaking her head. "What possible reason would she have to do anything to me? I've only ever been a friend to her."

Nausea turned her stomach at the betrayal, but John reached out and squeezed her hand. "Let's just wait and see. Maybe it's not as bad as it looks."

Shannon made a face at him. "Seriously?"

"Okay, I know it looks bad. We'll get to the bottom of this, Shannon."

Who would have ever thought that John Palmer would be encouraging her to look for the good in people?

"So, what's the plan?"

John grinned at her, obviously pleased with her response. "Let's go talk to Duncan."

Between the four of them, it was decided that Preston would go out to the house, clear the driveway and scout the area. When Lisa got home, Shannon would ask her over to talk. John and Duncan would be inside the house, and Preston would watch from the outside.

Shannon didn't like the plan at all. She felt like she hadn't had long enough to think things out, and she was afraid she would flub something when they talked to her. John had given her a list of things to say and do.

"You'll be fine, Shannon. We'll be there as well. Are you worried about her hurting you?"

"No," she gasped, horrified at the thought. "I think that's the problem. She's a nurse, and my friend. She wouldn't hurt me for anything. These things that have been happening to me have been escalating, and I just don't see her doing it."

John looked skeptical, but he didn't contradict her outright.

"We'll take it slow, and be subtle," Duncan promised.

Forty minutes later, they pulled into Shannon's freshly cleared driveway. They had an hour before Lisa got home from her night shift at the hospital. Preston was nowhere to be seen, but she'd kind of expected that. He was probably watching them, though. They all piled out of Duncan's extended cab truck and trooped up to her door. They had time to kill. Shannon fed and played with the kittens, and did a load of laundry. John ghosted after her, and it was almost as if he was afraid to let her out of his sight.

Shannon fought tears constantly. It was one thing to think she'd caused a blip on some guy's radar she'd never seen before, but to imagine it was somebody she'd cooked for, and held when she cried over a lost patient, was disheartening. No, it was flat-out demoralizing. It made her question every friendship she'd made. Her eyes drifted to John as he fiddled with one of the monitors. Were she and John actually as connected as she thought? Or was this just a friendly arrangement in his eyes?

Shannon was frazzled and aggravated by the time Lisa pulled in the driveway a few minutes later. She gave her long enough to get into the house, then called over. "Lisa, can you come over here for a minute? I really need to talk to you about something."

"Sure, Shannon. Give me a minute and I'll be over."

John suddenly turned away and held the earpiece in his ear. "Go ahead." He looked at the monitors and tapped a couple of buttons. One of the cameras viewing the outside corner of the house came into view, and Duncan leaned in to look. Lisa walked across the screen and disappeared, and there was a knock at the door. John nodded to her, and Shannon walked over to let her in.

Lisa wore her standard blue scrubs, and had her hair up in a knot on the back of her head. Dark circles shadowed her eyes, but she smiled at Shannon when she walked into the house. When she caught sight of Duncan and John, though, she frowned. Her eyes widened dramatically when she saw all the camera equipment and monitors.

Shannon closed the door behind her, and turned to introduce the two men. "Lisa, these are two of my bosses, Duncan Wilde and John Palmer. Guys, this is Lisa Dixon."

"Hello."

Shannon motioned to a chair. "Would you sit down for a minute, please?"

"Sure."

Lisa was looking more and more leery. It was an awkward situation to walk into. She forced a smile and crossed her legs, leaning back into the cushion. "So, what can I do for you guys?"

Shannon sat on the corner of the couch closest to her. John snugged his chair in behind her, and Duncan stood at the fireplace mantle. Lisa may not have realized it, but they had positioned themselves to come to Shannon's defense if she needed it.

"Do you remember me telling you about that stalker I had? Several years ago."

Lisa frowned and nodded. "Of course. He's in prison, though, right?"

"Yes. But some things have been happening recently that made me think he was out."

"Oh, God—he's not, is he?" Lisa leaned forward, and seemed genuinely alarmed.

"No, he's not. But somebody is making me think he is. They're doing the same kinds of things he did."

Shannon paused, like John had told her to do, and let the silence stretch out. Theoretically, it was to make Lisa uncomfortable enough to talk, but she stayed quiet.

"Anyway," Shannon continued, "night before last I started getting text messages threatening to hurt me. They intimated threatening my boyfriend." She made a motion to John. "That cell phone was found in the Denver PD booking room this morning, under the counter."

Lisa paled, and her jaw slackened. "What?"

"The cell phone was found under the counter in the booking room. Lisa, did you work at the jail yesterday?"

The woman blinked heavily. "I did. They called me in for a couple of hours."

Shannon swallowed hard. She knew what she needed to ask. "And did you put a cell phone under the counter?"

"I did," Lisa admitted, readily enough. "Jimmy said that it belonged to one of his buddies, and he'd left it at his apartment. He asked me to leave it there for him to pick up."

Lisa seemed genuine. Shannon glanced at John, but she couldn't read anything from his face. Something occurred to her. "Wait a minute. Your Jimmy? As in, your schmuck boyfriend Jimmy that plays around?"

Lisa nodded.

"What's your boyfriend's name, Lisa?" John had rolled closer.

"James Wilkins. He's a road officer at Denver PD."

Shannon felt her own face pale, and she lurched to her feet. She jogged to the kitchen and snatched the business card from the refrigerator. *J. Wilkins.* She took it back to Lisa. "Is this him?"

"Yes, have you talked to him?"

Shannon felt the room dim around her. She dropped to the couch and leaned forward over her knees. A broad hand rested on her back. "It's okay, Shannon. We'll get him. It's okay, babe."

For a few minutes, all she could do was concentrate on breathing. The man stalking her had been right next door, at least part of the time. But how would he know the details about Gerbowski? The Pepsi can, and the rose petals?

John waited patiently at her side.

"I'm okay. Just shocked."

Lisa was crying, and seemed bewildered. Shannon still couldn't tell if it was an act or not. Her emotion seemed genuine, but Shannon had learned the hard way she wasn't always the best judge of character.

Duncan moved toward Lisa. "Ms. Dixon, do you know where Jimmy is now?"

She shook her head. "He was at the house for a little while last night, but he's gone now."

"Does he have a key to your house?"

Tears rolled down her cheeks. "Yes. Can you explain to me please what's going on? I'm very confused. I feel like I'm in trouble."

Shannon reached out and clasped Lisa's hand, in spite of John's earlier warning. "We think Jimmy's been stalking me. We're just not sure why."

Lisa shook her head in disbelief. "Why would he do that?"

"We're not sure, Lisa, but this is the best information we've gotten."

She looked up at Duncan as he stepped closer to her chair, cell phone in hand. "Lisa, what kind of vehicle does Jimmy drive? Do you know any of his personal information? Birthday, social, anything like that?"

"He drives a big black truck, four-wheel-drive—not sure what kind, though. And his birthday is June twentieth. Not sure about his social, though."

Duncan was inputting information to text somebody and nodding his head. "Good, good. When does he work next?"

"Should be this morning. We kind of pass in the night most of the time. He works days and I work nights or swing shift. Sometime we overlap in the morning and he comes to see me at the hospital or the jail if they've called me in." She looked at Shannon. "Did he flatten your tires?"

"I have no idea." It did make sense, though. "Lisa, I've never seen a truck like that in your driveway. Where does he park?"

Lisa made a motion with her hand. "Somewhere a couple blocks away. He said he doesn't want to run the chance of the people he's arrested figuring out where he lives or who he hangs out with."

John rubbed his hand across her back again. Shannon was so grateful he was here with her. She'd be floundering around completely if he wasn't.

Suddenly, he slapped a hand to his ear. "Preston? Preston! Answer me, damn it."

He powered the chair to the monitors, but Shannon couldn't see any movement anywhere. Duncan stepped up behind him and leaned over.

The bottom fell out of her stomach. Why wasn't he responding?

"Do you see him? What did you hear?"

John didn't even glance at her. "I heard a scuffle, and a couple of bangs, and then nothing." He held a finger to the earpiece. "Preston! Respond!"

Duncan slipped off his suit jacket. Shannon was surprised to see a leather harness wrapped around his broad shoulders, holding two black pistols, butt out. She'd never seen him wear anything like it before. But then, he was the boss. He ran the show. The other guys wore their guns regularly.

"What was his last position?"

"Northeast rooftop."

Duncan put on a headset and slipped out the back sliding glass doors. His limp was completely gone. Her heart pounded in fear, and it was all she could do to hold it together.

Lisa tightened her hands on Shannon's. "What's going on?"

John glared at Lisa. "We think your boyfriend is trying to hurt Shannon. At the very least, he's making her life hell. Do you have any idea why he would be doing that?"

Lisa shook her head repeatedly, crying all the harder. "I don't know why he would do that. He's a nice guy."

Shannon handed her the tissue box from the end table and Lisa blew her nose. John turned back to the monitors to watch for movement.

There was a ping to the outside of the house, and one of the small windows beside the big bay window shattered.

"Get down!" John yelled.

Shannon did as she was told immediately, pulling Lisa down beside her on the hardwood floor. They huddled together behind the couch, shielding their heads with their arms as glass continued to rain down. Shannon tried to look for John, but he was out of sight. "John?"

"I'm fine. Shannon, head to your bedroom. Get away from all this glass!"

Shannon didn't need to be told twice. Skittering on her knees, clutching Lisa's shirt, she pushed and pulled her way into the hallway.

"Lock up and don't come out until I tell you," he yelled.

She looked up at the very last second before she lost sight. John was at the window, Beretta out in front of himself, aiming through the shattered window and swirling snow. Shannon thought he actually looked vibrant, and alive, protecting her, and her heart swelled. But she didn't want anything to happen to him. "John, be careful!"

He glanced at her for a split second and grinned rakishly. "No problem, babe!"

Shannon continued down the hallway, Lisa right behind her. Inside her bedroom, she closed and locked the door. Lisa went up on her knees and pushed the bureau beside the door across the entryway, sealing them in. Shannon allowed herself to sit against the bed and catch her breath.

She didn't understand what was going on, but somebody had definitely fired two shots into the front of her house. Closing her eyes, she strained to hear anything from the front room over the sound of her own raspy breathing.

Something pinched in the side of her neck.

Shannon opened her eyes to find Lisa kneeling in front of her.

In her hand was a clear syringe, the needle bare. She looked at her neighbor in confusion, but her sight was beginning to dim. "What was that—"

Lisa grinned and backed away as Shannon slumped forward. Her last conscious thought was that John was going to be pissed.

*****

A frisson of unease chased across his shoulders as he lost sight of Shannon, but he couldn't be distracted. He scanned everything he could out the front, but nothing moved. "Duncan, update."

"Following a trail, no sign of Preston. Over."

"Roger. Two rounds just hit the front of the house, originating due east. Over."

"Roger. Trail goes in that direction."

"Roger. Out."

John fought to keep his own gun steady as he scanned the front yard, but he didn't see shit. Frustration ate at him. He wanted to be the one tracking that trail and chasing down the bad guy. He glanced at the monitors, looking for movement. Lisa had her back to the bedroom camera and she was leaning over Shannon, who was sitting on the floor beside the bed. That frisson of unease turned into an all-out quake as he realized Shannon was slumped over, apparently unconscious. Lisa was binding her hands with something.

"Duncan! It's Lisa. She's got Shannon in the bedroom."

He shoved his chair down the hallway as fast as he could, and slammed into the door knees first. The doorknob refused to turn, and he battered at the wood with his fists. "Lisa, don't do this. She's your friend. Lisa, Lisa!"

But there was no response. John shoved and pounded until his hands were bruised, but he couldn't get the door to budge. In frustration, he blew out the door lock with his gun, but the door itself still didn't budge. He screamed Shannon's name, but he knew she wasn't going to answer. "Duncan! Go to her bedroom window. They must be taking her out that way."

"On it."

Time completely stopped as he waited for some response from inside the room, but it was completely silent.

"Scanning. Multiple tracks outside her window heading away from the house. I think they've got her, John."

John rocked back in his chair as if he'd been shot, unable to even begin to assimilate the loss he felt. For a moment his vision narrowed to a pinprick before stabilizing. "We have to find her," he whispered. "We have to find her."

He powered out to the monitors and rewound the last minute. Lisa, substantially bigger than Shannon, had actually picked her up enough to get her head and shoulders to the windowsill, then black-gloved hands reached in to pull her limp body through. John tried to narrow in on the window, but the stationary camera only caught the corner of the sill. The assailant outside pulled Shannon through the window, then Lisa followed them through. The room was motionless for ninety-six seconds, then Duncan dropped into the room. John watched him shove the bureau out of the way that had been barricading the door.

Duncan jogged into the living room, his eyes connecting with John's in silent understanding. He dangled the tennis bracelet transmitter from his fingers. "This was on the floor beside the bed. But we'll find her. Anything on the cameras we need to know about?"

John dragged his gaze from the bracelet and shook his head. He turned the chair toward the front door. "We need to get after them. Did you find Preston?"

"Yes. He's groggy but getting his truck. He was darted with a tranquilizer. If he'd been smaller, like Shannon's size, it would have knocked him out for a while."

John skidded down the ramp, bumping into the front of Duncan's truck. Preston's Hummer idled beside it, and John maneuvered around to the passenger side. His disability had never frustrated him more than at that moment and he lifted himself into the seat and had to wait for Duncan to fold and pack away his chair. They were wasting precious time. As soon as he was inside,

Duncan was on the phone with Denver PD, tracking down Officer Wilkins' information.

Preston had blood running down the side of his neck, but he looked okay otherwise. Pissed, but okay. He accelerated out of the driveway and took two right turns, until they were in the alleyway behind Shannon's house. Tracks were all over the snow, and they followed them out of the alley, then lost them when they got onto the cleared street.

"Which way?"

John wanted to scream in frustration. They were literally seconds behind the people that had taken Shannon, but there was no sign of them on the busy streets. He glanced at Duncan in the back seat, but he shrugged his shoulders and continued talking to whoever was on the other line.

"South."

Preston turned left immediately in spite of oncoming traffic. Horns blared as he crossed the four-lane.

"Looking for a black Dodge Ram pick-up, Colorado plate Alpha Charlie Alpha six seven three. Address 450 Aspen Way, apartment 3B. PD has units out looking for him, and will meet us there." Duncan snapped his phone closed and leaned forward between the seats. "We're heading in the wrong direction."

"Fuck." Preston turned around and headed in the opposite direction, toward the apartment that had very little chance of having Shannon. The guy was a cop. John knew he wouldn't be so stupid as to take her back to his own place. He'd have a backup plan in place, for just this type of occurrence.

John rubbed his eyes furiously and prayed that Shannon was okay.

Chapter Nine

S hannon's head was throbbing, and her shoulders ached with the cold. She knew something was wrong as soon as she came around, so she kept her eyes shut in the hopes that she would be undetected. She listened to the sound around her, but couldn't distinguish what exactly she was hearing. There was a rattle and a bang, then silence for several seconds, then another rattle and bang. There was blinding light around her, she could tell, but she didn't dare open her eyes just yet.

Surreptitiously, she wiggled her wrists. There was a little bit of room, but not a lot. Slitting her eyes open, she dared to peek around. It looked like she was in an old storage facility of some type, like what they used for big businesses.

"You can quit faking it now. I know you're awake."

Shannon shuddered again with cold, and opened her eyes in the blinding light. It was definitely a warehouse, but the thing was long past being usable. Vast arrays of glassless windows stretched out in front of her. Discarded boxes were scattered on the floor, and Denver PD Officer Jimmy Wilkins sat on one of those boxes, chewing a piece of beef jerky. Shannon knew deep down inside it was bad that he had allowed her to see him. She'd heard that somewhere before. Why bother hiding if there were going to be no witnesses?

"Officer."

His handsome face twisted with regret. "Yeah, I think that may not apply to me anymore."

Shannon levered herself up into a sitting position, folding her legs to the side. A lump beneath her left thigh reassured her that all was not lost. Now, how to get her hands free. She looked around the warehouse, surveying the black truck parked at the far end near a big overhead door and the tent set up just a few feet away. They appeared to be staying a while. "Where's Lisa?"

Jimmy smiled, and continued to chew, but he didn't answer her.

"Can you tell me why you did this? Is it because I brushed you off?"

Her captor tipped his head back and laughed. "Well, I have to admit—the fact that you would choose a gimp over me was pretty maddening." Anger glinted in his eyes. "But I think things will end up in my favor in the end."

"So, what are we waiting for, then?"

He surveyed her with steady, cold blue eyes, as if deciding how much information to feed her. "We're waiting for Lisa. When she gets here, things will get interesting."

Shannon shivered and wished she had something warmer on than a fleece and jeans. They'd draped a blanket over her where she'd been lying, but it had fallen away when she sat up. She almost wished she'd stayed lying down. Snow drifted in from a hole in the roof, and she found the source of the rattle and bang. A piece of the roof tin flipped up and down in the breeze. The third time it flipped up, she thought she saw a face peer through the hole. She glanced away quickly, and prayed her mind wasn't playing tricks on her.

Jimmy chewed his way through the bag of beef jerky, watching her the entire time. Shannon tried to ask him questions, but he refused to answer anything else. Finally, she asked if she could go to the bathroom. Jimmy laughed out loud. "Sure. Go ahead." Then he just sat and watched her. Obviously, there were no facilities, or if there were, he certainly wasn't going to guide her to them.

Shannon gritted her teeth and fought off another cold shudder. "I'm cold. Can you wrap that blanket around me again?"

Jimmy didn't move. Shannon gritted her chattering teeth and tried to decide if she had enough room to work her hands down around her butt. Maybe, just maybe. She shifted up onto her knees and worked her bound hands down over her hips. Jimmy watched her but didn't say anything. Shannon worked her arms down the length of her legs and moved her feet through the circle of her arms until they were in front of her body. Holding the blanket in her hands, she whipped it around her shoulders and settled back Indian style on the floor.

With her hand on her ankle gun John had made her start to carry.

For the first time, tears came to her eyes. She now knew there was a chance she could save herself.

*****

John's head throbbed. They were at the office, gathering intel. All the guys that were free had come in, which he appreciated, but it felt as if every one of them were looking to him for direction. And he didn't know what to tell them. There'd been no ransom demands, or any communication at all, which scared him more than anything. If they asked for ransom, she was valuable. The fact that they hadn't asked told him the kidnappers weren't interested in money.

Duncan was on the line with Chief Quillen almost constantly, and each time they hung up he shared more learned information. Like the fact that Wilkins had been the one to take the call at the office, but no official report had been filed. And that Wilkins had been on the job less than a year, the same time Shannon had been in Denver. And Lisa Dixon's information was a dead end. There was no Lisa Dixon in the DMV database. Quillen was working on obtaining a search warrant to go through her house, but it was leased through a realty company.

Clayton Williams reported back that he'd spoken with Gerbowski three times in three days, and though he was not forthcoming with information, on the third day he was suddenly very excited. Prison officials were going over the recorded inmate calls to try to narrow down whom he had talked to, but so far, nothing.

John was beside himself with fear for Shannon. But the fear fought with guilt, too. He'd trusted Lisa too easily and Shannon had paid the price. He paced up and down the hallway listening for the phones to ring, but it was eerily quiet.

*****

Shannon glanced at the door long enough to see a beat-up old minivan pull into the warehouse. Lisa stepped out of the unfamiliar vehicle and grinned when she saw Shannon was awake.

"Oh, good. You came around. I was worried I'd given you too much."

She set several bags on a workbench, then rummaged inside. Jimmy crossed to paw through it as well and pulled out a wrapped sandwich. He peeled back the plastic and took a huge bite, then spat the food on the floor. "I told you to get roast beef, not fucking ham."

Lisa smiled sweetly at him. "It was all they had."

Jimmy flung the sandwich across the space and bent to the bags again, pulling out a tube of Pringles. He crossed the concrete to sit on the boxes where he was before, crunching away.

Shannon kept him in her periphery but turned her gaze to Lisa. "I thought you were my friend."

Lisa snorted and shook her head. "That was not your first mistake."

She swallowed. "So what was my first mistake?"

Her ex-friend turned around to lean against the bench, arms crossed over her chest. "You're first mistake was stringing Michael along like you did. It's been years and you're still all he talks about."

"That's not my fault," she protested, even as her mind reeled. This all came back to Gerbowski.

Lisa shrugged. "No, not really, but if I get rid of you he'll get over you faster. Then that clears the way for me."

Shannon shook her head at the injustice of it all. First she was stalked and now she was being blamed for it. "I've tried to get away. I haven't spoken to him at all. If I could wipe myself from his mind I would."

"I know, sweetie. I think getting rid of you is the only way to do it though."

"Can't you just tell him I died?" she pleaded. "We'll find a newspaper article or something to back you up."

Beneath the blanket she worked the handcuffs, trying to squeeze her hand through the iron loop. Her left hand had always been just a hair smaller, so she concentrated on it, but it was going to be impossible to get it through. She was dividing her attention between keeping the cuffs quiet and debating with Lisa, but Lisa had rationalized everything in her head to sound feasible. Shannon had to convince her otherwise.

"Just how do you think you're going to get away with all this? My bosses have taken the case and they won't stop until they find you."

Lisa snorted and unwrapped a sandwich. She pulled the tomato from the middle and flung it away, then took a bite. She grimaced at something but swallowed it down. She ripped off the cap from a bottle of water and took a long swallow.

Shannon's mouth watered with need and she opened her mouth before she thought. "Can I have a drink?"

Shit, shit, shit! I shouldn't have called her over.

But Lisa just shook her head. "Nah. You don't need a drink." She giggled, her eyes dancing mischievously. Wilkins laughed with her and slid off the boxes to cross the floor. He pressed a kiss to her lips and tucked her hair behind her ear.

"You're so mean," he told her. "But I love this side of you."

Lisa kissed him but her open eyes strayed to Shannon, obviously to monitor her reaction.

Shannon fought to keep her face smooth, but she was confused. Obviously Lisa was *with* Jimmy Wilkins, and Wilkins seemed to be okay with the fact that the entire situation they were in was so the way could be cleared for his girlfriend to be with another man.

Lisa pulled away from Jimmy and turned to Shannon, hands on her hips. "What are you thinking, neighbor, dear? That you were in my shoes, with two strong, vital men paying me attention? I have no idea what you see in that cripple."

Shannon shook her head and looked away.

Lisa stamped her foot. "Look at me, you sanctimonious bitch!"

Shannon's mouth fell open at the insult and her eyes snapped to Lisa's angry face. "What have I ever done to you? I've only ever been your friend, and this is how you repay me?"

Lisa blinked and Shannon thought regret might have flashed across her face. "It doesn't matter now. Michael is more important to me than any friendship. Any relationship."

Shaking her head, Shannon looked away from her former friend, wondering why she bothered. Obviously, she wasn't going to be around long.

*****

As he reached the end of the conference room, John fought to keep himself from ramming into the wall, just for something to do. His arms quivered with a need to bash something. Instead he pivoted the chair and shoved himself to the other side of the room.

Wrapped around his fingers was the bracelet he had given Shannon days ago, with the transmitter inside. Useless.

They were flying blind with crazies in the cockpit. Obviously they wanted Shannon for themselves, otherwise ransom demands would have been made by now. His throat ached with the need to cry out at the unfairness of it all. He'd finally found his somebody, his person that he could connect to more than anybody else, and she'd been snatched away.

When the phone rang on the desk on the far side of the room, he lunged for it. He snatched it up before any of the other extensions were lifted. "Palmer!"

There was a long beat of silence before a quiet, male voice came on the line. "Industry Parkway, the old Hartwell warehouse. You need to hurry."

The line went dead.

John couldn't turn the chair fast enough to the door. He scraped his knuckles on the doorjamb on the way out but ignored the pain as he yelled for Duncan. His buddy must have already been on his feet because he lunged out of the office, cane swinging.

John related what the caller had said, then immediately turned down the hallway. Everybody had gathered in the break room to await word and do what they could to help. He spat out the details and immediately began directing men. "Harper and Nashburg, I need eyes in the air around this building. I don't care how you do it but you need to be ready. Grab a mic on the way out." He searched the crowd for a mop of auburn hair. "Willet, I need every detail you can find me on that building. You've got, like, five minutes."

The man took off running.

"Do we bring in the PD?" Roger asked.

John paused and glanced at Duncan. With a slight shake of his head, Duncan reinforced his own thoughts. "No. If it comes down to brass tacks they may not fire on one of their own."

A murmur of agreement rippled through the room, and for a moment John was overwhelmed with gratitude. Knowing they could be in the gray area of the law, all of these men were standing behind him.

Within just a few minutes, Willet had gathered enough information about the abandoned building in the oldest part of the industrial park to begin to plan a rushed maneuver. It had been seven minutes since the call, and he was sweating bullets that everything was taking too long. But, eventually, the plan was set. No one raised an eyebrow when he said he wanted to be there for the raid, though Duncan did caution him that the terrain could make it difficult. They didn't know what would be on the ground. John shrugged his concerns away. He needed to be there for Shannon. Period.

*****

Jimmy slid his smart-phone into his pocket with a sly grin. "They're on the run."

Lisa nodded once and headed for the minivan. "Good. And you're sure they'll relate the information to the gimp?"

Jimmy nodded, though Lisa was turned away from him. "They will. If the PD thinks they can lead the rescue, though, they'll do that first. Then they'll tell LNF."

Shannon watched the other woman struggle inside the van for a moment before pulling out a long-legged tripod. She handed it off to Jimmy then climbed back inside the van. When she reappeared she had a compact video camera in her hand and a bright orange paramedic bag over her shoulder. Shannon's skin chilled at the thought of being drugged again and her hand tightened on the grip of her pistol. If she stayed completely still with the blanket draped around her there was no chance they would see, but she had to drag the slide back to chamber a round, and that would make noise. A very distinctive noise.

Her eyes darted frantically, trying to decide if she could bolt. Jimmy seemed to recognize her intentions, though, and wagged a finger at her. "No, no, no. Don't make me tie your feet. It will make it that much more difficult to play."

He grinned at her with heat in his eyes and, for the first time, Shannon worried that they wouldn't kill her, they would just play with her. By the look of things they were going to record the entire ordeal. Maybe it would all just be an act to have ransom demands met.

Fear clogged her throat and slicked her hands on the grip. If he came at her, she would have no choice but to shoot him. The thought of pulling the trigger on another human being was abhorrent to her, but she would do everything she could to protect herself. Never seeing John again was not an option. And though he wasn't Mike, there would be a certain satisfaction in getting revenge for what they'd been doing to her over the past month.

Lisa attached the camera to the tripod, removed the lens-cap and centered it directly on Shannon. She clenched her jaw at the invasion and tipped up her chin. If they were going to record her, it would not be as a cooperative victim.

*****

John silently urged Duncan to drive faster, though he knew the need for stealth. It was why he'd let Duncan drive. He didn't trust himself not to just plow the truck into the warehouse in search of her.

"Alpha 2, I have a visual. Over."

John pressed the earpiece tight to his ear so as not to miss anything. "Request you say again."

"Alpha 2, I have a visual. Tangos are located in the northwest corner of the warehouse. Three tangos in all, two standing, one seated. Over."

"Roger. Out."

He looked at Duncan, whose lips were pursed with concentration as he navigated the scrap yard left over from Hartwell Enterprises. During their heyday they'd been a glass bottle recycling company, but they'd gone under many years ago. Now the property was littered with derelict, unidentifiable equipment and overgrown bushes and trees. And while it provided them great cover, it was also difficult to navigate. Four of them were in Harper's Humvee. The Night shift guys were moving in from the east and would provide back-up when Day shift moved in. Chad and Roger Stottsberry were in the seats behind him, armored and ready to move in.

"Alpha 2, I have movement inside the building. Are you in position? Over."

"Negative," he growled. "We are not in position. Over."

"Permission to neutralize targets, over?"

John didn't even hesitate.

"Granted. Whatever you need to do to keep her safe."

His heart thudded and he gripped the dash in iron fists, urging the truck faster. Duncan seemed to be just as on edge, because in spite of the danger he sped up.

*****

Shannon's heart raced as Lisa pressed a couple of buttons on top of the recorder and a red light came on. Dread coursed through her as she realized they were getting ready to do something to her. Or maybe Lisa was recording a ransom demand. Hope flared in her chest. "Why are you recording?" she asked desperately.

Lisa gave her an enigmatic smile and stepped into the camera's view. Jimmy stepped behind the viewer and gave her a thumbs-up.

"Hello, Michael."

Shannon felt her mouth fall open as cold fear tightened her scalp. They weren't demanding ransom. They were recording her death.

"It's been a long time since I've seen you, and I apologize for that, but it's been necessary. All of the plans I've made are coming to fruition, and I hope that you will soon be able to get over the infatuation you feel for this woman. I've watched her for months and she is not the idol you think she is."

Shannon shook her head, not believing what she was hearing. Michael wasn't even eligible for parole for two years, so she had no idea why Lisa was even recording. He wouldn't be able to see the tape inside prison. But maybe two years was not such a big deal to Lisa.

Another thought occurred to her. If she wasn't there to contest the parole proceeding, he would probably have a much better chance of being released.

She tensed when Lisa turned to her.

"Michael, this woman has repeatedly turned you away, and now she's sleeping with a cripple." Lisa pulled a large eight-by-ten from a stack of items on a box and turned it toward the camera.

Shannon assumed it was a picture of John, but she couldn't see from where she was. Jimmy snorted from behind the camera and shook his head. His gaze connected with hers and he sent her a disgusted look.

The unfairness of the entire situation, the complete ridiculousness, made her want to cry. She was a good person. She didn't deserve to be treated this way.

Lisa lowered the picture and Shannon caught a glimpse of it. She was curled up in John's lap with her arms around his neck. The wheelchair took up half the picture because it was zoomed in. She gasped as she realized when the picture was taken. It had been in her bedroom the night Harper had been called in. Somebody had been standing outside with a camera and had captured the moment. She could only imagine what else he'd captured. They'd gone to bed not long after that.

She looked at Jimmy and he smiled.

Instinctively, her hand tightened on the grip of the pistol.

That had been a very private moment, when John had held her. She dreaded to think what else he had.

She had her answer when Lisa pulled another eight-by-ten from the stack. This time she turned and held it up to show Shannon.

As much as she wanted to control her emotions, tears immediately welled in her eyes and dripped down her cheeks at the blatant invasion. In this picture she was astride John in the bed, her head tossed back in release. His eyes were closed in pleasure. The only saving grace was that he had his hands covering her breasts.

I'm sure that's not the only picture he took, though.

Jimmy seemed to delight in her tears, grinning fiercely. Lisa seemed satisfied, too, because she turned back to the camera and held up the picture. "You didn't believe me when I told you she had moved on. Here is the proof. Jimmy just took this picture, and he has more if you need to see them."

Lisa dropped the picture to the stack, as if disgusted, then stepped back in front of the camera. "Michael, I love you and hope you'll be able to move on now that you've seen her betrayal. She's not waiting for you, as you've believed for so long. But I am." She put her hand over her heart. "I'm waiting for you and I'll continue to wait for as long as it takes for you to get out."

Shannon felt like Lisa was coming to the end of her speech and she scrambled for something to delay. The bracelet wasn't on her wrist anymore, so her hopes that John would roll in to the rescue were already slim, but she had to try.

"When did you meet Michael, Lisa?"

The other woman turned and surveyed her with cool eyes. "We met a few years ago when I worked in a hospital in Columbus. Michael had been attacked during a fight and knifed repeatedly. I took care of him for weeks while he was recovering. Before he left the hospital he said that he wished he could love me without regret. That I was his angel."

Shannon tried to keep her face calm and accepting, though she thought Lisa was off her rocker. Had she actually done all this in the hopes that he would stay with her once he got out?

"He called me his angel, too."

Lisa's face darkened with anger. "No, he didn't."

Shannon nodded. Maybe if she could get Lisa off the plan she obviously had in her head she could have a chance at surviving. "He did, actually. All the time. 'Honey' was another favorite."

Fury sparked in the other woman's eyes and she stepped forward as if to smack Shannon, but Jimmy grabbed her arm. "Don't, Lisa. She's just messing with you."

Well, in for a penny, in for a pound.

"And why are you doing her dirty work?" Shannon asked, trying to needle him. "You've given up your career to screw her, but she's doing all this for another man. What are you going to do when she's done with me? Go on the run for the rest of your life?"

His lips tightened and he hesitated.

"How did you even hook up with her? She's bad news."

Jimmy's lips tipped up in a smile. "But she's clearing the way for my brother to get out of prison for a crime he didn't commit."

Shannon jerked back in shock, shaking her head. Of all the things she expected to hear out of his mouth, that wasn't one of them. Mike had relatives, but she didn't remember Jimmy being one of them. "No, you're not. You don't look anything like him."

Shrugging, Jimmy cocked a hip, still holding onto Lisa's arm. "Doesn't change the fact that we shared a father. I wasn't in the court with everybody else, but I followed the trial as much as I could. When you testified about what had happened, I knew you were lying. Because my brother wouldn't have done that stuff. You had to have led him on, just like he said. Just like you did with me in the conference room."

"I didn't," she gasped, compelled to defend herself. "You were hitting on me but I wanted nothing to do with you."

He smirked. "Right. I know you had to play it that way in front of your boss, but I know what you were thinking. You liked the attention. And you kept glancing at him to make sure he saw. You've probably slept with all those rejects in there. Fucking a guy in a wheelchair is just foul. You're an awful good actress in those pictures, though."

Shannon clamped her jaw shut and forced herself to sit still, angry, frustrated tears filling her eyes. The complete sickness rampant in the family was appalling. She wanted to lurch to her feet and scream at him, but she refused to let go of the gun to do it. She actually shook with the effort to stay seated.

"Job security, right?"

She looked away, out over the expanse of the warehouse. It didn't matter what she said or did, they already thought they knew her. Nothing she said would change their sick minds.

Lisa turned away and reached for the bright orange medic bag. She sifted for just a moment before pulling out a syringe and several bottles of a clear fluid.

Shannon's heart stalled, then began to race. "You're making a mistake, Lisa. Getting rid of me won't get you Michael. It will just make him miss me more."

Lisa's hands fumbled a bottle.

"Why would you ever accept second best from anybody? You're a fantastic human being, a wonderful nurse. What are you going to do when you can't be a nurse?"

This time, her movements paused and she rested her hands on the bag. Shannon grasped for inspiration. "You were a fantastic friend, too, I thought. I loved being with you and joking around. This doesn't have to be the end of all that."

Lisa snatched up the bottle and syringe, and started refilling. "Jimmy, lay her down and hold her."

Shannon tensed as Jimmy started to walk toward her. Her thoughts raced and her hand tightened on the butt of the gun. Her heart, on the other hand, completely stopped beating. *It has to be now!* Tossing the blanket from her shoulders, she lunged to her feet. Or she tried to. She'd been sitting so long her legs had partially gone to sleep. She stumbled as he drew close and she lifted her weapon. He didn't even pause as he advanced.

But neither did she.

She scraped the slide back with her hand, loading the bullet. The little Beretta bucked in her hand as she squeezed the trigger, but she hit what she aimed for. His upper chest.

The smirk left his face, replaced by utter disbelief. He paused for just a moment, then shook his head and continued toward her. She fired again just as he reached her and toppled over.

Shannon lost track of everything as two hundred pounds of man came down on top of her, slamming her into the rough ground. Her head bounced off the concrete and the gun skittered across the floor, useless. Her breath slammed out of her lungs. Darkness edged her vision and she fought to stay conscious. She didn't know where Lisa was.

She shoved enough to shift Jimmy off her a bit, but couldn't get out from underneath him. As she struggled against his lifeless shoulders, Lisa stepped into her line of sight.

She stared down the barrel of Shannon's own gun. Tears tracked down the woman's face but resolve glittered in her eyes. "Goodbye, Shannon."

The gun fired and Shannon screamed, but nothing happened. When she opened her eyes, she couldn't believe the sight. Cameron Jennings had tackled Lisa, and now had her face down on the dirty concrete.

Chapter Ten

"Gunshots fired! I'm taking out the woman. What the hell?"

Adrenaline raced through John's blood as Duncan floored the vehicle for the last five hundred yards, then skidded to a halt outside the warehouse. Men were already running toward the commotion. Chad took long enough to park John's chair below him, then bolted into the darkness. John literally dropped into the chair and shoved off.

Crumbled concrete littered the ground around the building, not to mention crushed glass. He felt his hands being nicked, but he refused to stop until he got to Shannon.

Chad had just dragged Wilkins' body off her when he got within sight. She sat up and shook her head in response to a question he asked. With a final push, John entered the cleared area around the melee. Shannon looked up at him and tears flooded her eyes. Chad un-cuffed her hands and helped her to her feet. Though not quite steady, she ran to John.

She slammed into him full force, almost tipping him over backwards. He swung her into his arms and draped her across his lap. For the first time in hours, John took a breath as he clutched Shannon to him. She burst into tears and buried her face in his neck, gasping. John felt tears flood his own eyes and was man enough to just let them roll as he whispered to her over and over again that she was okay. He pushed her back for a moment to make sure that the blood coating her front wasn't her own. She shuddered as she looked down at herself, but shook her head. "It's not mine. I shot him. I shot him."

She burrowed into him again and he just let her cry.

When the PD came late to the party, she was still curled in his lap, though her sobs had quieted. Ambulances came one after another. Ex-Officer Jimmy Wilkins was pronounced on the scene.

Lisa Dixon was concussed and had a broken collarbone from being slammed to the concrete by Cameron Jennings. Cameron had a gunshot wound to the shoulder but would be fine when they stitched him up.

As the coroner lifted Wilkins' body to the gurney, Shannon suddenly ripped away from John and staggered away from the confusion to be sick. John held her hair away from her face until she was done, then pulled her into his arms to offer what support he could. Killing a man was never easy, and for a person like Shannon, not familiar with such harsh realities, it had to be especially hard.

Nobody knew why Cameron was there, only that he'd been the one to step in front of the bullet meant for Shannon. Harper had seen the whole thing through his scope and had pulled his shot in the split second before he'd hit them both with his high-powered rifle.

When the PD started asking questions and sorting details, Harper faded away. There was no need for them to know what had been planned.

The detective in charge was thorough but kind, and Shannon had no problems answering his questions. The detective's job was made easier by the camera that had recorded the whole incident, including the scene of Lisa standing over top of Shannon, ready to kill her.

Once Shannon got over the first wave of sickness and caught her breath, she was done. She pressed a kiss to John's cheek and slid from his lap, but stood beside him as they answered questions. The contact that Duncan had been talking to all day, Chief Quillen, arrived and paved the way for a lot of the details to be smoothed over and expedited. Within just a few minutes, they were given permission to go home.

One of the men had driven Duncan's vehicle inside the warehouse, so it was a lot easier to leave. John's hands were gritty with glass, but he didn't say anything as they all bundled into the truck for the ride back to town. He sat in the backseat and kept his arm around Shannon all the way. She nestled into his chest and drifted off to sleep.

The knot in his chest loosened inside him as he thought of what could have happened, but didn't. Everything had turned out as perfect as was possible in a situation as crazy as this one. Yes, a man had died, but by his own actions. He knew Shannon would be feeling all kinds of guilt over what she'd done, but he hoped she felt vindicated as well, and more secure in her own ability to take care of herself.

He felt useless as fuck. He'd trusted Lisa when he shouldn't have and Shannon had been stolen out of his grasp. He hadn't been able to track her, or find her, or even fucking get to her rescue in time because of the damn chair. She'd killed to protect herself, which he admired, but he would have taken that responsibility off her hands in a heartbeat. It would have been a drop in the bucket considering all the years of service he'd had.

"Do you think she wants to go home?" Duncan asked softly.

"Yes," Shannon murmured against his chest.

John was surprised she was awake. She was still curled into his side, quiet, unmoving, but apparently cognizant.

Within just a few minutes Duncan pulled into her driveway. He circled the vehicle to retrieve John's chair.

John's face heated as they waited for him to shift off the seat and drop down. All of the attention should have been on Shannon, and her comfort. Instead, he was making her wait on him. He must have made some involuntary movement because she reached out and grabbed one of his hands, turning it palm up. She gasped at the sight of his ripped-up palms and seeping blood.

"Jeez, John. Why didn't you say something?" Duncan growled.

His skin glinted with glass. When he looked at Shannon's face, he was dismayed to see her eyes full of tears again. "Aw, Shannon, I'm fine. It's no big deal."

She shook her head and pursed her lips, then stepped behind his chair. "I know it pisses you off to be pushed, but you're going to let me this time, John Palmer. Do not touch those wheels. Duncan, thank you for the ride."

"No, problem, Shannon. I'm just glad we made it there when we did. Don't worry about work. Take as long as you need. And John," he continued, "I expect you to be with Shannon while she's off. There'll be two guards posted for the next forty-eight hours, as well."

John snorted but didn't argue. Of course he'd be with her. Actually, the guards would be welcome. The two of them could rest without worry.

Shannon rolled him up the ramp as Duncan pulled out of the driveway. Somebody had cleared it of snow while they were gone, but he gritted his teeth in humiliation. He was damn heavy and she'd been through ten hours of hell. Forward motion slowed at the top of the ramp and he reached down to help her, but she snapped at him to not touch. Biting his tongue, he crossed his arms over his chest, struggling not to completely lose his shit.

*****

Shannon paused to retrieve her cluttered key-ring from the pocket of the borrowed coat. Harper had secured the house when he reconned and given the keys to John. When he handed it to her, she'd gotten choked up at that glimpse of the familiar. And as she pushed him inside the entryway, she felt it again. She never thought she'd see home again. Tears dripped down her cheeks, but she brushed them away and straightened. John was hurt.

She didn't realize until afterward where they'd kept her, less than five miles from her own house. She'd seen the glass on the ground, but it just hadn't registered. Heck, John had probably had a hell of a time even getting to her with all the debris littering the warehouse floor. Her throat tightened at what he'd obviously gone through to get to her. She looked at the wheels of his chair. Glass glinted there as well.

"John, we have an issue."

He turned his head to look up at her, and something about the way he looked, pissed and grumpy, made her heart ache. She pressed a solid kiss to his forehead before she motioned to the wheels of his chair.

"Fuck!"

She grinned at the familiar expletive and shook her head. "I think what we need to do is, you need to sit here for a minute while I go strip off these clothes and grab tweezers. Once we get as much as we can out of your hands maybe you can shift to my desk chair and we'll work on the wheels."

His solid jaw was clamped shut and he looked furious that she had to do all this for him, but he gave a tight nod. "Go ahead and hop in the shower. I'm not moving."

As quickly as she could she went to her bathroom and ripped off her bloodstained clothes, shuddering at the clammy feel. Thoughts of Jimmy coming at her again clouded her mind, but she shoved them away and stepped under the spray. John needed her. And she needed the *distraction* of John needing her.

Within just a few minutes she had scrubbed and washed her whole body twice. She also took a few seconds to brush the sickness from her mouth. In the bedroom she slipped on a pale pink set of sweats, then went to the bathroom to gather medical supplies. Tweezers, gauze pads, a warm bowl of water, a paper cup and a towel. It wasn't until she was leaving the room and saw where John had blasted the lock trying to get to her that she realized she harbored no fearful feelings of her bedroom, even though it was where she'd been taken.

John was in the same spot as before. He'd started taking the larger pieces of glass out himself, making a little pile on his jeans-clad thigh. Shannon swung the office chair from her desk on the other side of the room and positioned herself directly in front of him, her knees pressing against his. John glowered but held out his hands when she wiggled her fingers. "Don't get cut," he told her gruffly.

Shannon smiled at the words. He took care of her better than anybody ever had before. Even when she was trying to take care of him. "I'll be fine. Just hold still."

For a solid twenty minutes she hunched over his hands and plucked slivers from his bloody palms. He never said a word. The calluses he had built up maneuvering the chair had also kept him from feeling as much pain as a normal person probably would, and the bleeding was minimal. "I think it looked worse than it actually is." She looked up at him with a smile and was taken aback by the intensity in his dark gaze.

"I thought I'd lost you," he ground out.

Her eyes filled with tears, but she wiped them away on her shoulders. "Not right now, damn it. I'll never get through this without breaking down if you don't talk about something else."

He clamped his jaw shut and looked away, though she thought she caught a sheen of moisture in his eyes.

Blinking rapidly, Shannon took a deep breath and rinsed his hands in the water, running her own fingertips over the skin. It felt clear, but she had a feeling she'd missed a couple deep ones. She cleared her throat as she set the supplies away. "I think you're good enough now to shift to this chair."

John looked at the armless desk chair and frowned. "I don't know."

"I'll brace it while you shift over. Just remember not to touch your wheels."

A maneuver easier said than done. Even though she braced as hard as she could, John was a lot bigger than she was, and at one point they both almost went to the floor. But John's strong arms saved them. Finally, he was settled in the seat.

They both then went to work on the wheels of his chair, which had a lot more glass in them than his hands had.

"I'll have to get Chad to bring over my backup chair. This rubber is going to be Swiss cheese."

Shannon snorted and nodded her head. "Wonderful ride, I'm sure."

"Not!"

They laughed together and Shannon appreciated the normality. When his wheels were as clean as they were going to get them, he shifted back into his seat. Shannon surveyed the cup of green and brown glass and shook her head. Definitely not what she had planned to be doing tonight.

She waved a hand at him. The dark blue t-shirt he wore had bloodstains on it from contact with her shirt. "Why don't you go take a shower?"

He nodded slightly and rolled away. "Stay in the house, okay?"

Shannon threw the cup away and rinsed the water from the bowl. His warning was not needed, though she did plan to check on the kittens in the garage.

Pickle was especially glad to see her, twining about her legs over and over again as she carried the kitten box inside. She picked up each of the little cats and fondled them beneath their chins, setting them to purring before she placed them back in the box. Boohini clawed his way to the top, demanding his share of the love, and Shannon sat down on the kitchen floor to cuddle. It seemed so mundane to be petting a kitten after the ordeal she'd been through, but she soaked up the quiet, broken only by his diligent purr. Her world began to right itself.

When John rolled into the kitchen twenty minutes later, she was stir-frying at the stove.

"I hope you're hungry. I made a lot more than I'll ever eat. Seems like the hunger just caught up to me."

"I'm very hungry, actually. And it's the adrenaline rush fading that's made you hungry."

She steamed rice in the microwave and threw a couple of eggrolls from the freezer into the toaster oven. Within a couple of minutes they were eating. Shannon actually ate more than she expected to, and enjoyed it thoroughly. Almost directly afterwards, though, tiredness began to set in. She glanced at the kitchen clock and was shocked that it was going on seven o'clock at night. She and John had been home for hours, though it felt like minutes. It was almost like she'd been wading through sludge.

John spoke, snapping her out of her reverie. "I think we should go lie down."

Shannon nodded, tired beyond reason, but she didn't move. John rolled to her side and motioned to his lap. With a sigh, she lay across his legs and wrapped her arms around his neck. Time completely stopped as she curled into him to absorb his heat, inhaling the woodsy scent of the body wash he used.

She must have dozed off because they were suddenly in her bedroom, and John was urging her to her feet to get under the covers. Shannon did as he directed, then reached out her hand. "Will you lie with me?"

"Yes."

That one little word made her incredibly happy. A few minutes later, when John snuggled in behind her, she sighed in relief. She could relax now. Tension leached from her body as his warmth invaded her bones, and she drifted away.

*****

John woke to Shannon curling into him, her hand across his belly. The house was silent other than the tick of a clock in the hallway. He looked down at her face resting against his chest. The moonlight filtering in gilded her features silver, and the tracks of tears glistened on her cheeks. "What's wrong, babe?"

She rocked her head against his chest. "I just…didn't actually think I'd have to kill anybody. I mean, you told me I might, but I never really considered it, you know?"

He heaved a heavy breath. Thoughts of young men saying the same thing to him years ago filtered through his mind. "Killing a person isn't easy, but you have to be willing to step up and realize that your safety is paramount. If you hadn't pulled that trigger, you would be dead right now. The end. The most important thing you can do is get back to your family."

"So, who did you have to come back to?" she asked softly. "That it allowed you to protect yourself that way?"

John's throat clogged with emotion, and it took several long seconds for him to be able to talk. Nobody had ever thought to ask him that before. "Well, I didn't have the family, but the kids I was training did. I fought so that some of those kids wouldn't have to feel what you are now."

Shannon's tears flowed faster then, and he knew she'd just

have to work it through in her head. She hadn't done anything wrong, but she needed to believe it herself. After several minutes of emotion, she drifted back into a deep, restful sleep.

The tension that had furrowed her brows was gone, and she looked peaceful. The fact that he had eased her humbled him. He hadn't done anything to justify her belief in him, but he would take this last little escape for now, until the guilt overwhelmed him.

He watched her for hours, until the sky began to lighten outside and she shifted.

Her eyes fluttered open and her lush lips spread in a smile. "Hi."

"Hi," he whispered back. Awareness trickled down through his body as she shifted, rubbing her breast against his side. Deliberately or not, he couldn't tell.

Until she drifted her hand a little lower.

Craning his head around, he raised his brows at her. Rather than answering him, she rolled out of bed to pad to the bedroom window, twisting the rod on the window blinds to seal out the morning light. He was a little curious about her actions, but marked it up to insecurity.

As she walked back to bed, she slipped her sweat pants down over her hips, then her sweatshirt over her head. Her dark nipples were already pebbled from the coolness of the room, and she shivered as she slipped back under the covers beside him. John lifted her up to drape over his chest, and she took it one step further by straddling his hips. The awareness that had curled through him intensified, and he felt himself harden between their bodies.

Shannon rested her chin on her interlaced fingers and gave a subtle wiggle. John clutched her hips in his hands and ground her into him. She gasped and moved again as if she couldn't help herself. The heat of her core aligned with his hardness.

She pulled away and pushed the blankets back to expose his body. Grinning seductively, she grasped the elastic of his underwear and dragged them down his legs and off his feet.

John felt a flash of insecurity and she knelt above him, glorious in her nudity. He wished he looked just as good for her.

But she didn't let him linger on his uncertainty. Her gaze latched onto his hungry cock and she paused, then licked her lips. "My mouth just watered."

He grinned in spite of himself. "Really? And what are you hungry for?"

"You. And to feel alive."

She reached forward to wrap her hand around his hardness. John moaned and let his eyes fall shut so that he could focus on the feeling. Her thumb located his slit and began to rub gentle circles against it. Her other hand drifted between his legs to fondle his balls, lifting and tugging.

He was in heaven. And hell. He didn't deserve this after the way he'd let her down. The fact that he wasn't there for her just reinforced all the fears he had initially. Even though she appealed to him more than any other human being ever had, he had nothing to offer her other than trouble and work to take care of him.

"Hey, whatever you're thinking about, you need to stop. We were on a roll."

John looked down the length of his body and felt his cheeks heat. He needed to get his head back in the game, so to speak. "Sorry."

Shannon leaned forward to kiss him and smoothed his brow. John closed his eyes and just absorbed her touch, so thankful that she hadn't been seriously hurt.

His dick started to take interest again and he flexed his hips up into hers. Shannon gasped against his cheek and lifted enough to grin down at him. "I love it when you do that."

Holding her hips in his hands, he centered her exactly over top of him. Her moist folds spread and wrapped around his shaft, as if to welcome him in, but he didn't enter her. Instead, he guided her hips in a forward and backward motion. At the top of the slide, he worked the head of his cock against her clit. She gasped and sat up enough to rest her hands on his pecks. "My God, more, please."

For several minutes he did that, until she moaned and grew

impatient over top of him. Her nails dug into his chest as he dragged her hips faster over himself, but he had to pause. His own climax wasn't far away, and her excitement fed his own. He refused to come before she did this time. Panting, he tried to catch his breath. Shannon wiggled over top of him, until he growled at her to hold on a minute. He actually lifted her out of contact with his body and dragged oxygen into his lungs, slowing down.

Shannon moaned and kneaded his chest like a cat, leaning down to press kisses to his mouth and down his neck. John's cock continued to reach for her heat, until he couldn't deny himself any longer. Tilting her hips, he pushed her down onto his aching length.

They both cried out at the incredible union. It was all he could do to hold off his straining release. Pushing her shoulders up, he sat her astride him. He moved his hand to where they were joined and worked the pad of his thumb into her wetness, finding and circling her hard nub.

Shannon cried out and bucked her hips. John's hand followed her movements, working in tandem with her. And when she cried out in joy, arching over top of him, John was ready. Her rippling orgasm forced him over his own edge, and he was lost to everything around him except her body depleting his.

*****

She fell across John's chest, quivering from being used and manipulated so well. Chair or not, legs or not, John was a master lover. He'd made her body dance, over and over again.

And forget.

But the memories started to filter back, flashing before her eyes like a movie on a screen. Mere hours ago, she'd been on the verge of being murdered. Now she'd just experienced passion like she'd never tasted before.

It was a struggle for her brain to process the dichotomy.

Tears leaked from her eyes and rolled across the bridge of her nose to land with a splash on his bare chest. She felt him shift beneath her, and he tipped her chin up. "What did I do wrong?"

The tears came harder then. "You didn't do anything wrong. At all. You've done everything right."

He snorted. "Not even. I damn near got you killed."

Shannon jerked upright in alarm, her tears clearing. "No, you didn't! If it hadn't been for you, I would have been dead."

John shook his head on the pillow, looking mulish.

"I'm serious. If you hadn't made me start carrying my pistol, I would have been shit out of luck. As it was, I just barely got it out in time." She waved a hand. "And we were all sucked in by Lisa. Never in a million years would I have suspected my friend of being out to kill me."

He didn't say anything, but she could tell by the look in his eyes he wasn't hearing her.

Shannon left the bed and padded to the bathroom. When she came back she put on the same pink outfit she'd had on before. John was sitting up in the bed, getting ready to transfer into his chair.

She grabbed his underwear from the floor and held them out to him. Fury darkened his expression and he snatched them from her hand. "I can get my own fucking underwear!"

Shannon turned away so that he wouldn't see the fresh tears in her eyes. She'd only been trying to help. John seemed particularly aggravated right now, though, and she didn't know why. "What's wrong?"

He clamped his jaw and refused to look at her as he settled into the chair and turned for the bathroom. "Nothing, Shannon."

Nothing, my ass. The shattered door lock caught her eyes, and she thought of the glass in his hands. He'd done everything he could to get to her, and he hadn't been able to. Hell, he'd been the one to send her into her bedroom to get out of the gunfire.

Knowing John, he was wallowing in guilt right now.

Shannon shook her head at his stubbornness. He'd done everything he could to protect her. It wasn't his fault they'd all been taken in.

Restless, she headed to the living room and switched on the

news. But nothing was said about her abduction or even the fact that the Denver PD had been dispatched en masse. National news was the same old crap.

She had so many questions floating around in her head right now and she didn't know which way was up. John being shitty left her floating in insecurity. She looked at the clock on the DVR. Almost eleven o'clock. She was wide awake and didn't know what to do.

*****

Everybody was in good spirits as they walked in the door of the Frog Dog. Shannon had been rescued safely, one of the bad guys was dead, and the other two were in jail. A good day's work by Lost 'N' Found Investigative Services. All while rubbing the PD's nose in their incompetence.

Ember called out a 'hey guys!' and motioned to the back wall. Their table was open again. Chad shook his head. They'd been here twice and he already considered this "their" table. The four of them settled into the same chairs they had last week.

Ember arrived within seconds and asked for their beer order. Zeke glanced up at her and smiled, asking for a Frog Dog. He didn't stutter or hesitate, and she raised an eyebrow at him, then moved on to the other guys. She smiled and disappeared.

The crowd tonight wasn't nearly as large as last week, but they weren't as friendly either. There was a group of guys a couple of tables over rumbling about the lack of service. Ember appeared to be the only one serving tonight, and she was hustling. She brought their order then moved on to the aggravated table of men.

Zeke turned to watch her, but she handled them with charm and ease, then moved on. Chad had to admire her finesse.

They had several rounds that night. Ember stopped at one point, dragged a chair from an empty table and plopped down into it, sighing raggedly. "Any of you guys want to wait tables? I'm pooped."

"Where are the other waitresses?" Chad asked.

She shrugged, rubbing her tired eyes. "Wish I knew. One said she was sick and the other didn't even bother calling in, she just didn't show."

"Can you call…an…anyone else in?"

She shook her head at Zeke's question. "There's no sense now. The night's almost done."

The rowdy guys a couple tables over were calling for her, so she pushed to her feet, resting her hand on Zeke's shoulder. "You guys need another round?"

They all shook their heads and watched as she went to the rowdy table. One of the more vocal guys reached out a hand to cup her butt and pull her closer. She swatted at him, but he pulled her in tighter. She began to struggle. "No!"

Zeke was out of his chair and across the room before Chad could even blink. The drunk restraining Ember looked up at the glowering giant with the scarred face and immediately let her go.

"You need to leave before I feed you to the bears outside."

Within seconds they were shoving to their feet and dropping cash on the table. With a final, nasty look over their shoulders, they were gone.

Ember laughed and wrapped her arms around Zeke's massive chest. "Thank you! Those guys have been bothering me all night."

Chad laughed at the deer-in-the-headlights look on Zeke's face, but made a motion with his hand. Zeke wrapped his arms around Ember and squeezed her back. Even from across the room, Chad could see how stunned his buddy was.

Ember pulled away with a last, lingering smile and went to start bussing the other tables that were leaving. Zeke returned to his chair and dropped down, obviously shocked.

"Dude, you didn't stutter at all."

Chad clapped him on the back and Terrell popped him in the shoulder. "You didn't even give us time to provide backup."

He grinned and took the last swallow of his beer. "I just didn't even…think about it."

Ember waved them off that night as if they were friends, and Zeke seemed just as reluctant to go. Chad wondered what it would take to get the two of them together.

Chapter Eleven

Shannon woke to a light stroke on her cheek. John sat in front of her. The light from the dying fire highlighted his frowning face. "I'm sorry I snapped at you earlier."

She yawned hugely and stretched on the couch. "And I'm sorry I handed you your underwear. That was my mistake. It'll never happen again."

He glared at her, but she could see his dark eyes dancing with humor. "Smart-ass."

"Hard-ass."

He barked out a laugh and grinned at her.

She sat up on the edge of the couch and pushed her hair away from her face. John reached out and tugged at a curl, as if he couldn't help himself.

"Why did you snap at me like that? It hurt."

He dropped his hand to his lap and winced. "I feel like I let you down, with everything. I guess I'm feeling defensive. Useless, to be blunt."

Shannon shook her head, unable to believe the wrongness of that statement. "You have to know how wrong you are. I wouldn't be sitting here right now if you hadn't done what you did to prepare me. You stepped in to protect me before I even realized I needed it. Remember now, if you hadn't seen those spikes in the driveway, they'd have tried to grab me then. They were watching, and knew when they missed."

John sighed and nodded. "I know. But I think if any of the other guys had been here they'd have taken care of you the same way."

"But I didn't want any of the other guys here. I only wanted you."

He frowned at her and shook his head, as if that wasn't what he wanted to hear. "I don't know why. I'm a crippled, bitter, grumpy ass who swears too much."

"I know, but I've been half in love with you for months."

His eyes flared with heat before he looked down at his lap. "No, you're not."

Shannon smacked him on the knee. "Don't tell me I'm not in love with you."

"Ouch! Why did you hit me?"

Shannon gasped when she realized what she'd done, then squealed with outrage when he started to laugh at her. She reached to pinch him on the chest, but he grabbed her hands and spun her around to pull into his lap. He pressed a kiss to her temple. "You're getting violent recently. Why is that?"

"Because you frustrate me beyond all reason." She tugged at her wrists and he let her go. She wrapped her arms around his neck and pressed a kiss to his lips, rubbing the short hair at the nape of his neck.

He melted under her mouth. Cupping the back of her head, he took control, making her shudder with awareness. He pulled away and pressed a kiss to the tip of her nose. "Only half?"

"Huh?" She blinked at him in a daze, not sure what he'd asked.

"Why are you only half in love with me?"

"Mm, I said I was half in love with you for months. But then you moved in here and I really got to know you. Now I'm completely in love with you."

He pulled back to stare down into her eyes, and she let him see the truth in her heart.

He looked away.

"I don't know if I can reciprocate that. I mean, I'm nuts about you. I love having sex with you, obviously. But I don't know what love is, you know? I don't know if I'm feeling the same thing you are."

Shannon tried not to be hurt at his words. She pulled back and dropped one hand down to hold his on her lap. "And that's fine. I won't rush you into saying something you don't feel. But I know in my heart that I love you, wheelchair and all, cussing and all.

None of it makes me want to be away from you. You were the family I thought about when I fired that gun."

His dark eyes rested on hers for a long time, until he leaned forward to kiss her. "Okay, let's give this some time to digest, okay? You may feel differently when things settle down and you realize you don't have to depend upon us anymore."

She shook her head at his stubbornness, but didn't say anything to contradict him. It really didn't matter what he said. She'd be waiting when he was ready.

*****

They were restless that day and decided to go into the office to figure out exactly what had happened the day before. There were so many unanswered questions.

Duncan seemed surprised but happy to see them, clapping John on the back and wrapping Shannon in a huge bear hug. She knew he had to be relieved after pulling off what sounded to have been the biggest single endeavor the service had ever tackled.

"You doing okay?"

She nodded, so appreciative that she'd landed in the job she had, and most especially with the people. "I'm fine, believe it or not. Pretty satisfied with myself, and you guys coming to my rescue. I think everything played out the way it needed to."

Duncan nodded and moved behind his desk to his chair. He settled gingerly, and she wondered if all the excitement from the day before had hurt him. When the men had run in, he'd been right there with them, and she couldn't remember him limping at all. He waved a hand when he noticed her concern. "Don't worry about me, Shannon. Have a seat."

She did and crossed her legs. "Where is Lisa?"

"She's in jail a couple of counties over. Because of her affiliation with the local jail they thought it best to house her away. She's been charged with abduction and the prosecutor's office will surely file attempted murder charges when they view the recording. I watched it myself a few hours ago and I have to say Shannon, you did everything perfectly. You acted exactly as you should have. The shooting itself was clearly self-defense."

Tears came to her eyes and she slumped back into the chair, overwhelmed with appreciation at his words. A part of her played it over and over in her mind, convinced there could have been another way out, without all the loss. "Everything happened so fast. It's a blur in my mind."

Duncan nodded, his lean face sympathetic. "But your interview with the detective was perfect, too. You gave him all the information he needed, which was corroborated with the recording. I'm sure you'll probably have to go to court, but it should be a slam-dunk case."

The thought of going through another trial turned her stomach.

John reached over and grabbed her hand. "Don't worry about it now, babe. It may never happen. She may plead out and go straight to prison."

Shannon nodded, though with her luck they would fight to the end.

"Clay is still in Ohio talking to Gerbowski, who is swearing up and down that he didn't know anything about the whole ordeal. We have evidence to the contrary, though, found at Lisa's house. He'll be charged with conspiracy, and shouldn't be out of prison for a long time. We think that they moved to grab you now because he has a parole hearing coming up in six months."

Shannon frowned. "No, it should be two years before his first hearing."

Duncan sighed and leaned back in his chair. "With overcrowding in the prisons, and the fact that he's been an exemplary inmate, the state moved his date up."

Her blood chilled at the thought of having no notification, and him being on the streets again, possibly terrorizing another woman. If she could guarantee that wouldn't happen, she would go through it all again.

"Once we had Wilkins as the primary suspect for letting himself into your house with Lisa's key, the rest of the things started to fall into place. The can that started it all was a couple years old, but the print could have been collected at any time. They have contact visits at the prison, so once the plan was in place, they could have smuggled in a fingerprint transfer. Much easier to conceal than the can itself. It would have been a piece of cake to transfer the print to the can." He shrugged. "Wilkins stole the cell phone when he did a transport a couple weeks ago to Canon City. The prints at the tree outside your house matched Wilkin's uniform boots perfectly, and the carpet fiber we found on the dog looks like it will match up with the carpet in the trunk of his cruiser."

John tightened his hand on hers as every standing question was answered. "What about Cameron? How did he play into all of this?"

Duncan scrubbed his hands over his gray head and rubbed at his face. "Well, Mr. Jennings is still a bit of a question. Right now we think he didn't have anything to do with them. He wasn't there in the warehouse, right?"

Shannon shook her head. "No, not with Lisa and Jimmy. But I think he was on the roof watching us."

"His cell phone called this office at exactly fifteen thirty-four yesterday."

John's hand tightened on hers. "That was the call I took telling me where she was."

Duncan nodded at his partner. "Exactly."

"So, he was watching out for me?" Shannon was overwhelmed with all of the information flowing at her. And she felt bad for thinking Cameron had been a creep. He'd taken a bullet meant for her. At the very least, she needed to thank him.

"I was going to go over to the hospital and speak with him if I could. I know he had surgery to repair his shoulder last night. You want to tag along?"

With a glance at John, she nodded. "Definitely."

As they were walking out of the office, Duncan handed her a large manila envelope. "I don't think the PD will miss these."

Shannon glanced inside enough to see the glossy pictures, then fastened it shut again. Gratitude overwhelmed her and she had to wrap her arms around Duncan again. "Thank you."

He winked at her. "Let's go see our wild card."

So, an hour later they were directed to a room in the ICU. The nurse on duty looked at her critically. "Are you Shannon? He's been asking for you. Hopefully when he sees you he'll settle down."

As soon as the nurse swept back the curtain and Cameron's groggy eyes latched onto Shannon's, he broke into quiet, rasping sobs. The sound broke her heart, and in spite of her lingering wariness, she stepped forward to take his uninjured hand. John moved in to stop her, but she shook her head at him.

"I thought I'd lost you again. They wouldn't tell me what had happened and I couldn't leave." He looked her up and down. "Are you okay?"

"I'm completely fine, thanks to you. You stopped a bullet for me. But why would you do that?"

He pulled away from her grip and wept into his hand. Shannon handed him several Kleenex and waited until he got control of himself, mopping his face and wiping his red-rimmed eyes. "I signed on for the Navy even when my fiancée warned me she wouldn't be there when I got home. I didn't believe her, because we'd been together since junior high. I thought she'd be my home base, you know? We didn't know she was pregnant when I left. She had a miscarriage. And there was nobody here for her. She committed suicide six months into my deployment."

Fresh tears wet his face, but he wiped them away. He reached into the bedside table and handed his wallet to Shannon. She flipped it open and gasped.

The girl inside could have been her younger sister. Though her hair was blond, the resemblance was remarkable.

"I walked into the agency that day and thought I'd seen a ghost. And I'll be honest with you, I think things got kind of confused in my head for a while. I thought you must have been related to her. I wanted to talk to you but couldn't get my words straight in my head."

Shannon showed John and Duncan the picture and even they

shook their heads at the resemblance.

"There was a cop following you, which I thought was strange. I was worried so I watched him, and later that morning they snatched you. I waited until I knew where we were and I called the agency, but they didn't get there in time. I knew by how aggravated the woman was becoming that things were moving, so I went down to get ready. But you took the cop out before I could get there. The woman picked up your gun and fired, and I thought for sure she'd gotten you. I didn't even feel the bullet until somebody rolled me off her. Then I think I passed out."

"I knew you'd been hit but I didn't know how badly. I thought you were with them for a while."

The younger man winced. "I'm sorry about that. I didn't mean to come off like a stalker. I just didn't know how to cope with Janelle's loss." His eyes started to tear up again, but he took a deep breath and got himself under control. "We had our whole lives planned together, you know? And I let her down by leaving her behind."

Shannon left the hospital room feeling sorry for the man who had been a creep. Cameron was under psychiatric care for his loss, and he would continue to be for a long time coming.

She felt deflated as she rode back to the office in the crew seat of John's truck. All of the details had been tied up, for the most part. She looked at the back of John's close-shaven head in front of her and wondered what he would do if she ran her fingernails down the plain of his neck. It was a very sensitive spot, she'd found.

Something drew her gaze to the rearview mirror. His dark eyes had gone almost black with awareness. He'd known what she'd been thinking.

*****

John pulled up in front of the office and put the truck in park, but let it idle to stay warm. Duncan was twisted in the seat, blathering on to Shannon about state laws protecting the guilty. John wished he'd just shut the hell up and go.

Looking at Shannon in the mirror as she talked to his buddy, John realized he didn't have the balls to tell her goodbye. The danger had passed and there was no reason for him to stay in her house anymore, other than because he wanted to.

He'd had wants before, and been denied, but none of them had been as strong as what he felt now. He wanted to watch her smile at him over breakfast, he wanted to watch her stock the fire in that damn see-through nightgown. God, he wanted to see her look at him with that emotion in her eyes that nobody else ever had before.

"Get out, Duncan."

His buddy looked at him in surprise but didn't object. With a promise to see them both in the morning, he slid to the pavement, set his cane and walked into the lobby. Shannon looked at him curiously in the mirror, but he didn't say anything.

John put the truck in gear and pulled a u-turn, then looped back into the parking lot. He slid the gearshift into park again. "Can you come up here, please?"

After a second, Shannon rested a hand on his shoulder and stretched her leg over the center console, stepping to the passenger seat. She settled onto her bottom and tightened the coat around her. "What's wrong?"

Now that he was on the spot, John floundered for what to say. He wasn't a bare-your-heart kind of guy. "I don't like people."

She raised her delicate brows but didn't say anything.

"In general I have no tolerance for them. They piss me off and drive me to cuss. Most of them don't have the sense to find their way out of a paper sack. None of this applies, of course, to other Marines."

One side of her mouth lifted in a smile.

"And it doesn't apply to you. You're the first person I've ever been with who doesn't make me want to shoot somebody out of boredom. You have spunk and heart and you're sexy as hell, and you don't mind my shit. And lady," he said with a sigh, "I come with a lot of shit. I have a lot of baggage, and though I don't mean to spew it on you, I know I will. I'll tell you I'm sorry now and every day for the rest of my life."

He reached out and tugged her to lie across his lap.

"But I'll also tell you I love you every day, which I do. I do not fucking deserve you. I know that. I've not done anything in this life to be given a gift like you. But I will cherish you, and honor you, as much as I possibly can. You make me feel like a man, and I cannot tell you how much I need that."

Her pretty hazel eyes welled with tears then dripped down her cheeks. He felt his own throat tighten as he brushed her tears away with his rough thumbs. She cupped his jaw in her hand and pressed a gentle kiss to his lips.

"Okay."

He pulled back in surprise. "Just 'okay'?"

She nodded. "You didn't tell me anything I didn't already know. I know you have baggage, I know you're going to be a pain in my ass, but I love you more than I ever dreamed possible. You're abrasive and harsh, but you cuddle a kitten like you were meant to do it. You cuddle me like you were meant to do it. And you'll cuddle our kids the same way. You make my body sing and my heart race. I want to spend the rest of my life with you, too."

There was no way he couldn't *not* kiss her then. As he cupped her head in his hand, he marveled that he'd been given this piece of heaven.

*****

Shannon chased Pickle and the Little Gray out of the bedroom. Her family would be there in just a few minutes and they weren't even dressed yet. The turkey was roasting, but she needed to check it.

John rolled in from the bathroom, fresh from a shower. His hair was slicked down and water glistened on his chest. If they were caught with their pants down, so to speak, it was going to be his fault.

She looked at the diamond bracelet on her wrist and couldn't help but smile. When he'd asked her to sit down beside him at the kitchen table, she'd been curious. But when he'd held the length of diamonds between his fingers and made a motion for her hand, she'd cried.

"This isn't a tracking device," he promised gruffly, which made her blubber all the more.

One kiss led to many more, and then she straddled his lean hips in the chair right there at the kitchen table. It was exciting and sexy, knowing that they could be interrupted at any minute. They eventually moved to bed, where she'd loved the crap out of him dressed only in his jewelry.

Her hard-ass was learning to love. And she was enjoying teaching him.

###

Note from the Author~

I sincerely hope you enjoyed Book 1 of the Lost 'N' Found Series. I would appreciate it if you would:

LEND IT- to friends and family.

REVIEW IT- at the site you purchased it from. Positive reader reviews have a huge impact on the success of a book.

RECOMMEND IT- to anybody you think would enjoy it.

A portion of the proceeds of this book will be donated to the Wounded Warrior Project. If you would like to make a personal donation, you can find information at http://www.woundedwarriorproject.org/

Thank you so much for reading.

About the Author~

I am a wife and mother of two. I currently stay home to take care of the farm and family, which I love. I was a deputy sheriff in Ohio for nine years, and I found myself tapping that experience as I wrote *Second Time Around,* my first book. No, I didn't tackle and cuff my husband, although there was that time in K-mart... Anyway, it was quite a change going from writing technical reports with diagrams, witness statements, inventories, etc. that would stand up in court to writing contemporary romance. I've always written, though, and it was always a dream to do something with that huge, leaning stack of spiral-bound notebooks.

Second Time Around was my first release and Embattled Hearts is my eleventh. I thank you so much for taking an interest in my work...

Stay tuned. There's a lot more coming!

Also by J.M. Madden

Second Time Around

Burning Moonlight in the Urban Moon Anthology

Wet Dream

The Awakening Society

A Needful Heart

Tempt Me- Book 2 of The Awakening Society

Love on the Line

Love on the Line II

Please, connect with me online:

www.jmmadden.com

www.jmmadden.blogspot.com

FB- https://www.facebook.com/jmmaddenauthor

Twitter- @authorjmmadden

Or

Send me an email- authorjmmadden@gmail.com

Excerpt from A Needful Heart

Matt hoped for, yet dreaded, the possibility that Gina would brush against him as she strode down the hallway to the next exam room. The hope nagged at him. The dread, on the other hand, gnawed out his stomach and almost swamped him. What if she did brush against him? What if she glanced up at him with that gut-turning smile she had and said something to him, and expected some kind of response?

His worries stalled as she bypassed him completely and went into the small lab room directly across from where he leaned. He blew the stale air from his lungs and tried to settle his thudding heart. The peaches and cream scent she wore wafted to him, teased him with her freshness and sent a fresh jolt of awareness down his body.

Once a month for the past four years Matt had brought his neighbor George in for check-ups following a liver transplant. While George waited to be seen, Matt devoted his time to watching Gina and storing up images of her in his mind to tide him over till the next month. The shape of her ass in pink scrubs as it swayed down the hallway, the way her curly hair blew under the vent at the far end, the way her smiles came so easily when she greeted people and the way her ice-blue eyes crinkled at the corners.

Every time they left the doctor's office, Matt was frustrated and furious at himself for not talking to Gina about something other than George's next appointment or the pills he was on. But nothing ever came to mind. She'd tried to start conversations before, and he had totally locked up. She had to think he was the village idiot. Or the Shelbyville, Indiana, idiot.

Clenching his fists in frustration, he vowed to himself he was going to say *something* to her coherent, even if he had to stay here all day to do it. He needed to talk to her just to prove to himself that he could. Besides, it wasn't like she'd respond. Her pristine little life didn't have room for a roughneck like him in it. She'd give him a generic smile and dodge around him like she always did, and maybe he could get over this thing he had for her. Determined, planning words in his head, he stepped into the lab room doorway.

Just as Gina started to exit.

Head down, she was scanning a chart in her hand, totally oblivious. She plowed into him folder first. Papers flew and her arms wind-milled as she tried to keep her balance. Matt reached out to grab her but missed her arm. Horrified, he could only watch as she crashed to the hard tile. One of her tiny hands went down first to try to break her fall, and Matt heard the snap as soon as it hit. Her cry of pain made his stomach clench.

Oh, fuck! I've broken her.

He was on his knees in an instant, but the damage was done. Gina's eyes were awash in tears as she struggled to sit up. He put a trembling hand behind her back to support her. "Gina, I am so sorry," he began. His chest was tight with fear at what he had done and the urge to throw up was almost more than he could swallow down.

Her fly-away brown hair shone in the light as she shook her head and looked up at him with a tight smile. "No, Matt, it wasn't your fault. I wasn't watching where I was going."

She moaned as she cradled her right wrist. It was quite obviously broken. Matt had had enough broken bones in his life to know the sound. Then the instant nausea, the disbelief.

Man, why hadn't he just stood against the wall?

Gina cradled her arm protectively as footsteps approached. Dr. Hamilton stepped in, saw her on the floor and dropped to her other side.

"What happened?" he demanded. Gently, he took her wrist in his hands to examine it.

"I knocked her down," Matt admitted.

Gina laughed, or tried to. "No, you didn't, Matt. You were just standing there. *I* ran into *you.*" She gasped as the doctor turned her arm over.

"Definitely broken. We'll get a splint to bind you up so you can go to the hospital. Any other injuries?" The older man peered into her eyes over the tops of his bifocals.

Gina turned her head and tested the rest of her body parts, but everything seemed to work correctly. "I think just my wrist. I put my hand down to catch myself."

Madison, one of the other RNs, came in the door and almost tripped on the group on the floor. "Oh, my God. What happened?" She knelt down and rested a hand on Gina's knee. "What did you do, Gina?"

"I fell and broke my arm. Klutz that I am."

Matt rumbled deep in his chest, fists clenched. Why was she taking the responsibility? It was his fault, not hers. He must have looked truly alarming, because Gina reached out and rested her good hand on his arm. "I did it, Matt. Not you."

For the first time, Gina got a good look at Matt's face under the bill of his cap, and it worried her. He was pale, a tic in his jaw was pounding overtime and every one of his impressive muscles were clenched. The expression in his eyes made her think of a wild horse. Spooked. Shaken. "Matt, look at me." She waited until he did. "You did not do this. I did. Just like the five other times I've broken a bone. It was all me."

Something must have gotten through to him, because he eased back a bit on his haunches. Some of the fierceness left his bold face. He looked down where her hand rested on his tattooed arm, and Gina couldn't tell if he was surprised to see her touch him or what, but the expression on his face broke her heart. If the adrenalin wasn't beginning to wear off, and her arm wasn't beginning to throb, she would have probably taken more time to explore it.

"We need to get you to the hospital, Gina," Dr. Hamilton manipulated her arm into a soft splint as he spoke, and Gina gasped at the pain. Her eyes welled with tears as he gently strapped it on. He checked the circulation in her fingertips and guided her to hold her hand up, across her chest.

"Ok, it seems good. Let me get one of the nurses to run you over to the hospital."

"I can walk over. It's not that far." It was only actually a quarter of a mile, but Gina dreaded every step even as she made the offer.

"I'll take her."

Matt's voice brought all eyes to him. His skin took on a ruddy cast at the attention, but his eyes stayed determined.

"George still has to be seen. I'll take her over and come back for George."

Dr. Hamilton hesitated, his kind eyes shifting between Gina and the big man. "I don't know…"

"I'll take her," he repeated, and Gina could hear the determination in his voice.

Dr. Hamilton reached out to clap him on the back but changed his mind at the last second. "Ok. Thank you, Matt."

Before she knew what happened, Gina was gently lifted her to her feet and guided down the hallway. Madison retrieved her purse from the break room, promised to check on her later, and out the door they went. Matt made her wait at a bench out front and jogged to get his truck, a big black dually. He bumped the curb and pulled it right up to the bench.

Gina laughed at his total disregard for propriety, but she appreciated not having to walk any further than necessary because every step caused a ripple of pain to slide up her arm. He was so very gentle as he handed her up into the truck. Gina knew if she faltered, he would catch her in a heartbeat.

"You don't have to do this, Matt," she told him faintly. The pain was really beginning to get to her.

"I'm already doing it."

In less than a minute, he had pulled up in front of the emergency room doors. Gina tried to juggle her purse and grab the door handle with her left hand, but all she managed to do was drop the bag upside down on the ground. Contents scattered everywhere. Her lip gloss and mascara rolled away under the truck, and her credit cards fanned across the concrete.

"Damn it!" Frustrated tears filled her eyes.

Matt appeared in front of her as she prepared to drop to the ground to retrieve her things.

"Just hold on a minute," he grumbled. Leaning down, he snatched up all the items and shoved them in her purse, then zipped it closed when he was done. Gina was dismayed to see her cell phone in his big hands, in several pieces. "This didn't survive. I'm sorry."

The new, shiny, red phone had been an extravagance, and it made her sad to see it broken. Great, just great.

Slinging the purse strap over her shoulder, she left the pieces lying on the seat. She had other things to worry about right now.

Matt held onto her good arm as she slid down out of the cab, and Gina appreciated the help. It was bad enough having to go to the emergency room like this. Sprawling on the concrete was not something she wanted to do in front of so many people she knew. Delores Jones manned the front desk, as she had every day for twenty years, and Gina sagged into her arms gratefully as she came through the doors. Concern darkened the older woman's eyes.

"Oh, girl, what did you do to yourself?"

"Tumbleweed strikes again," Gina mumbled, cradling her arm. "I fell."

"We'll get you fixed right up, honey."

As Delores hustled her into the emergency, Gina turned to thank Matt for bringing her, but he was already gone.